THE INGRID PITT

BEDSIDE COMPANION FOR
VAMPIRE LOVERS

THE INGRID PITT

BEDSIDE COMPANION FOR
VAMPIRE LOVERS

BT BATSFORD LTD • LONDON

Printed by
Butler and Tanner, Frome, Somerset

for the publishers
BT Batsford
583 Fulham Road
London
SW6 5BY

ISBN 0 7134 8277 X

A catalogue record for this book is available from the British
Library

Pictures: courtesy of Joel Finler, Gary Parfitt and the author

CONTENTS

FOREWORD

Dear Ingrid

Sorry I have been so long in getting back to you regarding your book.

What I read of it was erudite, witty and the very last word on the subject that it is possible to write. But I'm afraid it just became too horrifying for me to read on. I got as far as Vlad and then I simply had to STOP.

Maybe my imagination is too vivid or perhaps I'm just too squeamish, but I just couldn't handle the images – which probably augers well for its success.

So sorry to be a wimp..., but there it is! But, that doesn't stop me from hoping that you will have an enormous hit on your hands.

Ken x

KEN RUSSELL

special thanks

I can't think of any book that has been completed without the help of kind souls inclined to give advice, useful information or guidance. I would like to acknowledge friends who assisted with patience and understanding, enabling me to make the gentle stroll through the ages and poke a stick at vampires from all over the planet....

My special thanks must go to Ken Russell and James Herbert, Paul Cotgrove, Marcus Hearn, Don Fearney, Gary Parfitt, Don Glut and Hammer films.

Dracula seems not to have wiped his mouth after his meal...

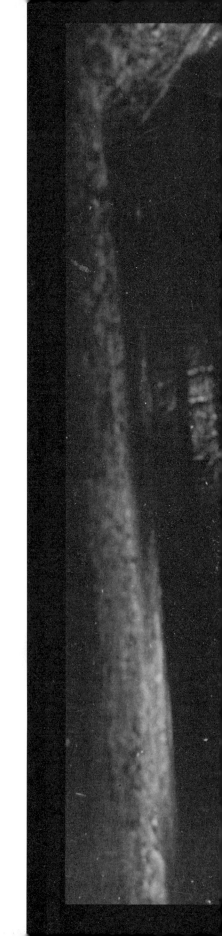

INTRODUCTION

There's nothing like a good deathbed scene – that moment before the death-rattle, the dramatic slump and the brightly lit tunnel into the next world. Few real-life final farewells can match the flawless invention and dramatic scope of the screen. From the eye-gyrating, heart clutching, soundless scream and fade-out of Max Schreck's *Nosferatu* to the frenzied, blood-gushing, bestial agony of Sadie Frost's Lucy in Coppola's *Dracula*, there's a new twist to the stake with every demise.

Remember the close-up on a suddenly nerveless hand, the glass, snow-filled ball rolling down the steps and smashing; the husky, whispered 'Rosebud' that signals the start of Orson Welles' Gothic *Citizen Kane*? Then there's Horatio Nelson, shot to pieces but determined to have a deathbed wedding by compromising his number one with his sailor's farewell: 'Kiss me, Hardy!'

And Sidney Carton heading for the guillotine with a nonchalant, 'It is a far, far better thing I do, than I have ever done – it is a far, far better rest that I go to, than I have ever known!'

That's the way to go! With a heel flick and a nose snub at the inevitable. The dramatic last chance to upstage the critics before the curtain call on the other side of the cheesecloth.

The manner of departure highlights one of the problems with celluloid vampires. There is no final – *final* farewell. It doesn't matter how horrendous the actual departure is, there is always the knowledge that, if you stay around long enough, the staked and pulverised undead representative for Transylvania will spring, beautifully coiffeured, immaculately tailored, carmine incisors gnashing, from the vamp-trap. It's a contract to cavort for another 90 minutes before getting the disenfranchising hawthorn stake through the crisp, white shirt front once more. It may be enough to provoke a warm glow of satisfaction at the come-uppance meted out to the gruesome being who flaunts the rules, but you know it can't last. There's not been a film maker yet who can let a good idea die. Dracula is never dead, only undead until the next elaborate cinematic ritual conjures him back to post-production life.

The vampire grew up with the film industry and from Dracula to Lestat via Nosferatu and Carmilla, the image of the undead has been defined by what hits the silver screen. Is that a problem? Not necessarily.

The problem is one of definition. What, exactly, is a vampire? Is it the cool, elegant Lord Ruthven or the unmanicured, halitosis-ridden Count Orlock? Is it something that goes squelch in the Transylvanian night or a more urbane figure that strolls down Piccadilly, wearing John Lennon shades, with an eye to a pretty ankle or a bouncing bustle? The love-lorn Carmilla or the libertine Lestat?

Did the aristocratic vampire have an active social life before Bram Stoker stuffed himself with crab thermidor, tucked Henry Irving into bed and nightmared Dracula into existence?

Can Bram Stoker be condemned as a plagiaristic literary vampire, sucking the life-force from an entity first transfused into life by the dashing Lord Byron? What was the truth about Dr. John Polidori's publication of the first modern-style vampire story in 1817, just a year after the opium-spotted holiday in Switzerland at the Villa Diodati with the vampire role model Lord Byron, the poet Percy Bysshe Shelley and Mary Shelley, the creator of *Frankenstein*? Where does *Varney The Vampire* come into the picture and what does he bring to the vampire legend as we know and love it?

Every major writer from Baudelaire to Yarbro has poked and prodded at the precedence of the Undead and each has added and enriched the final product in all its bloody incarnations to a point where the original life-threatening propensities have reached a vortex of confusion. Dracula, Orlock or Lestat occupy the mind and speculate on the shape of things to avoid. To treat them with less than the literary respect they deserve would be, for me in particular, to chew on the fingers of the hand that fed me. My problem with the written vampire is that it is usually portentous, pompous and past my understanding. What I have attempted is to take a look at the vampire legend without reverting to the morbid style of the king, Bram Stoker. A dish of Rice rather than a platter of Polidori.

The vampire archives are so stuffed with books, plays and films that it would be impossible to cover everything – assuming I knew what everything was. My intention is to swirl a cloak through bloody nooks and bat-filled crannies and record the way I see the perpetually burgeoning genre. To challenge the voice that whispers at the back of my head that things used to be better in 'my day'. I like Dracula's 'I'm me - stuff you!' that Bram offers. It's probably because I've got a father complex.

Before I get around to a post mortem on the unliving body of the fractious Count, a look at the vampire before he, or she, became a celluloid interpretation of the necromantic scene seems a reasonable way to progress.

The framework for the vampire story was firmly welded into place in the nineteenth century. Tales of blundering, rank-smelling bodies stomping around distant villages were rife and most thinking people were willing to accept the proposition that there were vampires amongst us. Then the twentieth-century's Anne Rice came along and, without destroying the legend, brought it forward and spruced it up so that it now stands, fashionably clad and immorally acceptable, on the brink of a new century.

The advent of the 'slash and faint' movies of the Eighties made the metamorphosis to a grander life-style necessary. Can you imagine the sophisticated Lestat spending his Saturday nights in a Whitby graveyard with the mithering Lucy or the technology-obsessed Mina?

But the vampire's genesis was far away from the North Sea squalls of the Yorkshire coast or the mosquito swamps of New Orleans. Exactly where is hard to nail down. India, China, Greece and the island of Java all have a claim. But so do other less obvious places. A trawl through some of the possible locations for the natal country of the blood-sucking bogey-man turns up some interesting stories.

PITT IN PICTURES: HORROR OR PORNOGRAPHY

I am often asked if I particularly wanted to get into the fantasy side of the film business. I'm not so sure that there isn't a big dollop of tautology in that question. The film industry is inseparable from fantasy. You only have to look at film budgets which are now reaching, or have reached, the $200 million mark to know that. The horror side of the coin is quite commonplace in comparison. I come from a background which should have slanted me towards the macabre. I was born into the biggest horror show of the century, the brutalities of the Nazi regime, and anything after that was like a walk on the banks of the Euphrates.

My choice was relatively simple. Pornography or horror. I thought I knew more about horror.

I discovered movies in my teens. The life I saw on the screen left me dazed and wanting more. Most of the films were American. The rewards for appearing in films seemed to be enormous. I devoured every word and picture in the film magazines that worked their way down to school level. I wanted that high life I read about in the magazines. Whenever I could get away I hung around the 'theatres' which were gradually appearing all over the place. The majority were little more than porno shows

or strips and they weren't interested in a teenager with a figure like a piece of string and a father fixation. The more legitimate theatres were still looking for a role. Under the Nazi regime the theatres had to toe a very rigid 'cultural' line. The older actors and directors were still very uptight about what was right and proper and what was entertainment. The younger set, also without inner guidance, either threw themselves into impossible *avant garde* productions or bad imitations of American ones. And none of those wanted me either. Then I heard about the Berliner Ensemble run by Bertold Brecht's widow, Helene Weigel. It was the top and I had been rejected by just about everyone at the other end of the scale. Youth has its uses. One of them is the capacity to take rejection and come back for more. I dolled myself up in actress gear and practised my smouldering Marlene Dietrich look. It took me half a dozen attempts to get past the assistant director whose job it was to fob off the likes of me. Perhaps Helene was impressed by my persistence because finally I got an audience with her. I had tried out all sorts of audition pieces and none of them had worked. I decided to throw the textbook away and go for it. I gabbled some nonsense and made facial expressions that would have scared a

gorilla to death. Helene took pity on me and waved me to a halt.

I was in! As a coffee maker. I didn't care. I knew that my natural overwhelming talent would soon assure my name in lights and I would be on my way to the fabled land of Hollywood. My mother didn't see it that way but, after a lot of argument and sulking, agreed that I could try the Ensemble for a short while. If it didn't work out I was to go and learn a proper job. I agreed. There was nothing else I could do. But I had my fingers crossed so it didn't count.

After the Berlin Wall was erected I was cut off from the Western Sector. At first it wasn't too bad but it became more and more restrictive and I was forced to leave. My departure wasn't exactly planned. A happy accident really. It led to me walking up the aisle with an American Army officer, the birth of my daughter, Steffanie, and living in America. My husband wanted to be a general and I wanted him to be a husband. I hated being the good little wife without anything to do. He went off to the Bay of Pigs and I packed my bags and headed for the hills! I joined a theatre group touring the States. The company eventually went belly-up and I was out on my neck with a few clothes, a little baby in a carry-cot and a beaten-up Oldsmobile. I decided that the time had come for me to return to the old world and give them the benefit of my talent and my experience. I didn't have the airfare but with the help of the taxi drivers at Kennedy Airport, who cleaned up my old banger, I flogged it to a German family who had just arrived. My intention was to go to Italy but I was tired and didn't feel like hanging around the airport in case the car broke down and the Germans returned and demanded their money back. So Steffanie and I took the first flight out. That happened to be going to Madrid!

DISCOVERED

I never believed those stories about actresses being discovered in a fish and chip shop (Christine Norden) or in Swab's drugstore (discovering Lana Turner seemed to be Merve Leroy's greatest claim to fame) but it actually happened to me! I was living in the famous Calle Doctor Fleming in Madrid. I had never seen a bullfight and let someone persuade me to go along one Sunday afternoon. It was awful. At first I was quite taken by the spectacle. All those handsome young men in skin-tight trousers parading about in the hot afternoon sunshine displaying their lunch-boxes, got me thinking libidinous thoughts. Then the *picadores* started planting colourful *picas* in the bull and the blood started to flow. While the *banderilleros* did their stuff I was still caught up in the razzmatazz and let myself go with the flow of excitement all around me.

I was sitting at the front and had a clear view when the *torero* planted his sword between the blood-soaked shoulders of the bull. It wasn't a good kill. The poor bull staggered around, a dirty great sword sticking out of its neck, blood gushing out of its mouth, its lungs sliced in two. It sank to its knees, struggled to get to its feet again but couldn't make it. Then it fell on one side and lay still. All in glorious, smelly-rama Technicolor. I couldn't believe it. I have seen a lot of pain and fear in my time but never anything to equal what had just happened. My reaction was photographed by one of the news-hounds and appeared next morning on the front page of Spain's leading daily paper, *El Pueblo*. Ana Mariscal, film director, saw the picture and decided she must have me to play the dippy Americana tourist in her up-coming film – *Los Duendes De Andalucia*. Fortunately the photographer had taken my name and was able to contact me. A few days later I was in the studio having a screen-test. Ana said she loved me and overlooked the fact that my total Spanish vocabulary ran to half a dozen words. I got the part and frantically rehearsed, phonetically, for my first shoot. I wasn't exactly confident but I was hopeful that I had more or less mastered the dialogue when I arrived on the set. Only to be told that the script had been changed. Slightly. I nearly threw up. Ana calmed me down and assured me that everything would be alright. There was nothing I could do but trust her so I stood where she told me, avoided the furniture and mouthed a load of incomprehensible gobble-de-gook when I was told. The rest of the cast were great. They were so anxious that I should get it right that they stood off camera, mouthing my words, hoping to mesmerise me into getting it right. It couldn't have been too bad. The film played for years in Spain and other Latin countries. It also helped me to get a toe-hold in Spain. I realised that if I wasn't to waste a golden opportunity I had to learn Spanish – but fast! I was the original 'Learn Spanish in 30 days' whizz-kid. I picked up a few modelling jobs and appearances on television. Then I met Arturo Ituralde who suggested I might like to front a TV show called *Aqui España*. It sounded great and was just what I needed to hone my newly acquired Spanish and let the industry know I was around. A band called Los Bravos and a singer called Julio Iglesias came on my show. I suggested to him that he should learn English and break into the international market. He, like Fernando Rey who got the same talking to, did as told and prospered...

Then came what, at the time, I thought was a golden opportunity to show off my comic talent. A film called *El Beso en el Puerto* (*The Kiss in the Harbour*). The leading man was Spain's leading pop star,

Manolo Escobar, and the movie played for three years opposite *Becket* in la Gran Via, Madrid's High Street. I can go anywhere in Spain and bands break into El Porompompero, the hit song from the film.

From my great comic debut I went straight to a short-lived job with the Teatro Nacional de España. Short lived because now I was getting offers of other jobs in the film industry. Not all of them exactly Oscar-challenging stuff but several steps, I sincerely hoped, in the right direction. The pay in the theatre is artistic satisfaction. If you want to feed yourself and whelp – forget it! Almeria was the Mecca for all the film companies looking for authentic outdoor scenery at a cut price. I persuaded them that I was a local asset. I could swear fluently in a dozen languages and worked cheap. And ride a horse? Of course! My mother had been an accomplished horse woman and optimistically named me Ingrid, which in Swedish means victorious on horseback. (Where I grew up horse riding facilities were in short supply. Any horse that had ventured near us would have ended up in a cooking pot rather than as a plaything for the kids.) The film companies needed women who could ride and fall off horses and I was over qualified in at least the latter department. I loved working on Spaghetti Westerns, American Westerns, any Westerns. There were so many Westerns being shot in Almeria they sometimes got their Indians mixed up and just exchanged their rushes. I got to work with great guys like Charlie Bronson, Bob Fuller, Burt Reynolds, Thomas Milian, Fernando Rey, Jose Bodalo, Stephen Boyd, etc. etc. The productions were good fun and the production companies were willing to spend a bit of money. There were so many films going on that it was like the Indian film industry. You could fall off a horse on one set in the morning, get thrown down a flight of stairs on another in the afternoon and be beaten up on a third in the evening. I was a qualified stunt girl by now and still had to do my TV show. Sometimes I was so bruised I couldn't climb up on my high chair to do my chatter. It couldn't last. When I finally got a chance to work on a film as a proper actress I could have wept if I hadn't already been crying over a fresh set of bruises.

the first horror film

I heard, between being thrown by a horse and being drowned in a river, that 20th Century-Fox were looking for a young woman exactly like me and off I went to Tinseltown. The whole story turned rather sour when I got to the Beverley Hills Hotel and found the cupboard in my room full of men's suits. I demanded another room and waited. The 'casting agent' turned out to be a casting couch attendant and I was on the street without a job, a place to live or money. It wasn't a new storyline for La La land and I should have been around long enough not to have got sucked in. I got a job in a Spaghetti House on Sunset as a plum cake baker and cooked the occasional spaghetti. This is how I met Willy Wilder, the great man who totally changed my life forever. Willy Wilder, I thought, was a great American director. He wandered into the saloon looking for a slice of my incredible plum cake. It was only after the third slice that I discovered that Willy was in fact Billy's somewhat less talented sibling. The film Willy talked to me about was to be made in the Philippines. I played the part of a peroxide blonde, married to an artist and having a *techtel mechtel* with the guide taking us on a recce in the jungle. Nasty things start happening and it becomes

obvious that something very obnoxious is lurking down by the river. The film was called *The Omegans*. It appeared to be about some other-dimensional beings that manifest themselves in the form of phosphorous paint. This phosphorous paint dried out anyone who was daft enough to come into contact with it. Budget-wise it was a great monster. No prosthetics, no morphing, no special effects. Just a dab of luminous paint or a flash of light and a lot of talk and you had this terrifying, invincible monster.

The film had a whole heap of problems. I lived on a house boat by the side of the river. At times it was hard to tell where the rain stopped and the river began. We had to be ready to shoot the moment there was a dry spell. Sometimes we just sat around for days and watched the rain. It was incredibly scary. They have headhunters in the Philippines. Before a man gets married he has to offer a head to the father of the bride... I demanded a bodyguard who slept on the floor in front of my bed. He also got rid of the leeches I picked up standing waist-deep in the river for hours on end while the technicians prepared to shoot a scene. He'd put a lighted cigarette on the leeches and they'd fall off. The whole thing was very nerve-wracking especially when I used to take a jeep and drive through the jungle to get to a village with a telephone to ring my nanny and speak to my child. The bloody woman would never be there. It drove me wild... but that's another story.

The whole scenario came back to me recently when I saw Robert de Niro in *Cape Fear*. It is the scene when, in the pouring rain, he heaves himself over the edge of the boat and makes his way to where the family are sitting in the salon. I had exactly that experience. Unfortunately it wasn't de Niro coming to get me but the assistant director to tell me we were packing it in for the night. I must say Willy was fantastic. Never a mean

Willy, not Billy, Wilder! On the set of *The Omegans* in the Philippines

word, no bad temper, always loved what he was doing. I wasn't too keen on squatting around in the sodden greenery with mud up over my wellie tops, but there you go – you have to suffer for your art. There were compensations. Like riding the rapids in the carved-out tree trunks used as boats. The jungle was incredible. At Pagsanhan, under a 500-foot waterfall, I had to launch myself into the dark green water for the bath of death – as it is written in the script.

I loved working on *The Omegans*. I loved the man who gave me a handshake instead of a contract over plum cake and kept his word. After I left Manila I only once spoke to him on the phone from Hong Kong and never saw him again...

Back in Spain I discovered that during my brief sojourn in the Philippines the film industry had virtually died. It was put down to the Spaniards getting too greedy and pricing themselves out of the market. I don't

know what the truth of it was. All I knew was that a great source of employment had disappeared. I spent a lot of time asking everyone I met what I should do now. Spain had also discovered restrictive work practices and formed a union – and they didn't want foreigners pinching their jobs. If I wanted to stay it meant marrying a Spaniard! That was not something I fancied. I hadn't made a lot of money on *The Omegans* and what I had was rapidly running out. Everyone suggested I should spend what I had left on a ticket to Los Angeles. I didn't really need convincing. Now I had played leading roles I wasn't keen to 'progress' to being a stand-in or a walk-on.

I took a jet to the City of the Angels. There I met a man who told me he had this big time agent Kohner and I should go and see him. I took him at his word. At the back of my mind was the thought that I would star in a film or two, buy a house on Sunset and ship my family out. Kohner was a bit of

a disappointment. I wanted film and he offered me what was then the despised medium of TV. I needed the bread and the first series I was offered starred John Mills and Ralph Meeker. It was quite a nice part, the lover of a travelling judge with a gun slinger sidekick ready to draw any time the opportunity presented itself. But I was made for better things. Kohner came up with *Ironside*. *Ironside* was a top TV series and I was warming to the idea of television. I wasn't warming to Hollywood though. It was alright but everything had a price and unless you were willing to meet it you didn't have a chance. And there were no guarantees that if you paid a premium you were going to get the goods. My salvation came at a card game.

The legendary stuntman, Yakima Canutt, was still the top man at this time, 1966-67, and carried a lot of weight with the studios. Ralph Meeker rang me up and invited me to a poker game at Yakima's house. I was feeling lousy but I still believed that if you stood close enough to the glitter some of the gilt would rub off. When we reached Yakima's house things began to look up. Sitting at the big green baize table in the conservatory were three or four men – and John Wayne. This, I decided, was going to be my night. Ignoring my blocked sinuses and Rudolph the Reindeer nose, I primped and giggled and let it be known what a cool cat I was. Nobody, especially the Duke, noticed. I was getting decidedly pissed off. All they wanted was someone to pour the drinks. Even Meeker hadn't fluttered an eyelid in my direction since we entered the room. So I plonked myself down in a vacant seat and wanted in. Very soon my meagre pile had all but disappeared. Only Yak's intervention stopped me losing the lot but I was getting the distinct feeling that I was inhibiting the lads in their bonding. And in the cheroot

smoke-filled room my sinuses were taking their revenge.

Yakima got me a taxi, Big John Wayne wished me luck and Meeker ignored me. I guess the streaming eyes and runny nose coupled with a voice that sounded as if it was being strained through several layers of wet coconut matting put him off. As I settled miserably into the corner of the taxi Yak leaned in. 'There's a big picture MGM are setting up in London,' he said. 'There's a great part in it for you. Brian Hutton's directing it. Tell him I told you to get in touch. It's called *Where Eagles Dare*.' I thanked him but put the idea of calling anyone aside while I considered the pleasure of just curling up and dying.

Next morning the flu was with me but the voice wasn't. Luckily my enthusiasm had returned so I got Kohner to set up the meeting with Brian Hutton at MGM. They were all most helpful. Brian was cutting a film he had shot in Mexico and agreed to see me at MGM. I couldn't talk and whispered that Yak had sent me. I took my best still out and wrote 'Heidi' all over it and put it in front of him, smiling sweetly.

Later I called him in London and suggested I should come over and see him. He said he always liked pretty girls to come and see him and that decided me. A great reason to go back to Europe with a great excuse. I had been without my baby too long. It was time to return to Europe and take a chance. I turned up at the Windkast production office in Tilney Street. It was decided that I would do a screen test and that I was to stay at the Hilton Hotel. I couldn't afford it but no way was I going to lose a golden opportunity. I had met actor Stephen Boyd again on the plane coming over and we had a few dinners together at an 'in'-restaurant, the Trattoria Terrazza. Stephen suggested I watched him play poker

Heidi – the face that launched a career

at the Pair of Shoes, which was just around the corner from the hotel. Of course, I had to recite my history as a big time poker player and dropped the names of John Wayne, Yakima Canutt and Ralph Meeker into the conversation as if we shuffled the boards on a regular basis. I guess I overdid it a bit because by the time we bellied up to the table I had agreed to take a hand or two. It soon became obvious that, although I talked an excellent game, I was a little short of match experience. I soon had to jack my hand in and claim that luck wasn't with me that evening. Everyone was very polite and didn't question my use of the word luck.

When it was time to go I was relieved. Now I could go back to the hotel, pack my belongings and do a moonlit flit. I barely had the bus fare to the airport. As we passed the roulette table Stephen stopped and put a few chips down in one of those complicated arrangements that gamblers do because they think it gives them a better chance of winning – and he won! He tossed me some chips and suggested which options to take. I did as I was told – and won! This was it. The magic formula. I couldn't lose. As I was about to bet the barn, he leaned forward, scooped up the pile of chips in front of me and thrust them in my grateful hands. 'Quit while you're ahead,' he advised sagely. I forgave him the cliché. In the last ten minutes I had gone from desperation stakes to several hundred quid – and in the Sixties that was a lot of money.

I now had the funds to stay and do the screen-test. It was awful. Although it wasn't allowed, I sneaked into the projection booth and watched. I should have gone back to Madrid. I called Brian and begged him to let me do it again. He just said 'That'll teach you. Go home!' I couldn't believe it. I had ruined the best opportunity I'd ever had to land a big budget international film with MGM!

Back home I kept ringing the production office and got the news that the film was now setting up in Austria and that an application for my work permit had been refused. Also they were seeing 299 Austrian hopefuls in Salzburg. I couldn't stand it. I finally found out that another application had been made to Equity and the Home Office. It looked hopeful.

Then came the day when I went to the hairdresser and as my hair was being washed, my daughter Steffka came in and told me to get to the airport – I had the job and had to leave immediately. My God – I'd made it! I'd got the job! A multi-million dollar international MGM production with Richard Burton, my idol, and Clint Eastwood. I could hardly breathe. I grabbed Steffanie and dashed up the stairs, two at a time.

When I got to London there was a snow storm and the car picking me up couldn't get to Elstree to collect my costumes. I went straight to Munich. As I walked into the foyer I saw Clint Eastwood propping up the bar. Jeezuzz, I thought, I could do with a drink and sidled up. 'You must be Heidi,' he grunted between his permanently clenched teeth. He later asked me to come to the Bambi ball in Munich but I was scheduled to shoot the next day and had to sort out my costume. I wondered if he believed me and would ask me some other time. I sat up most of the night cutting a blouse down and making a waistcoat smaller. Next day, after a hair-raising drive along icy mountain roads through driving snow I arrived at the location in Lofer. Brian Hutton opened the car door, smiled and said 'Hi kid – so you finally made it.' I just gave a forced smile. I was so incredibly happy that my heart was acting like an oversized Mexican jumping bean. I was told to go and wait in a shack that was doubling as a distinctly primitive

Green Room. As I opened the door I was set upon by a pack of dogs. My cursing and kicking was interrupted by a deep resonant voice from the darkness. 'You must be Heidi.' Clever, I thought. Now get the bloody dogs off me! It was Richard Burton and the dogs belonged to Liz Taylor who was visiting the set.

It was my big break, but I don't think I really exploited it the way I should have. First there was the billing. Elliott Kastner promised me the valued 'introducing Ingrid Pitt', but it wasn't in the dopey contract the great Mr. Kohner had negotiated in seconds on the phone and Elliott had forgotten about it. Then there was the hair. Mary Ure wanted to be the only blonde, so I got the dark stuff.

The bad dyeing process nearly cost me my crowning glory and I looked like a mouse all the way through the film. Shooting went well except for the usual unavoidables and cock-ups – like the snow melting on the last day of shooting and having to be painted in on the negative, which added a million dollars to the budget, I believe.

When it was finally released I was asked to tour the world making personal appearances. Wow-wee, I thought. Big mistake! While I was out there modelling Heidi's dirndl for the world's press I wasn't capitalising on my part in the film. I should have been in LA dragging my tail around the studios. Then I met Jimmy Carreras.

21

hammer daze

My part in *Where Eagles Dare* had put me on the list for premieres, cocktail parties and three-minute spots on television. I was doing my stint at the premiere of *Alfred the Great* when, at the after-film party, I happened to sit next to Jimmy Carreras. I hadn't a clue who he was and I can't remember going gee whiz and slapping my thigh when he told me he produced horror films. My horror films in Spain and the Philippines were still with me like a bad case of indigestion. But he was a producer and I was a budding matinee queen so I let him know I wouldn't turn him down if he asked me to star in one of his little pictures. You've got to remember, I'd just done this huge Hollywood saga and I was still thinking like that. "Drop in and see me tomorrow," he said. "Ten o'clock."

I'd heard it all before but I wasn't doing anything and I'd just bought myself a new maxi-coat and a floppy brimmed hat so I togged myself up and braved the wind and snow and made for Wardour Street. I was rushed straight into Jimmy's office. I had developed the full brashness of youth by now so as soon as I stood inside the door I took my floppy hat off and let my long blonde hair tumble over my shoulders. Just to let him get the full inventory I eased out of my long coat to reveal my very mini-skirt and tight – but tight – sweater. Get the picture? Jimmy did. 'I've got three parts for you,' he said. I tried not to faint or fall at his feet. Three films – just for wearing a floppy hat. I was soon a little tiny bit miffed. It was just one film but three roles – Carmilla, Mircalla and Millarca. Okay, so it wasn't a series but it was a start.

The Vampire Lovers was scripted by Tudor Gates from a famous short story, *Carmilla*, by Sheridan Le Fanu. When I left Jimmy's office I went straight to the book shop and bought the book. I was a little disappointed in it, to tell the truth. It seemed very languid and talkie. When I got Tudor's script I could see the potential instantly – although it didn't strike me as being a film about lesbianism. I thought it was a story about a young lady, loving by nature, who had a particularly unfortunate dietary problem. It was great fun making the film in spite of the fact that there was a potential recipe for disaster built in. All those would-be-leading-ladies on one film could be a nightmare – Dawn Addams, Kate O'Mara, Pippa Steele, Madeline Smith and me. I reckon we must have been a pretty mature bunch of pulchritude. I can't remember there being any bitchiness or 'her dressing room's bigger than mine' complaints. A lot of the credit must go to director Roy Ward Baker. He was a real sweetie and never got into a flap or made demands that couldn't be met. It could have all been so different. Neither Maddy nor I had bared our all on celluloid before. It didn't particularly worry me but I think Maddy had a few reservations. I had the attitude that, hell, I've got a good body so why keep it covered up. When I'm old and wrinkled I'd be able to say to my grandchildren 'what d'you think of the old bat now?' And it's worked out just like that.

I'm often asked why I didn't do the sequels, *Lust For A Vampire* and *Twins of Evil*. The main reason was that I was getting lots of other offers and couldn't fit it all in. Happy days. There was also that fact that after *The Vampire Lovers*, where Carmilla was the main character, the other two had diminished roles. And I was making *Countess Dracula*. I really thought it was great. Wonderful sets, fabulous costumes, a story that would peel tiles off a mortuary wall and a prime director, Peter Sasdy. The sets were purloined from the historical mega-epic *Anne of a Thousand Days*. Some of the costumes had come that way as well. It could all have been so great. Unfortunately, there was a little problem of what exactly we were making. Carreras wanted another Hammer Horror – Sasdy wanted an historic set piece. It wasn't easy. At times I found myself the whipping boy between the producer and the director. Sasdy has a lot of talent but I don't think *Countess Dracula* is a film he used a lot of it on. He didn't even like the title. Perhaps he was right in that respect, but if you're shooting a Hammer film you've got to put up with the title and the poster having very little to do with what hits the screen. There was also the problem with the blood. It seemed a bit ridiculous to me that I exposed everything for a blood-bath then prodded fairly futilely at the jiggly bits with a practically dry sponge. I wanted to have the virgins strung up overhead, have their throats cut and let the gore shower over me. That's what Erzebet Bathori, the character the film was based on, did. If only!

moving on

Hammer were pretty much finished by this time. Slasher films, gushing the blood *Countess Dracula* lacked, were coming into vogue and the Hammer output was beginning to look horribly dated. A valiant, but doomed, attempt to capture an audience easing into micro skirts and kipper ties was *Dracula A.D. 1972*. By A.D. 1983 it was dated and almost unwatchable. It's taken another 15 years to mellow the prime colours and kinky hairdos to bring it back into fashion.

In spite of the evidence that Hammer were flagging, rival company Amicus decided that horror was their thing and they were the natural successors. *The House That Dripped Blood* was an exploitation title even

if the film was more conventional than the title. Originally I was going to do the first of the four-story compendium. Then I talked to Peter Duffell, the director, and Jon Pertwee and they convinced me I should do the final episode: The Cloak. It was a fairly serious piece but Jon and Peter soon fixed that. We all gathered round at Jon's house in Castlenau and kicked the film around over lunch until it finished up the way you see it now. One of my favourite films.

A little aside: when we were at Jon's house there was this little boy on a three-wheel bike that kept crashing around the furniture and running over my foot. I tried to line him up for an accidental clout around the ear but never quite managed it. That little boy has grown up into tough leading man, Sean Pertwee. Too late now to belt him one, I guess.

British Lion arrived belatedly on the horror scene. Maybe *The Wicker Man* wasn't strictly horror. I'm sure Christopher Lee would argue it was something else, but Pagan rites and a finale depicting the public burning of a British bobby seems to fit the bill for me. (And the fact that both Chris and I, fresh from Hammer, were in the cast.) What I remember most about making the film was the cold. It was supposed to be the time of renewal, spring, but someone had got their calendar wrong and we were shooting in winter. All that prancing around naked in the churchyard was very goose-pimpling. Poor old Eddie Woodward had a particularly bad time of it. If you're doing the bit around the gravestones it's fairly simple. You stand in your positions huddled under blankets, fur coats and hot water bottles until someone calls 'Action!', then you dump your protection, wriggle about until you hear 'Cut!' and then dive back under the blankets. Not our Eddie. His endless barefoot jaunts across the Scottish hills dressed in a chemise took some doing. It seemed like an eternity before the 'Cut!' was sounded and he would come running and stick his bare feet under my frock, freezing my thighs in the process. I was heavily into yoga in those days and would sit around in the lotus position pretending not to have a goose-bump anywhere on my body. Greater love hath no woman than she will sacrifice her warm thighs for a fellow thespian. Britt Ekland also had a problem. I've heard it said that she refused to do the naked dancing because it was rude. To be fair to Britt, it was

South American adventure.

probably something to do with the fact that she was pregnant at the time. After all, she is Swedish and they're not normally reticent about getting their kit off in a good cause.

Nobody Ordered Love is a film I've become obsessed with lately. It's obviously a case of absence makes the heart grow nostalgic. I've never seen the finished version and the more time passes the more I want to see it. It was quite a nice story about a past-it actress trying to do away with her up-and-coming rival. Played out on a film set about World War One, it had a nice Truffaut

atmosphere to it. Then the money man pulled out for reasons unknown. Although it is rumoured that the main man talked through a mouth full of cottonwool and wanted to make offers you couldn't tell the tax man.

Anyway, a film was cobbled together and put out on the Rank circuit. Now it gets a little murky. The producer/director, Robert Hartford-Davis got a bit of wind in his water, stuck the tins of film under his arm and headed West. There he married and tried to keep a low profile. Not low enough, it seems. He died in mysterious circumstances and the tins of film went missing. Since then I've tried on every occasion to find the movie, but, like a couple of other films of mine, it seems to have gone beyond recall.

There were a few other films about at this time. *Parker*, *Transmutations*, *The House* directed by Mike Figgis which set him on his path to Hollywood glory, and *Hannah's War* – but we don't talk about these...

By this time I was getting ideas above my station. I wanted to write. I had already done the odd tract or so on Native Americans but now I had a yen to see my name on the cover of a book.

I was having trouble with a man I had carelessly married a couple of years earlier. He was a big wheel in the film industry and had told me that if I left him he would 'see that I never worked again'. All good melodramatic stuff. The sort of thing someone says in the heat of the moment but is powerless, or hasn't the will, to carry out. Unfortunately, I had picked the wrong guy. There was a deafening silence from my agent as the word got around that I was worse to touch than poison ivy. I eventually had a film set up to shoot in Turkey. I'd had the jabs, bought the suntan lotion and was waiting for the ticket when my producer turned up at my house. He had been warned off! If he

Ingrid with James Philbrook in *The Prehistoric Sound*

employed me his film wouldn't see a screen anywhere in the bought-up, bolted-down world. I didn't blame him for chickening out. He had investors to satisfy. I didn't need to be put through a mixer to know I had to get away for a while. I met somebody who convinced me that the Southern Hemisphere was the place to be so I hopped aboard a Boeing 707 and jetted off to Argentina.

southern adventure

I loved Argentina. And still do. In quick succession I did spots in various films which have been all but aka'ed out of business. The first was a sort of South American *bandito* type film. Generals overthrowing the government, setting up a repressive regime and then in turn being overthrown by a mouthy girl whose father had been

The author
and Judy
Huxtable in
Robert
Hartford-
Davis'
*Nobody
Ordered
Love*
1972

wronged. This was followed by a werewolf story with religious overtones. Before they could hit the screen Isabel Peron got the chop and generals with a puritanical streak took over the country and proceeded to murder anybody they didn't like. *Las Madres Lloronas* still turn out every week at the Plaza de Mayo, with placards showing the faces of their missing children and demanding that something is done about the people who murdered them. The films disappeared and were not seen for years, although I have had letters recently from people saying that they are turning up on TV and in pampas cinemas throughout Argentina.

Somehow the Generals equated me with the mouthy girl in one of the films and I was warned to get out of Buenos Aires. I flew back to England on the last flight before they closed the airport. Three months later I was back at Ezeiza airport with an appointment to see an admiral who had taken over the film industry. I ran several projects past him but he had so many hang-ups that an adult film was out of the question. We finished up with a compromise. We would shoot a film called *La Nina Gaucha*; I would play a wicked housekeeper and my daughter Steffanie would be the little Gaucho girl of the title. When it was finished we were going to be allowed to dub it into English for European and American sales. A pipe dream! For one thing they have a completely different approach to film making. Different – not necessarily inferior – but not for distribution outside Latin America. But I went along. I had an Argentinian backer by this time who had just left his wife and wanted something to take his mind off the break-up. We started shooting and it was going well. Time came for our backer to open the vaults. *Nada*. I went to see him. He was in tears. His wife had taken the children

away. He couldn't think of business at that moment. Monday would be a good day. So I had a bad weekend telling Hector Olivera, the producer, that the cheque was in the post. He wasn't exactly pleased with the situation but neither was I. It was even worse on Monday. Over the weekend, backer and spouse had re-plighted their troth and grabbed a jet to Paris. Not (would you believe it – yes, you would) leaving a cheque to cover the costs of filming the epic. I managed to placate Olivera by promising to leave my daughter in his tender care while I flew back to London to raise some cash. Everybody I spoke to said they would love to help out – in, say, three or four months. Right then they had long pockets and short fingers. Olivera was, meanwhile, still filming but when I arrived back in BA, fundless, he pulled the plug. I tried to convince him that if he gave me the film we had already finished I could get the rest of the money in London. He wouldn't listen and we parted company. There didn't seem much point in staying on in South America. Anyway, it was becoming downright dangerous. When I first went there it was pretty bad but by this time it was frontier stuff. Maybe the contract out on me in England would have expired by now... Regretfully I booked a flight across the Atlantic.

home again

If there was a change it was for the worst. My old *alma mater* seemed to hold out a little hope. They were making a TV series, *Hammer House of Mystery & Suspense* and producer Roy Skeggs suggested I wrote a vehicle for myself. That was very ego-soothing. The result was *Osmosis*. Another woman with a problem who finishes up dead. Hammer scheduled it for the following year and, wouldn't you know it, the

American backers Fox made a hurried withdrawal.

I did a few TV shows and occasionally some brave soul would give me a bit in a film but I mainly worked out my frustrations on stage and writing. A theatre production company, TRIP, was founded and toured the provinces with such blockbusters as *Duty Free* and *A Woman of Straw*. I did manage to pull a stroke that set the trend for others to follow. British Caledonian were an enterprising air travel company operating out of Gatwick. I convinced them that backing a travelling stage company gave them access to every town in Britain that had a theatre. They liked the idea and we looked like being a success. We even did a tour of South America very successfully. When we returned, triumphantly I felt, we were met with the news that British Caledonian were going out of business. Another company I had put the death hand on. But I still had my writing. I bashed out *Cuckoo Run, Pigeon Tango, Katarina, The Perons, Bertie the Bus, Bertie to the Rescue, Eva's Spell* and a number of other books in quick succession. *Cuckoo Run*, published by Futura, was picked up by a Spanish TV company as a basis for a series. The boss of the station bought an option on the spot for a pittance and promised that as soon as he returned to Madrid he would formalise the agreement and send more loot. He returned to Madrid all right, but instead of sending a contract he dropped down dead. I was beginning to get the feeling that maybe, unknowingly, I was a real live vampire.

While I was getting myself ensconced in the fantasy scene I was also having the occasional outing in my other favourite genre. *Who Dares Wins* was a direct result of the SAS storming of the Iranian Embassy I remember it well: a sort of mini 'what were you doing when you heard Kennedy had

been asssasinated'. When the black-clad figures swarmed over the embassy I was watching a John Wayne film – *True Grit*, I believe. I'm afraid the Duke lost out to our boys in balaclavas. It got to producer Euan Lloyd too. He lived around the corner from the embassy and watched the whole event as it happened. He was so thrilled with it all he went and registered the title the next day and won the rights to make the film before the cockney sparrows had tuned in their chirrup.

That was how the film got off the papyrus and onto the screen. How I got the part of the baby-bashing terrorist is entirely due to Ian Botham! Euan was about to leave his office in Twickenham Studios when I called him and asked him round to lunch. He agreed. When I opened the door he pushed past me with a curt 'hello, where's the television?'

He sat enthralled as Botham carved an entire totem pole in cricketing history. This was the 1981 third test at Headingly when he scored 149 not out – when the English team stood, in well practised stance, with their trousers round their ankles. Beefy belted shots to all points of the arena and England staggered into the limelight, unable to believe what had happened.

Euan was also in staggering mode. As he passed me on his way to the door I ventured a 'what about the film?!' Dazedly he nodded. Easiest film I ever got. No audition, no arch dialogue – just a barrage of boundaries from Botham.

A couple of years later I got another 'nasty' part from Euan – *Wild Geese II*. This wasn't so happily resolved. I got the job alright, but by this time I fancied myself as a bit of a writer. The script called for me to be shot – again. I rang Peter Hunt (the director) and suggested that when I was cornered by John Glenn I should flip my skirt aside to reveal a knife strapped to my thigh. In an

The vampire aristocracy – super-imposed Pitt and Lee

exciting, beautifully choreographed knife-fight later I could be stabbed dramatically in the cleavage and expire spectacularly in a welter of blood. Hunt loved it. Ten minutes later Euan rang. The script was the bible and if I didn't like it I could wander off into the sunset. I climbed down hastily and got shot as per the script. And then Richard Burton died, and so did the film. Edward Fox took over just in time and everything else didn't matter...

By now I had swallowed the writing bug. Timidly I approached Hammer with my latest offering, *Dracula Who...?*, a story about a vampire who is tired of waking up to find someone trying to stick a dirty great tree trunk through his pristine shirt-front and decides to get out of the business and become a vegetarian. His wife – the Countess – wants none of it and pursues him across space and time in an effort to bring him back to the old ways. But they find someone else is muscling in on the fangs business and nearly get caught in the fall-out from the problems the unknown vampire conjures into being.

A few years ago my ex-husband died and people who hadn't spoken to me for years suddenly found the power of articulation. Now I'm getting back into what used to be called 'the groove'. Not to be confused with 'a rut'. Things look on the up and I'm still waiting for the next big break that will put the star back on the dressing room door.

Well, that's more than enough about me – let's talk about vampires.

Dracula (Gary Oldman) in Coppola's major 1992 remake

PART ONE: VAMPIRISM AROUND THE WORLD

When students of the vampire want to make a point and prove that Dracula has a provenance that can be verified in historic archives, there are always two mouldering examples disinterred from the catacomb of time and dangled before a mesmerised audience. The first is a Wallachian Prince with a penchant for using pointed wooden stakes as suppositories – Vlad Tepes, or as he is known down at the local SM Club, Vlad the Impaler. The second is a Hungarian Countess with an unproven theory that she could arrest the ageing process with unguents not normally available on the local apothecary's shelf, Erzebet Bathori. Lizzie's speciality was tearing virgins to death and bathing in their blood. Unfortunately, there has never been a suggestion that either of these wicked people returned from the grave to bother their neighbours. It seems, then, that although they more than justified the requirement for vampire-hood during their life, they failed after death to become undead. That was left to the likes of Peter Plogojowitz and Arnold Paole. They were dead but refused to lie down and gave their family and friends a hard time until... but we'll get to them later.

The origin of the vampire is lost in the mist of myths, but it was post Jurassic Age and pre-*Jurassic Park*. Bram Stoker was a little coy on his creation's antecedents but Anne Rice, as befits a modern woman, had no hesitation in basing the vampire's homeland in Egypt. Greece, as the acknowledged centre of civilisation, at least by the Greeks, bequeathed us early accounts of lycanthropy, but made no claim to the shape-changers being seriously senior citizens. Over the centuries, the Greek shape-changers have rolled over to accommodate the triple icons of the modern horror industry, the werewolf, vampire and everyone's favourite split personality, Dr. Jekyll & Mr. Hyde – to say nothing of Elizabeth Taylor.

out of africa

Vampire-like creatures can be found on the African continent. One such is the *obayifo* of the Ashanti. The *obayifo* is omnivorous and will have a go at anything with a gill of liquid sap in it. Anyone can be a *obayifo*. You don't even have to be dead; just have the ability to leave your body at night and whiz around in a phosphorous glow. Its ability to blight a crop or bring on chronic anaemia is legendary and tribes prefer to pack up and move to another place rather than attempt to

An artist's
impression of Vlad
the Impaler

The all-star vampire
line-up: Kirsten Betts,
Madeline Smith,
Ingrid Pitt,
Kate O'Mara and
Pippa Steele

dominated by the constant damp, deprivation and poverty of a woodman's life. Each type of supernatural oppressor had its own territory. Ghouls tended to live in holes in the ground by the cemetery where they could keep a weather eye open for new arrivals. They weren't beyond ingratiating themselves into a local family, even marrying a stalwart son and having children. Usually the first indication that something was amiss was when the husband noticed his beloved wasn't eating her gruel with the enthusiasm he liked to see. Suspicion would turn to certainty after he witnessed her in the cemetery with others of her kind stocking up on calories from the dead bodies they had disinterred. A bit of argy-bargy would ensue in which the ghoul wife did her newly enlightened spouse a lot of no-good – then he would strike back, the ghoul would be defeated and the triumphant husband would go to the local fertility dance and pick himself another bride.

Demons were a whole different cauldron of nastiness. They were just evil through to their little green soul. They lived in trees, under bramble bushes, in caves and under bridges. There was no pretence about them. They waited until a tasty young *Fräulein* passed by then jumped out on her and dragged her to their bolt hole and did whatever their speciality was. Some just sat on their victim's chest and drank blood. Others had a thing about mammaries and ripped the *Büstenhalter* aside and chewed on the free-floating orbs. A few were even more sexually oriented and sported enormous phalluses, often prehensile and crammed with fangs, with which they tore the unfortunate *Fräulein* apart. Other demons just wanted to sow their seed. Their courting habits were no more refined but at least the ravaged lived to tell the tale and bear the demon-child. This was usually hideously

misshapen, covered in fur, with a mouth full of bone-crunching teeth and it invariably ate its legal father before making the rest of its mother's short life hell.

With these as co-denizens of the wooded glade the German vampire – *das Vampier* - was almost socially acceptable. Not exactly the type you would take home to *Muttie* or go on a second date with but at least you had a chance to refuse his advances. And, in some cases, if she played her cards right, a suitably endowed woman could have a vampiric makeover and take on the pivotal role. A case in point is the famous *Weisse Frau*.

Die Weisse Frau, White Lady, started life as the drudge in the household of a miller with ideas above his station. He had long lusted after the sort of life enjoyed by his local war chief (*Kriegs Häuptling*). It was a dream that he had little expectancy of fulfilling until he caught his daughter in amongst the sacks of flour, doing what came naturally, with a well set-up son of the local gentry. The miller expressed great sorrow at the desecration of his beautiful daughter whom he had hardly noticed until then and had treated worse than the donkey that turned the heavy millstones. He took his case to the young swordsman's father. All the old boy wanted was a quiet life so he put his son and the miller's daughter through a form of marriage and went back to oiling his leathers.

The young scion of the forest baron soon tires of the uncouth miller's daughter when her belly swells and she is no longer exciting on the flour sacks. Just before the baby is born he brings in a replacement and slings his pregnant wife out to face life at the mercy of the ghouls and demons. She manages to reach her father's house, the waters break and she delivers a healthy baby. She believes that now she has the fruit of their union all she has to do is turn up at her husband's pad

and he will welcome her with open arms and they will dwell happily in a forest glade for the rest of their natural lives. That's not the scenario as far as the young master sees it. He is too young, talented and libidinous to settle down with Hildegard, the miller's daughter. Weeping and wailing she returns to her father's mill. He's not happy to see her either. His short-lived dreams of being socially acceptable have foundered on her inability to keep the local squire's son hot and he is not amused. Homeless and hungry she staggers along a trail through the trees. The sound of a galloping horse silences her snivels. Into view comes the love of her life, riding flat out on a big black charger.

Holding the baby up so that he can see it and be persuaded to come back to her, she stands in the middle of the track. A very bad move. The hot-headed lad has business elsewhere that can't wait and, with a merry laugh, rides straight at her. A flicker of surprise crosses his delicate features when his wife makes no attempt to leap aside, but what the hell. It's quicker and less acrimonious than getting a divorce. The baby is killed but the mother manages to drag herself back to the mill. Her father sees a chance to profit from the damage done to what he sees as his property and goes to see the Baron. The Baron isn't interested. He's got some hi-tech halberds to inspect. As the miller walks back to the mill

Opposite: "Yoo hoo!' Murnau set a trend that others followed in 1922 in *Nosferatu*

Delicious... Herzog's 1978 remake of *Nosferatu* with Isabelle Adjani and Klaus Kinski

a couple of foot-pads, no doubt hired by the villainous son of the Baron, slit his throat and throw him in a stream. The stream carries his body to the water wheel at the mill where his daughter finds it. It's the end for her. Her baby dead, her marriage going through a terminally bad patch and now her loving and doting father done to death, the only answer is to do away with herself. She jumps in the stream and drowns.

When the Baron hears what has happened he is a bit upset. It means that he will have to go twice as far for supplies in the future. Upset he may be but not half as upset as he is going to be. Within days there are rumours of a mysterious White Lady seen wandering around in the forest. The brave souls who have tried to engage her in a little polite conversation soon have cause to regret their garrulousness. Within days they drop down dead. The visitations became bolder and more frequent. There are stories of pigs sucked dry of blood. The baron's son has managed to find himself another wife, one with money this time who can afford to keep him in the style to which he is accustomed. She is also pregnant. As the day for the birth approaches, sightings of the *Weisse Frau* became more frequent. The father, who isn't so stupid that he can't put two and two together and come up with the malignant spirit of his first wife, takes all the old tried and trusted precautions against vampire invasion, garlic, wreath of briar, stems of Edelweiss etc, and sits outside the birthing room with his sword ready to defend his family. The baby is born, but before the happy father can sheath his sword and get into the room the birth cries of the healthy child turn into the death screams of the mother. The Baron's son again draws his sword and bursts into the room. The sight that greets his eyes haunts him for the rest of his days. The White Lady stands by the bed.

On the bed lie the remains of the mother, covered in blood and torn limb from limb by the supernatural strength of the vampire. Worse still is the bloody, partially devoured corpse of the baby hanging from the spectres' mouth. With an anguished cry the bereft father leaps forward and swings his sword at the figure of his ex-wife turned vampire. She shrieks with laughter and disappears up the chimney in a cloud of green smoke. The mutilated body of his baby son falls at the feet of the distraught father who sinks down into the welter of blood and curses the folly that brought him to that place. He needn't have worried. Whatever the *Weisse Frau* was giving out it wasn't forgiveness. Within days her grief-stricken ex-husband withers and dies.

It isn't the end of the White Lady. For years she was to be seen flitting through the trees like a giant moth. Sightings of her invariably led to a premature death and the rate of deaths in childbirth went up when she was around. There are still the odd appearances but in recent years there have been other and more immediate horrors to occupy fertile minds and she has been upstaged to a certain extent.

While the *Weisse Frau* can be viewed as a romantic, however bloody, love story, another creature from the *Wald* can only be described as 'ugh'. The *Nachzehrer* is a nasty, wart-covered creature that spends most of his life in his grave sucking his thumbs and sending out mental hate mail to his kith and kin. He knows this is wrong – thumb sucking beyond the growth of adult teeth makes for an overbite, and willing death on others is plain anti-social – so he has developed the sly habit of keeping an eye open, usually the left one, in case he gets attacked. After a while as the least robust of his ex-circle die off, he gets less and less satisfaction from telepathic feeding. He still hasn't got the guts to dig his way out through seven feet of compacted soil so he starts eating his shroud. When this proves protein free, he is not beyond actually chewing on his own flesh. This has a diminishing return. The more he chomps, the less of him there is to cannibalise others. At last he is driven to the point that comes to all of us sooner or later, the time when he has to get up off his backside and go out there and get his shroud dirty. He's not too fond of the idea of blundering around in the woods *à la* Boris Karloff, advertising his coming and giving the locals time to form themselves into a Militia, sharpening up their stakes and giving him a good going over. As with all good vampires, he is an adroit lycanthrope so he changes into a boar. A clever disguise as long as game is out of season. Soon the rest of his relatives are found in various attitudes of terminal surprise without a drop of blood in their veins.

Once the *Nachzehrer* has broken out of his grave his former shyness is forgotten. The sense of power transmitted to him by actually clamping his jaws on a pumping artery and tasting the hot red blood on his lips, makes him a bit of an exhibitionist. When things get a little dull, and he's had his fill for the night, he has been known to rush through the village shouting out the names of the quavering villagers huddled under the sheets and hoping that they will miraculously be struck stone deaf. If they don't get some rapid intervention from the gods of the forest they've had it. Anyone, who hears his, or her (a *Nachzehrer* is staunchly unisex in its dealings), name called withers and dies within days. Why the vampire should do this and deplete his sequestered supply of rich warm blood is a mystery which only he could explain, but as few people care to have an edifying conversation with this slimy piece of crud I guess we'll never know. Recruitment into the *Nachzehrer* coven is restricted. Like being born royal or a web-surfer. You can't choose to be elected. There are benefits to this, of course. There are no annual subscriptions and membership lasts until you are out-fumbled by the dire and dirty. The deficits unfortunately, appear to outnumber the benefits. There's the accommodation, for instance. Restricted room under seven feet of dank soil, disintegrating shroud mixed with decaying flesh cuisine and a thumb sucker's overbite are just some of the disadvantages.

On top of that there are the locals who object to being farmed and fornicated and sometimes try to spoil the fun. The latter-day Van Helsings, if they catch on to what is happening before the *Nachzehrer* gets to the gallivanting stage, have a number of options they can put into place to curb his lifestyle. At the dead of night the villagers go to the graveyard and listen at the grave of anyone they suspect of not rotting as efficiently as they should. The vampire invariably gives himself away by being a noisy eater and chewing on his shroud. The vampire hunters now swing into dynamic action. Quickly they dig down and expose the cowering revenant. A sharpened finger bone is driven into his watchful left eye so that he can't put the evil eye on their efforts. Next they cut off his thumbs and bind his arms to his side so he can't switch from thumb sucking to finger sucking. This part of the exorcism is really just a show of petulance. Now comes the real stopper. A gold coin is placed in the vampire's mouth and then his head is chopped off. Depending on how tired they are, the avenging villagers have the choice of either burning the body or slitting open the stomach and forcing the head, face down, into the rotting intestines. What happens to the gold coin isn't mentioned. Probably a perk for the stomach slasher and head burier.

Then all they have to do is expunge all records that the vampire ever existed and return to the hearth of their family, happy in the knowledge that they have averted a fate worse than death... Until more shroud chewing sounds come from the cemetery!

Then there is the *Doppelsauger*. This is very much like a *Nachzehrer*. Coffin habits are almost indistinguishable: eats its own flesh, will try the shroud unless a method is devised to stop it, kills off its erstwhile relatives telepathically and becomes manic when it is forced to feed above ground. Means of dispatch are also similar: coin in the mouth and head lopped off with a sharp spade. Where the *Doppelsauger* differs from a *Nachzehrer* is in its incarnation. A *Doppelsauger* is not born. The latent *Doppelsauger* can go its whole lifetime without coming out of the closet. Opportunity makes for a successful transition. If it is weaned properly and never gets a chance of suckling milk from a breast again there is no problem. If there should happen to be an available nipple which comes within its grasp it is enough to turn the straight baby into the feared creature of the night – the *Doppelsauger*.

There are ways to unmask or expose a latent vampire. Spotting warts and blemishes in mystical patterns on the body are one way. Full, Mick Jagger-like lips are another, and that old standby for identifying a vampire when all else fails – flexible limbs.

Finally, there's the *Alep*. It's not the last vampire in the pit of the undead but it's interesting. It's a vampire that thinks it's a demon, or vice versa, and wants to be a chevalier. As blood-drinking is its ultimate aim, the *Alep* could be classified as a schizophrenic vampire. It could also get into a sub-division as a were-pig. The usual hunting ground for a proselytising *Alep* is a leafy country lane. It ambles along in a swirling cloak with a large floppy hat on its head which hides its blood-red, iris-less eyes and lipless mouth. Its particular predilection is for young, virile ploughmen. These it engages in conversation and offers advice. It is an expert at repairing pieces of equipment that have seen better days and never accepts anything in return for all the favours it confers. All the creepy old revenant wants is to be invited home for a fireside chat and bite to eat – preferably from any babies that might be under the same roof or, if that's not an option, from the friendly ploughman. This is where the *Aleps'* diversity shows up and makes other, straight-into-the-jugular vampires, look a little restricted. When the *Alep* has fandangled its way into a household it waits until everyone is asleep then turns into a snake and slithers around sucking the blood of its vulnerable hosts through their nipples. In most circumstances it usually restricts itself to the children and males of the household. This is not meant to imply that the *Alep* suffers from any homosexual tendencies. Rather the opposite. Children and men it regards as fodder, purely and simply. What it really wants is a chance to seduce the beautiful young spinsters of the parish and have a meaningful and mind-blowing relationship.

Sated by its recent repast, the *Alep* returns to its arbour in the leafy lane and chats up the local milkmaid as she trudges home with a couple of pails of milk suspended from her yolk. Gallantly it doffs its hat and offers to carry her burden and chats amicably to her as it escorts her home. At the door it excuses itself and departs. Mysteriously the milk in the pails is, at this point, discovered to be sour but no-one ever seems to make the connection with the friendly gent who carried the buckets home. This carries on for a few days, the flattered milkmaid falling further and further under

Lionel Atwill and Fay Wray in macabre goings-on in Germany in *The Vampire Bat* 1932

the spell of the smooth-talking faker. Another phenomenon occurs. The cows produce less milk and finally run dry altogether. The *Alep* is sympathetic and offers to help out. This usually means it has to move in. Things go from bad to worse, dairy-wise, and the milkmaid is glad of a sympathetic shoulder to over-react on. Now the *Alep* reveals a side which few other vampires possess. This is obviously its schizoid demon part showing through. It lures her into bed and they have a real moist, wall-banging night. Unfortunately the moisture is mostly the milk-maid's blood and the banging on the walls is mainly due to the *Alep's* enthusiastic and acrobatic love-making. Once its lust is satisfied the sexually exhausted *Alep* laps up any warm blood which may be dripping from the woman's body and goes out and looks for another ploughman to provide a good solid lunch. If the object of his fatal desire turns out to be frigid and it doesn't get to first base it doesn't curse virgins and stomp off up the hill muttering. It waits until its proposed victim is asleep, turns into a mist, probably green, and enters her body through one of her orifices. Once inside, it does what it wants to make it happy and then evacuates the body and runs off snorting in its favourite disguise of a were-pig.

Aleps have to work at getting into the club. One initiation rite requires that it eats the placenta of a still-born baby. It is also helpful if they are the seventh son of a seventh son, although this can sometimes have the disastrous effect of producing a saint. Having lycanthropic tendencies helps, but what really does it is being born with hair in the palm of the hands and a full set of teeth in the mouth. Instant *Aleph*ood!

Such a powerful vampire, especially one with such interesting side bars, is not easy to get rid of. The best thing to do is try and confuse it. One method of doing this is to buy a new pair of shoes. The old shoes are nailed up over the door, the toes pointing upwards. The new shoes are placed carefully beside the bed with the toes pointing towards the door. The *Alep* oozes into the room in one of its various forms and is brought up short by the display of footwear. While it is puzzling out what it all means, the sleeper, who was only pretending, jumps up and throws salt into the intruder's eyes. Blinded by the salt, the intended victim, now turned attacker, can leap onto the *Alep* and drive a sharpened stick into its brain through its streaming eye sockets. After that it's business as usual, decapitation, quartering and burning. And another way to get rid of the *Alep* is to steal its hat!

the vampire church

Would the recurring plagues of vampirism that haunted the fourteenth, fifteenth and sixteenth centuries in Middle and Eastern Europe have happened without the flux of Christianity? Probably not. Vampires would have stayed as a bedtime story for peasant children, carefully angled to give the adults the means to control them by frightening them to death. The Church, first in the role of guardian challenging the ignorant fear of the masses and then later as the co-conspirator and press-agent for the self-effacing vampire, set about defining the monster that knew no Christian God and was, therefore, in league with the devil. It mattered not a jot to them that the vampire sprang from communities that pre-dated the coming of Christ. In fact it strengthened the hand of the evangelising priesthood. It proved their point, if anyone dared to argue it, that Christ had saved the world from a future worse than death.

Death is what the Christian religion is all about. If Christ hadn't been crucified by the Romans he would probably only be remembered as a minor prophet – lucky to be included in the *Koran* as a footnote. Peter might have fared better. He did at least take his claims to Rome. In that case the symbol of life, the fish now used by 'Born Again' Christians, would be the mark of the new Judaism. But Jesus did die on the cross and the mark of his divinity, the event that marked him out as more than just another old-world Jewish prophet, was his resurrection.

The resurrection is as important to the Christian religion as it is to Vampirism. The qualification is death. The thing that marked out the early Christian Church, and latter-day Church as far as it goes, is its ability to take on old religions, do a quick make-over and then present the product as something essentially Christian. In many ways the church works like a giant corporate vampire. Regardless of the wishes of those it targets, it moves in and imposes its will and emaciates the body that it acquires. Just look at what happened to the Africans and Native Americans and all those virulent cultures subjected to the assault of the Christian church.

The evangelising started with the death of Jesus on the cross. As he walked in the *moonlight* he was arrested by troops summoned up by Judas. Peter promised everlasting fealty but Jesus told him that he would deny him thrice – before the cock crew.

So, after his trial Jesus is taken to Golgotha and nailed to a cross. He's still alive next day when the guards come to check his state of health. Crosses were at a premium at that time. Residents were overwhelmingly available for crucifixion and the state was happy to oblige. The Romans were good at book-keeping and had worked out how long they could afford to keep a cross occupied. Jesus was taking too long to die so the legionaries helped him on his way to his Father by plunging a spear into his side. It might be argued that the Jewish council, the Sanhedrin, and the Roman authorities were very civilised and did not bring witchcraft into the evidence that consigned Jesus to the cross. He had, after all, very recently raised the dead and fed a crowd of worshippers in very peculiar circumstances. Acts that a millennium and a half later would have resulted in the awkward situation of Christ's most fervent followers, the Inquisition, having to burn him on the same evidence.

All the actions are reasonably straightforward. Jesus is borne away by women of his family and laid in a cave carved out of the rock by Joseph of Arimathea. Joseph claimed he had earmarked it for his own interment but we have only his word that he was going to use it for that purpose.

Again, everything seems normal. Then Mary the Madonna and Mary Magdalene show up at the cave in the garden of Gethsemane. On the way there they pass a figure swathed in a cloak. They don't get a look at his face but notice that he appears to skim along – above the ground. Probably something they come across every day in that locality because it doesn't blow their mind or prepare them for something a little unusual that is about to happen.

When they get to the improvised tomb they find the huge boulder, that had been rolled across the entrance, moved aside.

Inside the cave is empty. Just a few bandages that had been wrapped around Jesus's body. Mary asks a couple of blokes who happen to be passing if they have seen Jesus around. Surprised, they ask her why she is looking for him in the place of the dead. A funny question to ask, but perhaps they had been out of town and hadn't attended the public execution.

The story is getting a little hair-raising. Who was the mysterious stranger in the garden? By whom and how was the huge boulder rolled aside. From all accounts it is not something that could be taken on lightly by a man, after hanging on a cross for a day or two and then being pierced with a spear, of less than robust health. Unless, of course, like a vampire, he had the reputed strength of ten men!

The vampire connection now gets even stronger. The closest friends of Jesus gather one night to discuss what they should do. With their number one honcho sidelined and not even a tombstone to mark the passing of a martyr, they are on the brink of jacking it all in and returning to their civvy jobs.

Then Jesus walks in, fit as a flea and ridicules them for doubting him. After all, he had only been crucified, stabbed, dead and buried. Enough to make anyone doubt, not just the cantankerous Thomas. But Peter and the rest of the lads are happy to go along with Jesus's admonition to get out there and

kick a few butts. Only Thomas, who had a date at the time Jesus was delivering his pep talk, wanted out, but somehow Peter got in touch with Jesus and arranged another meeting. This time they made sure Thomas was there. He was still a bit petulant and it wasn't until Jesus stripped off and showed his scars that Thomas agreed to go along with the others and spread the creed of the undead and encourage the eating of flesh and drinking of blood.

Jesus made a spectacular getaway, married his long-time sweetheart, Mary Magdalene, and got a royalty for every soul that was saved. Perhaps.

This is one of those 'which came first – the egg or the succubus?' riddles. Was the vampire, as a vampire, extant before the Christian Church moved in or did the trappings and paraphernalia of the Church provide a handy mould for the vampire horde? When the early Christian priest warped the rites of the pagan communities to fit his own sense of decorum was he aware of what he was doing? Of course he was. After all, the majority of them had spent most of their lives looking forward to fertility festivals and the annual burning, drowning or dismembering of the local social inadequates.

It was a two-way exchange. The Church acquired some well-loved and established festivals and the hoi polloi got stuffed. The converts to Christianity weren't fooled. They danced to the Christian drums but their feet leapt to the ancient rhythms. In the end it wasn't the Church that led the way but the congregation. They went to church, prayed to God, flipped a groat in the offertory box, confessed that they were mad, bad and dangerous to know and then went out and got on with their Morris Dancing until it was fertility time again and they could get down to some real country sports.

vampires – early examples

Once the vampire was hooked into the body of a mainstream, proselytising religion like Christianity it had to be defined. Not only defined but explained. Not an easy thing to do when one of the main ways of identifying a potential vampire is the non-corruptibility of the body in the grave. As saints were also believed to have an incorruptible body you can see the problem. Other problems stemmed from the fact that many of the priests professing to be experts on the new religion were still thinking and preaching in pagan terms. Inevitably this led to misunderstanding. If God's mouthpiece, de facto, was infallible, then Peter the Apostle and later Paul, presumably, knew what they were talking about. Maybe they did. This didn't mean that when the message got through to the foot soldiers on the frontiers the received wisdom was the same. Chinese Whispers prove that when 12 people are gathered together in one place, what number 12 says has usually got little or no relevance to what number one said.

When Clovis I, the Frankish King who murdered and corrupted his way to the throne in the fifth century, was persuaded by his sainted wife Clotilda that it was a good political move to convert to Christianity she was getting into something more far-reaching than she realised. Clovis, as he had already shown by taking on most of the top European conquerors of the age and winning, wasn't a man to do things by halves. St. Paul had laid down the ground rules and St. Peter had given the faithful a patriarchal father and taken them to the hub of the world, Rome. If Clovis was going to get into the founding house of Christianity he wanted to be remembered for something. He came up with the Salic Law. This was mainly concerned with inheritance and the

Opposite: The cross always works, though chopping off heads and stakes through the heart also seem to be universal remedies: Peter Cushing and Christopher Lee in Terence Fisher's *Dracula*, 1958

passing of titles. It seems that in spite of the good Clotilda's influence he was a bit of a misogynist and couldn't bear the thought of women getting their perfumed hands on the sources of power. There were also some observations on the workings of the Christian Church. This was probably just a sop to prevent his wife going on too much about what he was doing for the sisterhood. Now he could unctuously point to his relationship with the clergy and direct attention away from his main theme.

Predictably his rather casual approach to a subject that was beginning to be the driving force in more and more lives led to misunderstandings. The crumbling of the Roman Empire and its effects on the outer rim of Latin civilisation, leaving recently pagan communities with a half-understood religion, led to some pretty nasty re-interpretations of the Scriptures. Christ had cast out devils, he had encouraged men to eat his flesh and drink his blood and he had enjoined his followers to fight Satan with whatever means came to hand. The pagans knew about Satan. They were still keeping him on a fairly short leash in case the Jewish guy didn't work out. As most of the feast days for the evangelising Christian Church had craftily swallowed up the old festivals it wasn't too obvious when the newly liberated communities slid back to their old ways but were careful to pay lip service to the new. This meant they could piously murder and burn any poor soul that wasn't up to translating the pagan references into good Christian ethics. The priests had a high old time trapping and burning any poor sinner that didn't conform. Some old crone living in a hovel used her knowledge of herbs and incantations to cure someone whom the *cognoscenti* thought should be dead and this brought out a retaliatory streak more vicious than that of the Queen of Hearts in *Alice in*

Wonderland. Even mending your britches on the Sabbath could be disastrous if you were in the bad books of a priest or someone blowing in his ear. Luckily the Great Charlemagne, a couple of centuries later, decided to reissue the Salic Law with a few amendments. He then put his own man, Leo III, on the throne of the Vatican and ensured that his recommendations were carried out. It was a time when invasions, followed almost inevitably by plagues, were sweeping across Europe and the vampire had been lured by the Church to put its hands up as the source of most of them. Charlemagne tried to make some sense of it and proclaimed that anyone burning alleged vampires without good proof would themselves be executed. It held up until his death when he was succeeded by his son Louis I. Louis hadn't his father's zeal for fair play and the church edged its way carefully but inexorably towards the iniquities of the Inquisition.

The very fact that the church began to take such stern measures against vampires proved their existence and on the premise that there was no such thing as bad publicity the vampire took on renewed undeadedness and became the main talk of the dying classes of the Middle Ages.

By the end of the first millennium vampires had spread along the trade routes, the legacy of a now defunct Roman Empire. Northern and Eastern Europe took to the dark invasion most fervently. At times they seemed to be vying with each other as to who could produce the sickest and most monstrous bloodsucker. It was easier now to spot the monster. The vampire had gratefully taken on the role appointed it by the church and dedicated some of its favoured moves to its host. With renewed enthusiasm it went about eating bodies and drinking blood. It also took a leaf out of the

Christian testament by making converts. Real converts. Not the conceptional converts of the church but bodies with unwavering dedication to a way of undeadedness.

Slovenia offered a home from tomb for ambitious vampires. One vampire, a *Nalapsy*, even used the bell tower of a church as a hub for its activities. It was a nasty piece of work that would have been, and probably was, just as happy before it had Christianity to contend with. Probably had a gene or two of Attila in it. This vampire didn't just float around getting his teeth into a specially selected victim. This one wiped out whole communities, right down to the last dog and cat. Killing was done by laser-assisted eyeballs. One look from a *Nalapsy* and that was your lot. When the neighbourhood was strewn with dead bodies the *Nalapsy* glided in and bit off their heads and sucked them dry.

There's a rather moralistic tale of a *Nalapsy* who moved into an area where the population had been dramatically swollen by refugees flooding in from the south. Wars had forced them to try and find more amenable accommodation. They couldn't have picked a worse time. A *Nalapsy* had just taken up residence and couldn't believe his good fortune when he saw the rivers of potential meals flowing in so he moved in himself. Six days and nights it took him to get through his grisly repast. On the seventh day he sorted out a suitably overgrown cemetery and was trying to get a warm shroud up over his blood-bloated lips when the invading cavalry arrived. They were a little upset that the *Nalapsy* had robbed them of the chance to dip their sabres into the ripe bodies of the villagers and refugees, so decided to take it out on the poor old vampire who only wanted to find somewhere dark and gloomy to sleep off its trencherman meal. Luckily for the

horsemen, they had someone in the ranks who had run into vampires before and was able to bring them up to date on the most modern method of dispatching them.

First, hawthorn spikes were driven through the *Nalapsy's* temples, eyes, hands and feet. Seeds and pebbles were then forced into all the orifices of his body and his arms were bound and nettles put inside its clothes. Two of the strongest horses were unsaddled and a rope tied around each of the vampire's legs. Whipped on by their enthusiastic riders, the horses then pulled in different directions and, if they were lucky, pulled the malignant soul apart. This method was favoured because the *Nalapsy* was reputed to have two hearts and therefore two souls. If the horses didn't do their work properly and only pulled off a leg there was a probability that one of the souls might zoom off without anyone noticing and find itself a safe haven in one of the bodies it had already sucked dry of blood. Hopefully the nettles, blocked-up passages and the spikes in various parts of the body would hold up the *Nalapsy* long enough to get a good fire going and burn the body.

If there was any chance that one of the souls had got away and found a new home the bodies underwent surveillance over a period of a couple of weeks. Signs that all was not well with the cadaver were quite obvious. No rigor mortis, open staring eyes, a good colour and an over abundant growth of hair. If the hair fell in two perfectly shaped ringlets, that was the slammer. The recaptured *Nalapsy* was once more put through the trials of being man undead.

So far I've tried to get a sense of ongoing purpose into the ghouls, ghosts, demons, succubi, incubi and all the other wriggling, creeping crawling and caterwauling creatures that have fed and bred the vampire legends. Heads buzzing around trailing entrails or bloodsuckers trapped in waterfalls may seem a cosmos or two away from Dracula being lyrical about the creatures of the night. The point is that everything has to start somewhere and vampires evolved out of ancient tales of witches and warlocks. Lycanthropy wasn't an abstract notion – it was a fact. Witches had familiars in the shape of toads and black cats. And, of course, bats! There was a little confusion about just what the bats and cats and things got up to – or whether they were, indeed, the alter-ego of the witches or warlocks themselves. The Inquisitors lumped together the practitioners of the black arts as disciples of the devil. They got confessions of baby butchery, killing by the evil-eye, eating of corpses and, wouldn't you know it, blood drinking. The virtuous priests got the confessions by butchery, maiming, excommunication, the mutilation and burning (alive or dead!) of bodies and the withdrawal of the right to drink blood and eat the body of Christ.

The cases mentioned so far are just a minute portion of stories about supernatural beings whose main aim in life, or death for that matter, is to make it uncomfortable for the straight Joes out there ploughing the fields, tanning a hide or robbing a Sheriff. I've had to leave out dillies like the Irish would-be vampire, the *Dearg-dul*. The *Dearg-dul* is a beautiful woman that, at the equinox, rising in full splendour from her grave, has her evil way with as many men as cross her path before returning, sated, to her grave to await the next equinox. Then there's the *Cat of Nablishima*, a Japanese vampire that takes on the shape of its victims and then plays havoc with their lovelife. The *loogaroo* just has to get a mention. Haiti is perhaps better known for its zombies but the *loogaroo* fits in nicely. It's usually an old woman who feeds blood to the devil so that

he will help her out on the magic side of the business. The down side to her blood tapping is that the devil is a bit fickle and usually ends up feasting on his supplier.

All the stories have one thing in common. They call for a suspension of belief in the normal, humdrum, everyday life by stretching the imagination. And, because the Church condemned vampires, they, perforce, endorsed them as real, devil-serving entities.

MELROSE ABBEY

Not all vampires of the early Christian era were drawn from the ranks of the desolate and dissolute. A particularly active revenant was about in the twelfth century. Not only was he a hunting, shooting, fishing type before he died but when he wasn't slaying something or other he turned his hand to a little vicaring. So obsessed was he with riding to the hounds that he earned himself the *soubriquet* of the 'Dog Priest'. In modern times he would probably have turned his obsession towards the golf course. Overtly his day job was looking after the immortal soul of the lady of the local Knight Templar. The husband, hoping to purchase a penance or two by going to the Holy Land and delivering a few heretics up to the Almighty, was happy enough leaving his wife in the arms of the Church. Her main assets were safely padlocked and he wore the key around his neck. As soon as the crusader left, the priest convinced the pining lady that the best thing she could do to make herself feel better was to kick over a few traces. He was quite happy to endanger his immortal soul by helping out whenever he could. The lady gratefully accepted his offer and even let him use her husband's bits and pieces. Inevitably their rather casual, marriage-wise arrangement was the talk of the battlements.

Before long the priest had drunk his way through the cellar, worn out his master's britches, broken the wind of most of the horses in his stable and had saved the immortal soul of the lady by consigning it to Beelzebub.

Then, in the midst of his hedonistic life he had a few too many beverages, fell off his horse and broke his neck. The lady, understandably, was quite relieved. Her husband could reappear at the castle hearth any time in the next couple of years and claim his right to insert his key in her chastity belt. He wouldn't be too enamoured to find it hanging open and exhibiting signs of being frequently used in his absence. Whatever relief she felt was soon dispelled.

The departed priest turned up at the Melrose Abbey, his spiritual local and whose ecclesiastical jurisdiction he was nominally attached to, and found his entry barred. He didn't take this too well and shouted obscenities at the poor old abbot which got the old boy in a bit of a tizzy. But discipline won through and the foul-mouthed reverend roamed around the outer walls for a few nights, making it hell for the noviciates trying to practise unworldliness. At last the abbot got enough sincerity going inside the Abbey to convince the undead priest that he was going to get no sympathy from that quarter. He still wasn't convinced that being undead was a good thing. Unless, of course, he could still get what he wanted from the crusader's lady. The piety emanating from the lady's castle was a considerable amount less than had kept him out of Melrose Abbey so he managed to get into the bedchamber of the fair damsel. You can imagine her shock when hands, cold and smelling of the grave, began caressing her body as she slept. She awoke with her vocal chords activated and boosted beyond anything she had attempted before and the poor, bemused undead began

to get the idea that socially he was probably not as amatorially acceptable as he had been before he died. The thought hurt and he joined his former lady in screaming and carrying on to such an extent that other members of the household were awakened and burst into the room to see what was going on. They all started screaming and pointing and the ex-priest decided that he couldn't compete, so he gave them a sailor's farewell and flew out of the window.

Next morning the lady realised that she had to do something. It was all very well assuring the servants that there was nothing to worry about, but her husband was a

Welcome to my humble home, says Bela Lugosi

different matter. When he returned there would be a queue of people only too happy to tell him what had happened, and, without too much of a stretch of the imagination, what she and the ghastly ghost had been up to before he became one of the un-departed. Action was called for so she sent for the abbot who was instantly sympathetic. Hadn't he also been subjected to the abuse of his ex-associate? The abbot persuaded the lady that there was only one possible way to get rid of the hideous visitor. He would stay with her in her bedchamber and say a few appropriate words if the revenant churchman returned. The lady fell in with the suggestion but having already encountered the power of persuasion that the Church was able to command, called in a couple of her servants to demonstrate how pure her motivation was. Nothing happened for a while and the lady dismissed the servants but had to acquiesce when the abbot insisted on remaining until the cock crowed – a time when any self-respecting demon must return to its lair. It was just as well. His ex-colleague arrived on the hour, hooting and snorting and shouting wild vilification at his ex-superior. Probably thought he was taking up with the lady of the manor where he had been forced to leave off. Anyway, the abbot, being a pragmatist, had thoughtfully secreted a long-handled chopper in his habit. The priest realising that, even undead he couldn't afford to lose big chunks of himself, again made a hurried exit through the window. By this time the cacophony of screaming and shouting had roused the servants once more. They hastily made way as the abbot charged out of the lady's bedchamber waving his chopper and shouting the Lord's Prayer at the top of his voice. When he had disappeared it didn't get any quieter. The lady was giving it all her vocal chords could manage to reinforce her image as an innocent lady wronged.

Not being an experienced revenant the undead cleric headed straight for his grave. The abbot guessed that's where he was heading and trailed by servants, arrived just in time to see his prey dive into his grave and the ground close over him. Instantly the abbot realised that this wasn't as it should be and that he was dealing with something outside the scope of his day-to-day ministering. As he was deliberating with himself what he should do next, he heard the cock crow. This tidied things up considerably. The undead soul would now be contained in its grave for the hours of daylight and the clever and pious would have ample time to decide the next move. He quickly gathered together some workmen and a few of his flock from the Abbey. The diggers dug and the monks accompanied their endeavours with a few appropriate chants. When the body was finally disinterred the coffin was half full of black blood which gushed from the wounds that the abbot had inflicted on the revenant with his chopper. There was too much blood and the corpse was in too good a state, except for the chunks sliced off by the abbot, to be that of any old corpse. It was obvious that what they were dealing with was the uncorrupted body of a vampire. Vampirism was becoming very popular at this time and churchmen were in the forefront of scientific detection and destruction. The state of the corpse dictated the action. The body was taken up and carried away to an appropriate place, a fire was built and the body burnt. Just to make sure that there wasn't any nasty recurrence the Abbot ordered the ashes to be collected, shovelled into an earthenware jug, sealed with a blob of beeswax, a piece of cotton cloth in the shape of a cross with the word 'Pax' written on it impressed into the wax and the ashes taken back to the grave.

There the hole was strewn with rose petals and holy water, the jug placed at the bottom of the grave and the earth returned. Just to make sure, a cairn of rocks was placed on top and surmounted by a wooden cross.

The abbot, satisfied with his night's work, went back to the castle to report and was slightly miffed when her ladyship didn't want to hear about it. She was busy practising the story she was going to tell her husband and it wasn't easy trying to explain why the dashing priest would choose to return and select her for his haunting. The abbot returned to the abbey and told the tale to any passing minstrel or chronicling monk that he happened to meet and could be made to suffer for his supper.

The story of the beastly priest of Melrose Abbey is obviously not a story of a 'compleat vampyre'. There is no evidence that the Dog Priest sank his teeth into anyone or even tried to get it on with anyone other than the lady he was in service to. What is interesting is that the quality of the vampiric visitation has gone up. Usually the howling, screaming revenant is the result of some peasant not getting what was due to him in life and coming back and smelling up the place as a post-interment revenge. This story depicts a priest living the life of a squire who returns to try to carry on an extra-mortal relationship with his paramour. It also brings the church, in the feisty form of the abbot, into battle. The abbot of Melrose was the Van Helsing of his day. He was still preferring chopping and burning to the refinement of the stake which became the classic method of dispatching a wannabe vampire at a later date. But whatever the revenant reverend got up to in the privacy of his own tomb it was *dhampire's* play compared with Joan of Arc's playmate, Gilles de Rais.

Frank Langella in John Badham's 1979 version of *Dracula*

PART TWO
FAMOUS VAMPIRES

GILLES DE RAIS

Just what the 24-year-old Marshal of France was into is anyone's guess. He was a staunch ally of Joan of Arc and was a major contributor to the cessation of the 100 Years War. In many circles he was considered to be a model Frenchman. His off-duty activities were the same as anyone else's at that time: whoring, wining and dining, gaming and the occasional full-blown orgy with a little pederasty on the side. As a patron of the arts he had few equals and it helped to diminish the considerable fortune he had inherited. To try and restore his fortune he turned to the fortune tellers and alchemists who were always ready for a rich client with eccentric tastes. The more eccentric the better. With a little added imagination, supplied by the friendly local *shaman*, turning lead into gold seemed a reasonable proposition. Everyone knew about the Alchemist Stone and every alchemist pretended to have one. Gilles poured his fortune into keeping the chemist wealthy but hadn't time to supervise the actual conversion of base metals into riches beyond the dreams of reason. He was busy arranging parties for his friends and neighbours. Although not a vampire in the tradition of the fangs baring, cloak

swirling monster of filmland vampires, he qualified, nonetheless, as a medical vampire – a haematomaniac – of the premier division.

He had a particular penchant for eviscerating young boys and then wallowing in their entrails while he drank their blood. Hundreds of children were sacrificed to his bloodlust but, in spite of frequent representation at the Court of Reims by bereaved parents, nothing was done about his activities for years. He was able to remain secure after his part in kicking the Brits out of France and on the strength of his overbearing friendship with the Dauphin. While Charles lived he was home free. Nobody was going to point a public finger at the man who had put the king on the throne and owned estates that rivalled those of his sovereign. Gilles's problem was that he liked a spectacle. One where he could invite colleagues of a similar bent and rip a few children to pieces. And, even in the liberal 15th century, that cost money. And the alchemists were still producing excuses but no gold.

Something had to be done. Trade was out. What self-respecting chevalier could descend to the level of commercial interests? The black arts, sorcery, was the answer. De Rais started the trend towards business

conventions by putting on grand feasts. Tickets for these were much sought after and he kept the costs down by inviting his guests to bring along their own perversions. He even made a little money on the side by forcing his followers to cough up huge sums to underwrite some of his more extravagant orgies. Before long he had gathered together a salacious band of blood-drinkers and debauchers that were up to Olympic standard. Both Mount and Games.

Then the bottom fell out of his market. John of Nevers, who spent his entire life falling in and out of love with Charles VII, coerced by the more abstemious members of the de Rais clan, cut off his supplies. He only did it to spite Charles who was easily manipulated by de Rais. John, at the time, happened to be big in Brittany where, unfortunately for Gilles, most of the de Rais fortune was sequestered. Without money de Rais felt a draught in his bank-roll of typhoon proportions. Charles did a wonderful impression of a Cheshire cat and disappeared every time de Rais turned up at court and it wasn't long before all the people he had screwed on his way up were planning receptions for him on his way down. Especially the churchmen. They had looked piously heavenward while he was funding their living. Now they began to hear the screams of the children who were unwilling guests at his satanic revels. Before long the disaffected courtiers and the newly enlightened clergy got together and came up with enough evidence to really stuff Gilles de Rais, hero of France.

The Bishop of Nantes went straight to the heart of the matter. The murder and torture of innocent children meant nothing to the august churchman. He had been to quite a few get-togethers where the entertainment had been a bit – well – risqué. What really rankled was the fact that Gilles de Rais had the unbelievable insolence to whip a priest out of town when he tried to point out that there was a serious shortage of boys and he wasn't getting his share. Gilles was dragged into court on charges of heresy and murder. By a nice little point of law the Church couldn't deal with the murder charge and they weren't empowered to order a death sentence. (Shades of the Sanhedrin and Jesus). All they could do was point out that if the judiciary didn't do what was expected of them the Inquisition would look at each and every member in a most unflattering light. This sharpened up the court's perceptions of Gilles de Rais's activity considerably and they quickly returned a verdict that pleased the ecclesiastics. There is no doubt of Gilles de Rais's guilt. He boasted about drinking blood and frying livers. He was in the great tradition of the idle and powerful rich seeing their servants and peasants as no more than cattle. Indeed, in many eyes, not just your confessing rapists and pederasts, a well bred horse was worth a village of snotty-nosed peasants. The murder of the children was enough to convict him a thousand times over but not only was his trial a Church matter but there were a lot of vindictive courtiers who also wanted their penny's worth of blood-pudding. Once the torturers had their hot irons into him there was nothing he wouldn't confess to, and no crime that his tormentors wouldn't lay at his judiciously crippled feet.

Gilles de Rais was hanged in 1440 along with two of his fanciful chums. The fact that not more of his helpmeets were strung up alongside him has made many historians opine that the arrest and execution was the result of political intrigue. Although the bloody Marshal of France was in essence a sadist, the appellation of vampire sits reasonably well on his shoulders. That being true, it is one more step along the trail to the aristocratic vampire. You don't get bloodsuckers much more socially acceptable than Gilles de Rais.

vlad tepes

Gilles de Rais was the opening act. Following close on his cloven hoof prints comes the grand-daddy of them all, the Wallachian Prince, Vlad the Impaler. To be pedantic, Vlad also fails the test as an authentic bloodsucker. If there is ever a hospital dedicated to haematomania it will be called 'The Vlad Tepes Blood Clinic'. Wards will be named after Gilles de Rais and Erzebet Bathori, but it will have little to do with the myth and legends surrounding the vampires of the screen. Vlad was born around 1430 and claimed that the blood of Genghis Khan ran in his veins. To prove it he fought everyone who could put an army in the field. His speciality was sticking it to the Turks who, at that time were trying to take over Europe. He was a successful fighter and at some time or other was at war with one or more of his neighbours. Although officially he was Vlad of the Voivoides, his habit of impaling friends and foe alike earned him the nickname of Vlad Tepes – Vlad the Impaler. He also liked to sign himself as Dracula or some variation on this, his family name. Dracula meant different things to different people. Dracul can mean either Dragon or Devil. The 'a' at the end in Romanian means 'son of' and so those who were within staking distance were careful to accept Dracula as meaning 'son of the Dragon', the Dragon being an honour his illustrious grandfather had won in war. Those already accommodated on a stake and with nothing to lose no doubt preferred to interpret his name as 'son of the Devil'!

Tales of Vlad's inspired cruelty are legion. Some of them even have a moral. There's the tale of two monks. They visit Vlad's court and during the conversation Vlad asks one of them what he thought of his leafy domain. The monk, having had a close-up view of a staking or two, said he thought it was a great country and that Vlad himself was a vision of loveliness. Vlad thanked him and had him staked just to show he enjoyed a joke as much as the next despot. The second Monk decided that a soft tongue wasn't going to keep him from ending up like a showcase butterfly and told Vlad that he thought he was a cruel and terrible ruler and that he would pay for his sins in the life after – but that it didn't necessarily make him a bad person. Vlad, just to be perverse, rewarded the monk for his honesty and sent him on his way.

Nothing seems to be known of Vlad's sexual preferences but the nature of his extra-curricula activities would imply that he had some sort of problem. Or was it just a case of him being a man of his time? It was only 40 years since de Rais had been in business and Vlad wanted to mark his page in history by pushing the boundaries of what was unacceptable even wider.

It all started with his fear that if he was seen to be a little limp-wristed the Turks would be all over him like a measles epidemic. Just to make them think twice before pushing through the *Douane* without declaring their intent, he rounded up all the prisoners he could find, marched them to the border, had them cut down trees and sharpen them into huge stakes on piece work, then selected a piece for each of them, rammed it through their vital organs and planted them where the invaders couldn't miss seeing them. This tactic was so successful that he decided to explore this deterrent's efficacy when used on the general population. He started slowly. A few dozen

Things are hotting up in Mario Bara's 1960 film *La Maschera Demonio* (aka *The Mask of Satan)* starring Barbara Steele

and watched them slide down the pole. His henchmen soon got so expert that they could stake a man, woman or child in such a way that they wouldn't die for hours. Some were skewered through their navels, pregnant women were usually staked in this way; others had the point stuck up their bum and the sharpened end, driven by the weight of the dying person's body, went through their intestines, through their lungs and heart. A refinement to this method was to allow the condemned free movement of their hands and legs but no possibility of avoiding the spike. This way the stakee could afford the staker hours of endless entertainment as he or she clung desperately to the pole, knowing that in the end fatigue was going to overcome them and they were going to die an agonising death.

Vlad didn't like to hear criticism. A fact that most of the people he came in contact with understood without having to be drawn onto the stake. But there is always a spoil-sport who thinks he knows better. One invitee to the revels complained that the stench from the dead and dying on the stakes was so bad that it was destroying his enjoyment of his soufflé. Vlad, ever the obliging host, had him staked on a pole much higher than the rest so that he wouldn't be troubled by the stench.

Vlad was also keen on dismembering. Nothing made him happier than sitting under his castle walls, listening to the dying howls of his victims, breathing in the fetid air of corruption and watching a skilled butcher dismembering a few recalcitrant peasants. When he was in the mood he would draw off a pint or two of warm blood and quaff it down with roast buttock of virgin or a veal and ham pie.

As a young man Vlad had spent a lot of time banged up in a Turkish gaol. Later he had convinced the Sultan that he was too

at the time. Usually for some very good reason – like he wanted to see a good staking. Before long crime in the country ceased to exist. It was said that you could leave your jewels in the street and, if you were saved to come back the following day, they would still be there. The cessation of crime cut into the number of reasons Vlad could give as an excuse for an execution. So he did the obvious thing and gave up excuses.

Vlad's idea of a dinner party was to set up a table in a forest of newly staked victims

good a man to leave to rot and was given a post in the army. He was soon up to speed on the local torture techniques and was able to suggest a few variations of his own. This impressed his superiors and ensured rapid promotion through the ranks. He became so practised in the bloody arts that made the Turkish army what it was that when the throne in Wallachia became vacant the Sultan insisted that Vlad return to the land of his birth and take control.

The main opposition came from the nobles – the *boyars* – who had problems with their nationality and envied Vlad having his sorted out by a foreign power. Vlad was up to the job and the *boyars* were soon festooning the stakes especially set up for people of quality in the courtyard of Vlad's castle. With the main opposition gone Vlad appointed a new class of nobles. These were kept constantly aware that the slightest shadow of doubt about their loyalty meant a very painful encounter with a specially prepared tree. This kept them in line. Many of them, the ones with brains, got themselves jobs out of the country. Those that returned were usually feted generously before joining the Greek chorus on the masts.

All this talk of death, torture and smell tends to present Vlad Tepes as a rather dour character. Not at all. He had a rather salty sense of humour when the mood took him. He had a habit of going out amongst the peasantry in disguise. He would turn up at a house and beg for shelter. Once he had got his feet under the table he would regale the family with stories and gossip and encourage them to tell him their problems. As there was only one problem endemic in that part of the world they invariably trotted out a litany of complaints about the Prince. Vlad listened sympathetically and left the following morning with promises that, if he could, he would do something about their problem. Later he would return with some of his men-at-arms and carry the family off – to do something about their problems on a stake.

Another time, still in disguise, he met a peasant who looked a bit out of sorts. His wife had been giving him a bad time and kicked him out. Vlad looked him over. It was obvious from the state of his clothes that the wife as not exactly standing by her wifely duties. This, of course, was in another age when being a wife meant something. Vlad told the peasant to throw out his idle wife and get in someone who could look after him better. The man protested that she suited him fine. Vlad patted him on the back and told him to rely on his superior judgement in affairs of the heart. A couple of soldiers dragged out the errant wife and impaled her on the spot. The husband wasn't given time to grieve. On the same theory that if you put a thrown rider immediately back in the saddle they won't be frightened, the bountiful Prince brought on another woman and married the happy couple on the spot. Vlad was a little ostentatious, parading the peasant's ex on a spit in front of the new bride. This was the sort of encouragement she needed and, it is said, she never sat down for a meal but placed the food on her shoulders so she could eat as she hoovered. What she did with the broom is not recorded.

Then there is the much publicised by-play with the hats. A joke that Ivan the Terrible couldn't resist copying and, on the basis of this, declared that Vlad Tepes was a cruel but just ruler who, if he hadn't lost the true faith and converted to Catholicism, would have been perfect.

Vlad was holding an audience for a couple of Italian ambassadors who had turned up in his court to moan about the way the Prince treated people in general and

Italians in particular. Vlad listened politely and when they finished enquired why they hadn't taken off their hats. The Italians, being hot-blooded Latins and with the power of the Holy Roman Empire behind them, instead of whipping off the offending articles and doing some world-class grovelling, claimed diplomatic immunity. They didn't take off their hats for anyone – not even the Pope. It was a custom that they felt very strongly about. Vlad commended them for their zeal in maintaining the customs of their country and called in a couple of P.A.s. He told his visitors that he wanted to help them preserve the custom of keeping their hats on –   forever. His assistants produced a couple of six-inch nails and nailed the emissaries' hats to their heads.

The real belly laugh was Vlad's solution to his country's economic problems. Running a never-ending war and depleting the work force caused economic problems. Even so there were a lot of beggars and scroungers who somehow managed to slip through the net, and by persuading the more feeble-minded citizens to support them, they were not doing their bit for the country. A Beggar's Ball was the answer. In one of the old barns round the back of the castle Vlad laid out a great feast. The beggars came cautiously. The forest of staked bodies on every side wasn't too encouraging but Vlad's men laughed away their fears and led them on with barrels of beer and good red wine. At last the beggars were enticed into the barn. Their eyes popped out of their heads when they saw the tables laden with food and drink that the Prince wouldn't have sneered at. They didn't need any encouragement to fall on the bountiful offerings and consumed them with lashings of drink. Soon they were all sated and legless. At a signal from Vlad the doors were

closed and bundles of firewood, already in place, were set alight. The revellers were awoken from their drunken stupor when the flames began to lick their ears, but it was then too late. Vlad's men were immune to the pleas and curses and stoically waited for them to finish. When the fire died down and they opened the door, Vlad's problem with the scroungers of his society was no more. It was another example of good management that Vlad's fan Ivan liked to quote when he was receiving flak for some little unpopular holocaust he had promoted.

Vlad was also a moral man. He believed that marriage vows were immutable and laid down stringent penalties for anyone breaking them. It should be remembered that Vlad had spent a lot of time in the Turkish army and had picked up some fierce Islamic approaches to law and retribution. An adulterous woman could expect to have her sexual organs destroyed by fire, then her skin skilfully removed while she was still alive, then tied to a post in the village square with her skin exhibited on a table in front of her. Staking was considered too messy; without her skin the woman's body was too slippery and hard to handle. For a promiscuous maiden he had a special treat. Her naked body was exhibited, tied to a pole in the square. When the villagers had got tired of that a roasting spit was heated up. The girl was strapped to a table and an oversized, red-hot poker was pushed into her vagina, up through her entrails and heart until it came out of her head. Her body was then cut to pieces and fed to the dogs.

Unfaithful men were either just ignored as the pathetic victims of the hellish harpies who preyed on them or joined the next day's staking party. Occasionally, if the noble Prince was in a frivolous mood, he had the adulterer's legs tied to horses and then personally rode one of the horses while a favoured member of his party spurred the second mount in the opposite direction. Staking was always his favourite but sometimes even that would become boring. Then he allowed his fertile imagination to roam free. Slowly being lowered into a cauldron of boiling oil was quite favoured. Cutting off ears, noses and other appendages had limited appeal but could be carried out as a sort of noisy *hors d'oeuvre*. Sometimes he invited neighbours to dinner and then served up their nearest and dearest as the main course.

It couldn't last! As they say, all good things come to an end. Vlad's reliance on the Turkish Sultan for stability was undermined by the potentate's interests elsewhere. The Church began to kick up a ruckus – too many of their mendicant friars were disappearing in Vlad's domain for it to be more than just casual wastage. Vlad's strength was in the terror he inspired and in his connections in the outside world. As the Church became more belligerent the bordering countries began to get inquisitive. With Vlad in the saddle there was little to be done. So the Vatican supplied the answer and sent a couple of fervent clerics to sort out the problem. Vlad Tepes was cut down and his legend sprouted from the stump. Soon the tales of the Wallachian Prince who sported with devils and drank human blood was a conversation starter at every dinner party in the almost civilised world. And the story lost nothing in translation. Many said that he wasn't dead at all, but had retired to a monastic retreat where he had set up in partnership with no less an international celebrity than Satan himself. The staking, blood-drinking and mysterious departure – his body was never found – paved the way for the industrious Bram Stoker when he was looking for the origins of his monarch of the Undead – Count Dracula!

ERZEBET BATHORI

Let's be fair to poor old Erzebet Bathori (or Bathory), the Countess Nadasdy. She has had a terrible press and it's taken nearly 400 years for anyone to try and tell it as it really was. For instance, most authorities you read claim she tortured and murdered between 600 and 650 virgins. Never! Where do you get 650 virgins in a town of 30,000 souls and nowhere to go on a hot summer's night but the nearest hayrick? Her trial was a political ploy to discredit Erzebet so that the King could get his hands on her valuables. Anyway, she was abused as a child, so that should make it alright if nothing else does. Obviously she suffered from an overflowing libido. By the time she was 13 she had already been deflowered by one of the under-gardeners. It really wasn't her fault. The fact that if her abuser hadn't done what she wanted he would probably have finished up without any skin on his back has nothing to do with it. Those trying to rehabilitate the dotty old darling insist that she was nothing more than a fun-loving sadist who was just getting her kicks in the manner of the *mesdames* of the *manoir* at that particularly unsavoury time in mid-European history.

Six hundred and fifty? Never! No more than 50 – and some of them died because they couldn't appreciate a bit of fun.

So what are the facts?

Who knows? Various scholars have come up with as many variations on a theme as there are on a Beethoven sonata. These explanations of the psyche of the old monster are usually based on the original transcripts of her trial rediscovered in the early part of the twentieth century. The renewed interest in vampires during the 1960s and 70s brought the old transcripts back into the light of day and nothing has been detracted from the legend of the Blood

Countess in the re-telling of her decidedly eccentric history. I've not had the privilege of viewing the ancient parchments, although I'm sure that if I needed to consult them they would be available. I'm just too old and nasty to want to start learning to read old Hungarian so that I can get at the 'facts' as they were strained through the quill of a committed court recorder. I made a film in Hungary about ten years ago and, believe me, I can get my tongue around half a dozen languages but Hungarian isn't one of them. So I have to rely on what others, more committed than I, have to say about Countess Nadasdy.

Although Erzebet Bathori is usually claimed as Hungarian, she was a lot more cosmopolitan than that. She was born in Bratislava in 1560 which was in the Slovak Republic at the time. Right up to the present day Europe has been a melting pot of constantly changing flavours. It was easy to be a Slovak one day, an Austrian the next and a second-class Turk or Hungarian by Christmas. How much does it matter? We'll call her Hungarian with pretensions. She spent her childhood traipsing around the various castles and palaces that her well-connected family visited in a constant effort to make sure that they weren't marginalised and forgotten. It was a habit she continued into her adult life, although now, in Castle Csejthe, she had a base where she could practise her little diversions and perversions without getting the nosy neighbours riled. She needed their good offices so that she could plunder the stock of nice, blood-filled wenches that came to the area seeking employment. It was a brutal, lawless time. The Turks, who periodically overran Hungary and the surrounding countries, had a reputation for blood-letting and had raised the process of torture to a fine art. Within recent memory Vlad Tepes had turned the

tables on the Turks by using their own methods, embellished and enhanced, until torture was practically an art form. Over the intervening years, he had become not just a bloody monster, but someone with whom the *boyars* could empathise and would nod sagely to each other when his name and exploits were mentioned. Erzebet absorbed all this with her wet-nurse's milk and knew that a bountiful god had placed the rest of humanity on the planet just to satisfy her need to exercise control. There was only one smudge on her family escutcheon, but it was the same one that has fuelled war and pogroms right up to the Irish Troubles. The Bathoris were Protestant. They were powerful enough for this not to be a major problem, but it was nevertheless like a time-bomb ticking in the offertory box.

It wasn't something Erzebet thought a lot about. Highly intelligent and well educated, living the life of a gentlewoman, confined to her castle with *petit point* tapestry and keeping warm the only motivation in her sequestered life, she was being driven out of her mind with boredom. For a while the prospect of marriage to one of the most powerful men of the day, Count Ferenz Nadasdy, offered a way out. Erzebet was only 15 but already a mother with a well developed interest in physical matters. She didn't get what she was looking for from Count Nadasdy. He was just interested in the family estates she was to inherit and the added clout he would be getting as a dowry by being married to the cousin of King Stephen, the Prince of Transylvania and King of Poland. They were married in 1574. Ferenz had no time for a child-bride and having gone through the ceremony and done his duty by his new wife he departed for battlefields new. Spoilt and unfulfilled, the Countess Nadasdy turned her fertile mind to managing and running their massive estates.

The author in the 1971 film *Countess Dracula*, based on the horrific lifestyle of Erzebet Bathori

...and how are the mighty fallen... The face of Erzebet Bathori imprisoned for her crimes at the climax of *Countess Dracula*

Naturally this onerous task including the disciplining and chastisement of those servants who were less than diligent in their duties. The Countess found she had a particular talent for devising punishments to suit the crime. At first it was just the old, well worn chastisements that had always been practised and were considered good for the immortal souls of the servants – servants who were purchased and sold for less money than horses or cows. Thrashing with a cat-o'-nine-tails was something for the major domo to administer, being exhausting and beneath the dignity of the lady of the house. But it was good to watch and gave Erzebet ideas about other forms of punishment. Like sitting a lazy scullery maid on the fire or stripping off a careless seamstress and making her stand in the courtyard outside her window when the temperature was below zero.

For the next 25 years, practically abandoned by her husband, the Countess had little to do but devise suitable tortures for her offending staff. In this she was encouraged by various servants who were crafty enough to realise that their only chance of survival was to join their mistress in her black practices. Not just join but encourage and suggest better and more satisfying ways to make the lives, and deaths, of their colleagues, unbearable. But still, she was indulging in nothing worse than a lot of ladies of the Countess's rank and disposition did on a daily basis. What seemed to have released Erzebet's predilection for cruelty was the death of Ferenz and the advent of a new handmaiden, midwife Ana Darvulia, into her life. Darvulia soon cottoned on to what her mistress wanted and was more than eager to help. It was Darvulia who, if it is true, encouraged the Countess to use the blood of her victims as an unguent to ward off the effects of age. The commonly held belief that the Countess' interest in blood came from an incident when she accidentally cut the face of a maid and her blood spilled onto the face of the Countess and made it look more youthful, is probably apocryphal. She just had a need to hurt people and the spilling of their blood was just a symbol of that perversion. With Darvulia's help she invented better and better entertainment. She would start with needles under the finger and toenails. This produced a lot of sound but little blood. Cropping the ears was better. Pain and lashings of blood. This got the Countess started. Pins through the sides of the eyeball was a good one, but again: sound without blood. But it was building. Eyelids were quite bloody and turned the victim's face into a mask that got the old

lady's juices flowing. Darvulia spurned that relic from the old days, the Iron Maiden, and produced a much more satisfying modern version. The problem with the old Maiden was that it didn't matter how slowly you shut the door, the victim died without the voyeur being able to relish the visuals. What Darvulia devised was an iron cage with long, sharp spikes inside. Having survived the *hors d'oeuvre* of needles and judicious snipping, the tormented girl was levered into the iron cage and this was hoisted up about ten feet. Erzebet's chair was then placed underneath it and her sidekicks then thrust burning torches at the girl in the cage. In her effort to avoid the flames the girl impaled herself on the razor-sharp spikes. The blood, spurting from a dozen wounds, cascaded down on the Countess who would moan and groan and have orgasms. Why she had to get turned on in this manner is the province of a psychiatrist. After a heavy day in the torture chamber, the tired but happy Countess would totter off to her bedchamber, covered in blood and excrement, and zonk out until the next day when Ana Darvulia would arrive with a cheering cup of Earl Grey and a menu of delights that she had planned for the coming evening's entertainment. Life was so busy, busy, busy that the powerful noble woman had little time to waste on teeth cleaning or hair washing – even of the wash and go variety. The continuous round of maiming and killing never palled while Ana Darvulia was the energetic entrepreneur. But then she went and died. The Countess was distraught. Where was she going to get someone capable of supervising her need for labour-intensive horror? She needn't have feared. A local farmer's wife, Erzsi Majorova, who had been to some extent involved with acquiring suitable turns for Ana Darvulia's extravaganzas, stepped in and helped out.

Up until this point, under Darvulia's

supervision, the Countess had been careful to keep her household *peccadilloes* secret between the participants. That kept her safe. Darvulia wasn't going to say anything. Nor were the men involved in the heavy labour of making the hardware of torture and doing the general carrying of equipment. And the girls who made guest appearances on her stage were never in any condition to complain. Success and a new master of ceremonies bred carelessness. Local female fodder suitable for the Lady's entertainment was in short supply so Majorova looked further afield. So far the girls had been exclusively selected from the peasantry. Most of them had been sold to the Countess, as was the custom, from families that were glad to get rid of them. The mother's conscience was assuaged by assuring her that she was doing her daughter a favour by getting her into service. Any peasant who complained would get a visit from the Countess's men and be either bought off or beaten into forgetfulness. Where Majorova went wrong, intentionally or by mistake, was to procure, by force, the daughter of the lesser nobility. This caused a bit of a scandal, but the Countess might have survived if it hadn't been for her cousin, Count Georgio Thurzo. He came from the side of the family that had been effectively sidelined when Erzebet formed the powerful alliance with the Nadasdys. Thurzo had been sychophant icwith the new King Matthias for months trying to get his hands on cousin Erzebet's inheritance but with nothing to charge her with, the King was unwilling to take on such a powerful Protestant family. Even when he heard about the Countess's less than salubrious lifestyle he was unwilling to act. Almost resigned to being a perpetual carpet-bagging courtier, Thurzo couldn't wait to bring to the King the latest tale of Erzebet's somewhat unconventional lifestyle. Thurzo

trailed before the King the prospects of all those rich lands and strong fortresses scattered about the Ottoman Empire, being in control of one man, a loyal subject of his most wonderful Majesty. He modestly put himself up for the job.

Cautiously the King gave Count Thurzo the warrant to investigate. That was enough for Erzebet's unkissed cousin and he went into her castles and estates mob-handed.

What he found surprised even him! He had expected to have to gild the stinking lily. What he had to do was underwrite his reports to make them believable. He needn't have worried. Now that he had got into it the King could see a good profit from the venture and wasn't likely to pull the plug.

The Countess didn't know what all the fuss was about. When questioned by Thurzo and his bailiffs she quite happily answered his questions truthfully. She claimed that the crown had no jurisdiction over what she did with her bond servants in her own castles. Triumphantly Thurzo brought up the subject of the girls of noble birth who had been reluctant guests in her gruesome cellars. Erzebet protested her innocence. She had known nothing of this. They had been brought to her by Erzsi Majorova and she had assumed they had been bonded like all her other girls.

Thurzo wasn't having that and quickly convened a trial. This was just to get the deeds of her land turned over to him so that, as a family member he could make sure that they were safe. The second trial was more serious. She was accused of murdering 650 women and children. The most damning evidence against her was a book, fortuitously found by her cousin, the newly rich Count, naming 650 girls she had put to death and when. The diary was never admitted by the Countess to be hers but the weight of evidence was so heavily against her that it was almost a matter of overkill even mentioning it.

When the second trial began on 7 January 1611, the outcome was a foregone conclusion. Plea bargaining got the Countess off the executioner's block but nothing could be done for her accomplices. They were all executed, burning alive being considered the just reward for the Majorova woman who had precipitated the whole debacle by procuring above her station. Erzebet was sentenced to life imprisonment. In these enlightened times that might seem a fit punishment. What happened then is open to question. The widely held, and more romantic, story is that she was bricked up in a room in her castle and fed through a small hole in the wall. A later version is that Count Thurzo was given authority over her and she lived in relative luxury in her castle. Whichever – she lived for three years in this condition, before keeling over, and was then buried on one of her estates.

Countess Nadasdy had little to do with vampirism in its later form but she is reputed to have drunk blood and lived in a castle. Two of the top requirements outside fangs and a cloak.

the RISe of the REVenants
peter plogojowitz

By now Vampirism had been firmly taken over by the gentry and the church. This didn't mean that all vampires were high born or talked through a mouthful of communion wafers. The involvement of the good and holy meant that in future anything which happened in the vicinity of the cemetery came under close scrutiny by the local powers, corporeal and ecclesiastic. As the Balkan countries were in a constant state of hostility and ravaged by the by-products of war, famine and pestilence, there was always a lot of activity around the graveyards. So much so that priests were always digging bodies up to see that they were rotting at the correct rate. This did nothing to help contain the epidemics that decimated the lands but it did make things more exciting. Things like Peter Plogojowitz, for example. He was a farmer living in Kisolava in Serbia. In September 1728, after a short illness, Mr. Plogojowitz died. There was nothing extraordinary about the way he died, although his wife seemed to be relieved. Ten weeks after the interment Mrs. Plogojowitz was awoken in the night by a pounding on the door. When she opened it she was pretty surprised to see her late husband, covered in mud and looking a bit pasty-faced, leaning on the doorpost demanding entry. Obviously this was one phlegmatic lady. Not everyone would be willing to entertain the corpse of their late spouse in the middle of the night, no matter how pleased she was to see him dead.

1972: Robert Tayman as Count Mitterhouse in Robert Young's *Vampire Circus*

Plogojowitz soon dispelled thoughts she may have harboured that the reason for his return from the grave was that he couldn't die without her. He wanted his shoes. Again, this is one of those curious events that cries out for explanation but refuses to give one. Once he had his shoes tucked under his arm he was off. So was his widow. She hadn't been particularly enamoured of his habits when he was alive and she certainly didn't intend to have him back stinking up the hovel and demanding compliance in unnatural practices. As soon as the cock had crowed and she felt safe to leave she chucked a few things in a blanket and disappeared out of the story. Not Plogojowitz. He turned up next evening to find an empty house and not a word of explanation. This started his roaring and stomping, as the frustrated returning dead are apt to do, and he ran off to the house of his son. Plogojowitz junior lacked the diplomacy exhibited by his mother and instead of appeasing his ex-father with a glass of Slivowitz he gave him a dirty look and slammed the door in his face. This was not a good move. Within 24 hours the unsympathetic son sickened and died. The repercussions of getting into Plogojowitz's bad books were not missed by the villagers. They recalled that over the last nine weeks since Plogojowitz's death there had been no less than nine deaths. At the time they had seemed ordinary enough but with the new evidence to hand the villagers wanted a reappraisal. Rumours began to fly around. Family members of the dear departed whispered that they had been told on their kinsmen's deathbed of Peter Plogojowitz's appearing in the night, lying on top of them and throttling them. The stories, fed on fear, grew and circulated until there was a general consensus of opinion that Plogojowitz was the cause of all the recent misery in the village and something

had to be done. The local priest kept out of the general clamour to have the body of Plogojowitz exhumed. He had recently received a letter from the bishop warning him of the consequences of digging up bodies on the whim of anyone with a fanciful and macabre imagination. Reluctance to face the devil wasn't one of the characteristics his earthly congregation wanted in their religious leader. They told him they wanted Plogojowitz's body dug up and examined – or else!

The priest was even more sure he shouldn't have got involved when he saw what had been dug up. He wanted someone else to take the blame if things got too far out of hand so he sent for the District Magistrate. He wasn't much happier about being involved but couldn't think of a good excuse to get out of going. Being a cautious man by nature and a civil servant by trade he made sure that every move he made was noted down, and copies, probably in triplicate, were dispatched post-haste to his superior at the Imperial Court. And who could blame him. Not only was he subjected to the hysterical accounts of the walking dead from the villagers but the priest was trying to make sure that he was held responsible for turning a newly dead farmer into an active vampire.

The gist of his report was that he turned up too late to supervise the actual disinterment and had to rely on what the local priest told him of what had happened up to the time of his arrival in the village. Finally faced with the body he couldn't detect any smell arising from the corpse and there were no obvious signs that the body was, indeed, dead (except for the nose which had caved in and that could have been caused by the coffin lid when it was slammed shut). Hair and nails were new and shiny, although they appeared to have grown since

The Wicker Man,
not strictly a
vampire fest, but
still a role for
Ingrid to get her
teeth into

The kiss is sweet... but not as sweet as blood. Ingrid in *The Vampire Lovers*

Good day to you,
Countess

'Hey you! Get out
of my coffin!'
cries Lee

An unrecognisable
Ingrid Pitt

Christopher Lee
gets stuck in to
Caroline Munro –
*Dracula A.D.
1972*

Plogojowitz's death; the old nails were strewn about the coffin. The old skin, brown and papery, had peeled off to reveal a smooth white skin beneath and everyone agreed that the old boy looked better dead than he ever had alive.

The evidence that finished off any chance Plogojowitz had of spending eternity in a whole body was plain to see. Around his mouth was a large quantity of fresh blood – the remains of the feast he had enjoyed when he was roaring around the village giving everyone the dead eye. This put the visiting magistrate in a flap. He had incontrovertible evidence of a vampire infestation but knew it was something his superiors in Gradisk didn't want to hear. So he asked the priest what the usual practice was in these circumstances. Flattered to be asked for advice by the grand official from the Imperial Court, the priest gave instructions for a stake to be sharpened. He ran through a few of the more obscure psalms, prayers and incantations, held the point of the stake over the heart of the undead Plogojowitz and whacked it with a hammer. Both the priest and the official were aghast at the result. With a scream, the body, gushing blood from every orifice, sat up and for a moment appeared to be about to jump out of the coffin. However, the priest had done his job well and the stake held. The villagers made a night of it. They built a roaring fire and laid the body of Plogojowitz reverently on it. When the Reverend and the Magistrate left and the fire was at its height the villagers doubtless forgot their Christian upbringing and threw in a blessing or two for the more primitive Bacchus.

The fire that consumed Plogojowitz's body didn't bring an end to the problem of vampires in the village of Kisolava. Everyone knew by now that a person who died by the vampire became one. And there had been those nine deaths that could possibly be laid on Plogojowitz's grave. Now that the magistrate had, however reluctantly, admitted that Plogojowitz *might* be a vampire there was no stopping the village priest. All the graves of the unfortunate nine were reopened and those deemed by the church to be infected by vampirism staked and burned. Maybe someone was missed because a couple of years later another plague of vampirism broke out. It was very much along the lines of the Kisolava outbreak but by now the authorities were on the lookout and responded with alacrity and a government fact-finding committee headed by the level-headed Colonel Johannes Flukinger, was dispatched to investigate.

arnold paole

Arnold Paole was a Serbian NCO in the Austro-Hungarian army and had served in Greece and the Levant. Having a fertile imagination, the ancient monuments and evidence of a life far removed from the restrictive Catholicism of his village made him receptive to the folk stories of his temporary home from home. Back in Medvegna, Paole told highly embroidered tales of his adventures in foreign lands. The Plogojowitz incident had made vampires a big talking point and the gallant soldier was able to come up with a capper to the local stories. When he was in Greece he had been attacked by a vampire and nearly died. He was saved by a local witch who told him the best way to combat the ravages of vampirism was to eat dirt from the vampire's grave and smear vampire blood over his body. She even obliged with the location of a suitable grave to fill the prescription. Just to make sure that the vampire never bothered anybody again he cut its head off with a spade, drove a stake through its heart and reburied the body. Although he came from a family that had lived in the village from way back, Paole had little in common with others of his own age. Almost reluctantly he married the daughter of a local farmer and tried to settle down to a farmer's life. It wasn't very successful. Nor was his marriage. Finally his wife tackled him on the subject. He said that he could never forget what had happened in Greece and it made it very difficult to settle down.

Then in 1731 he fell off a hay wagon and broke his neck and his fears were seen to be real. For a month he laid quiet in his grave but then reports started circulating that he had been seen in the village at night, cavorting around and generally making a nuisance of himself. Livestock had also been found sucked dry of blood and there was a lot of unusual activity in the area surrounding the cemetery. No doubt the recent events in Kilosowa prompted the local priest to overcome his reluctance to be thought a fool by those in authority and reported what was happening to the government officials in Belgrade. The authorities duly dispatched a trio of army medical officers under the command of Colonel Johannes Flukinger.

When they arrived in the village they were besieged by families with complaints. There were even accusations that during the time they had been making up their minds whether to investigate or not, the vampire Paole had violated and killed four of the villagers. Flukinger wasn't going to be hassled by a gang of locals – he was a high-ranking officer in the Serbian army. After long meditation over a bottle or two of wine he ordered that the body of Arnold Paole be exhumed. As this was to be a scientific examination to determine once and for all time whether vampires existed or were just a figment of fevered imaginations, the three

medical officers insisted on being present throughout the whole operation. The result of the examination was pretty much the same as that of Plogojowitz – a scream when the stake went in, blood gushing from the body, hair long, nails renewed, old skin shed like a snake to reveal new skin beneath and the coffin deep in blood.

Now that the case for vampirism had been proved the Colonel swung into action. The bodies of the four people who had died since Paole became a vampire marauder were speedily exhumed and examined for signs of possession. Colonel Flukinger, in spite of what he had seen, was determined not to be rushed into making hasty assumptions. There was an added complication. Knowing voices whispered that it wasn't just the dead you had to be on your guard against. There were also the animals that had been killed and sucked dry of blood, allegedly by Paole. These, it was claimed, would also pass on the plague of vampirism to anyone eating the meat. It was a complication that the Colonel could have done without. For the moment he decided to stick with his original intention of examining those that had died, possibly from the attentions of Arnold Paole. The subject of whether or not vampirism could be passed on through contaminated meat would have to wait. Just to compound the problem a young woman called Stanacka claimed that during the night a young local farmer named Milloe, who had been dead and buried for nine weeks, had attacked her and bitten her on the neck. From being a healthy, physical girl she quickly faded and died a couple of days later. The Colonel was now beginning to lose his sense of reality. Vampires seemed to be coming out of the woodwork on every side.

The first coffin opened was that of a 20-year-old called Stana. She was three months pregnant and had sickened and died over a three-day period. No doubt encouraged by the romantic stories of combating vampires in exotic places that Paole had told around the village, she claimed, shortly before she died, that she had followed his example by eating earth from a vampire's grave and bathing in vampire blood. By this time the earth and blood remedy was beginning to look decidedly ineffective, especially as the body of Stana appeared to be perfectly preserved. The Army surgeons didn't shrink from their gruesome task and performed a thorough post mortem at the graveside. Their findings were frightening. The body was pliant and full of fresh blood; her intestines were a good colour and showed no signs of decomposition. Her hair and nails had grown and her skin was unblemished.

Coffin number two offered up a 60-year-old who had died after a short illness three months earlier. A couple of local onlookers called Colonel Flukinger's attention to the weight of the old lady Millisa. Alive she had been a lithe 45 kilos, dead she was turning the scales at about 80. There was no evidence that she had fallen foul of Arnod Paole but one of the villagers remembered her saying that she had eaten lamb shortly before she became ill. Wise heads nodded and the Colonel was forced to consider the possibility that meat from the dead animals had been spread over a large area and the contamination might be much more than they had ever dreamed. It made their efforts to find a common cause for the plague and eliminate the spread even more frantic. The body of a small child was found to have the, by now, familiar uncorrupted body that marked her out as a vampire victim. As quickly as the surgeons disinterred the bodies and sliced them up to determine the cause of death, the willing villagers, led by their pastor, were staking, beheading and burning the bodies.

Next they got around to the Milloes, senior and junior, and the son's victim, Stanaka. Stanaka's body still bore signs of her encounter with the revenant Milloes. It was enough for the doctors. They detailed the Milloes and Stanaka to suffer the standard release for their vampiric soul of staking, decapitation and burning. The military men laboured all day to make sure that no grave was unturned that might hold and shelter a vampire. When it was finished the Colonel retired to make his report. He seemed to have missed the significance of a similar infestation in Kilosowa and tried to make his summary of the situation as mundane and unsensational as declaring a dozen or so solid citizens to be vampires could possibly be. On 7 January 1732 he declared the area vampire-free and returned with his assistants to Belgrade to become the leading authority on vampires.

Plogojowitz and Paole became the prototype for many stories in the mid-18th century and dozens of books were written about them or featured them as characters in fiction. So exciting were the stories that they engendered copycat manifestations all over Europe. What is of particular interest is that they are the first 'authenticated' accounts of 'real' cases of vampirism. Before this some of the vital elements of the legend have been missing. Plogojowitz and Paole both came back from the grave and attacked a number of people who knew them by sight. When their marauding was over they returned to the grave and were there unearthed in a ripe and healthy state. Most convincing of all was Colonel Flukinger's revelation that other bodies allegedly attacked by the revenant twosome had also developed vampire characteristics. When they were exhumed they were also uncorrupted and did the blood gushing and screaming bit when they were staked. After this scientific examination and report who could doubt that the undead were about in Eastern Europe? The aristocratic Vlad and Erzebet had brought the possibility of vampirism into focus – even if, as we have seen, they weren't technically vampires. The seriousness with which the Serbian authorities treated the outbreaks shows that the idea had taken root in the psyche of the country and a scientific approach was being tried to explain what was being revealed. Now that the subject of vampires had become respectable an aristocrat rises out of the cavern of the undead. An alchemist, jeweller, astronomer, doctor, spy and general good egg – the Comte de St. Germain.

the comte de st. germain

The Comte de St. Germain wasn't just a run-of-the-mill vampire. In fact his connection with the hard-core vampire of legend seems to have emerged with Chelsea Quinn Yarbro's first novel about the enigmatic aristo, *Hotel Transylvania*. When St. German revealed himself to the Pompadour set in Venice he claimed to have lived for a couple of thousand years and had broken bread at the table of the family of Mary, Joseph and Jesus. The extravagant claim doesn't seem to have had his audience nervously backing out of the room or sending for the men in white jackets. Maybe this was because he had some high-powered connections... Like the Shah of Persia. It seems that the old Shah had a few baubles around gathering dust – as they do – and St. Germain said he would polish them up for him. The Shah accepted the generous offer and was more than happy when his jewels were returned, not only sparkling brightly but bigger and better than they were when the Frenchman walked off with them. Louis

XV learned about this marvellous trick and insisted that the Count did him a similar favour. He wasn't disappointed.

So just who was the Comte de St. Germain and why should he be included as a vampire's ancestor? In appearance he was tall, slender and around 45 years of age. He habitually dressed in black which set off his pale, thin face and made his sharp, beak-like nose seem more prominent. He wore a lot of jewellery, most of which had impressive crests, zodiacal and mathematical symbols on it. He had a deep, resonant voice which he used seductively as a tool of his trade. Although he was an avid party-goer and giver he was never seen to eat in public. He blamed this on a special diet which was not suitable for slurping in polite society. He also claimed to have discovered the elixir of life.

This claim was fortuitously authenticated by the Comtesse de Georgy. The old girl was in her seventies and just getting over the death of her husband when she met up with the Comte at a Paris party. Naturally she assumed that the man kissing her hand and calling himself the Comte de St. Germain must be a relative of the man she knew way back when. A son or something. After all, the man she had met in Venice when she was a mere slip of a girl had been exactly the same age as the black-clad figure before her. Making sure he had an audience to recount the meeting he then told her that he was, in fact, that selfsame 45-year-old who had wooed her all those years ago. The Comtesse was well acquainted with men making extravagant and baseless claims. She had been the wife of an ambassador and wasn't easily taken in. 'If you're the same man you must be the devil!' she sneered. This suited St. Germain fine; if you're destined to play the hero, go for the top. 'Don't call me that name!' he screamed, making sure he got the attention of anyone who so far hadn't been

Coleen Gray gets rather carried away by John Beal in *The Vampire*, 1957

party to the exchange, and ran from the room. There's nothing like a hysterical disclaimer to get tongues wagging. Before long rumours had St. Germain frothing at the mouth and growing horns and a forked tongue.

Now a fully blown legend, he moved across the Channel to England. His reputation had preceded him and he was soon doing the rounds, still carefully nurturing and embroidering his image as an alchemist *par excellence*, and a close relative of his satanic majesty. To this he now added playing the violin and singing in a powerful baritone voice. Just to make sure he missed out on nothing, he boasted an advanced medical knowledge, the fact that he could speak practically every language anyone wanted to throw at him and claimed to be able to tell the future. The Prince of Wales, not renown as a particular acerbic wit, proclaimed St. Germain as one of the greatest geniuses of all time. Frederick the Great, not to be outdone, cited him as a scholar of remarkable insight and one of the most enigmatic personages of the 18th century. The jaded Casanova wasn't so easily persuaded. His stock in trade was deception and he put down St. Germain as a mountebank but tipped his cocked hat to him as one of the best he had ever come across. A back-handed compliment if ever there was one.

In spite of his high-level protection St. Germain couldn't avoid arrest when he was found in possession of seditious, pro-Jacobite letters. This was the time of the Jacobite Rising in 1745 and it could have proved an interesting insight into St. Germain's claim that he could not die.

Quitting England, he turned up in the Court of Catherine the Great. She was a lady who could lay her own claims to inclusion in the annals of vampirism, if the stories of how she sucked dry the lusty men that made up her personal bodyguards have any basis in fact. She couldn't wait to bestow the rank of general on him. Why she should do that isn't clear but if the wily Comte had been around half as long as he claimed he must have learned a thing or two in the boudoir. Ranking him as a general on a scale of one to ten must give him an enthusiastic 9+ on anyone's erotometer.

After his fright with the Jacobites and his brush with immorality in the court of Catherine the Great, St. Germain became a moving target. Selling out his expertise and the notes in his little black book to the highest bidder, he became the James Bond of the eighteenth century. He began popping up all over the place in different disguises. He was Count Surmount in Holland, the Marquis de Montferrat in Belgium. Catherine's generous dubbing of General in the Russian army was also used. In whatever guise he operated his main aim, so he said, was to find sanguine, educated, cosmopolitan figures to fund his experiments. Experiments which promised the investor untold wealth, health and happiness. Just so that his proposals didn't appear to be too exotic to be true, for good measure he also threw in as security a paint making factory, which he owned.

It was about this time that he began to use one of his more obscure but highly significant titles – Prince Rakoczy of Transylvania. But, like a bad actor, he had overplayed his piece and when he laid out his wealth-making scheme to the Marquise of Brandenburg in 1774, he was cold-shouldered. Not to be dismissed, the versatile Count, or Prince as he was now claiming to be, went to see his old fan, Frederick the Great. Frederick had also got over his schoolboy's enthusiasm for the most energetic personage of the 18th century and hid behind a screen of court etiquette to keep St. Germain at arm's length.

Then came a glitch in St. Germain's remarkable story.

He died!

In 1784 while working his alchemic art in a laboratory which he had specially built, he just keeled over and died.

End of story?

Never!

At a party in Versailles, long before the *sans culottes* got their act together, St. Germain had banged on about the mood of the country turning ugly. It wasn't something the *Noblesse* wanted to hear. They sagely agreed that St. Germain had at last gone too far and curtailed his *soirée* invitations. What they thought when he turned up a year after his demise to once again warn Marie Antoinette that feeding the peasantry cakes wasn't a viable solution to the coming revolution, is not recorded. To the 'unspeakable surprise' of an old friend, Madame d'Adhemar, the revenant Comte paid a home visit in 1779. He still looked remarkably well for a man who had been dead for five years but, undaunted, the phlegmatic Madame chatted to him until he suddenly decided he had to leave, promising he would be back. Madame d'Adhemar claimed that he visited her on four subsequent occasions but remained remarkably reticent about what subjects they touched on during the course of their conversation. 'Hello. Still dead, I see,' seems hardly adequate.

The French Revolution of 1789 proved too volatile a stage for the dead but peripatetic Comte to miss. He turned up once more at Versailles and begged Louis XVI to either flee France with him or allow him to take Antoinette and the children to the safety of England. Again Louis doesn't seem to think there is anything strange in St. Germain turning up and doing a Cassandra act 14 years after he had been interred. Anyway, the upshot was that *le Roi* told *le Comte* that he was speaking nonsense, the people in the *rue* still loved him and it was only a few disaffected scribblers like Voltaire and Rousseau who were writing up a storm. It was still the tenor of his polemic when he was trying to explain to the *sans culottes* that he was good for the country and if they

would just be good boys and go home he would forgive them the bad manners they were displaying by not saying please when they invited him to stick his head under the blade of the guillotine.

Unfortunately, before he could fulfil the promise of more pocket money he was standing with a limp mace in his hand and a few thousand unfettered revolutionaries staring him in the face. St. Germain popped up again briefly in 1821 in Venice, his old haunting ground. He appeared to have been in one of his Nostradamus moods and offered Madame d'Adhemar a number of predictions. One of which was that he would be taking himself off to the Himalayas and wouldn't be seen for about a century.

We now fast forward to 1942. The Second World War was raging and an American aviator on patrol, of what and for what isn't stated, was forced to crash-land in the foothills of the Himalayas. He was pulled from his plane by a tall, gaunt man in black, old-fashioned clothing who spoke perfect English with a slight middle-European accent. The rescuer claimed to be the Comte de St. Germain. The name meant nothing to the pilot at the time. What's in a name? The man had saved him from almost certain death and that was enough for him. The man claiming to be the Comte of Longevity pointed the way down the mountain for the stranded airman to follow and then disappeared into the mist.

Was this the Count fulfilling his own prophecy?

Or was it the man who appeared on a TV show in Paris in 1972 who was the real St. Germain?

Does it matter?

Does St. Germain advance the claim for modern vampirehood or is he just an interesting sideshow?

He may have had a 'special diet,' but is

this alone proof that he drank blood? Quinn Yarbro's St. Germain, although impotent, got his kicks by drinking a small measure of blood from his victims, whom he first seduced. Although the victim had an orgasm, it was induced by the taking of their blood and not by any sexual athleticism on the part of the age-old vampire. And there is no evidence that those who were vampirised became vampires themselves.

But there is the longevity, affirmed by people of good standing, and his mysterious appearances before old friends and acquaintances — and, in the case of the American pilot — strangers.

The basis for St. Germain's claim to vampirism may not be strong in fact, but it does forward the image that would become established on the stage: a mysterious nobleman claiming to be a Prince of Transylvania, a corpse which becomes reanimated shortly after being dead and buried, a speaker of languages and someone who only appears at functions held after the sun has set and doesn't dine out.

St. Germain may not be a fang-wielding, stake-dodging vampire in the modern sense, but I like the sound of him and if I had to pick a number from one to ten on the vampire scale to indicate his standing in vampire-hood, I would rate him about a 6. I think the modern cinematic vampire owns a debt of gratitude to the old Comte who filled the gap between the old-style vampire and the monster created by Bram Stoker. But before Stoker can get his claws into the legend the newly socially elevated vampire has to cross the Channel and prepare the ground for Polidori and Le Fanu.

CROGLIN GRANGE

Croglin Grange, or Croglin Low Hall, was an unusual country house for its time. In 1850 the weekend cottage for the gentry usually ran to 20 bedrooms with hot and cold running servants scurrying in all directions and very few bathrooms. By this standard Croglin Grange was small — only one floor and four bedrooms. When Captain Fisher decided to take more commodious quarters in Surrey, he considered himself very lucky to let the Grange to a nice little family of siblings, two men and a woman. By all accounts the brothers and sister were paragons of virtue. Kind and considerate and always willing to lend a helping hand, they were besotted with the old house and loved the rolling lawns and mature bushes and trees. And the views. Through the trees, a short walk away, they could see the square tower of an old Norman church. They moved in during a particularly brilliant summer and whiled away the idyllic months strolling in the beautiful countryside and lazing under the trees, reading and painting. Each Sunday morning they attended the little church twice a day and were soon firm favourites with the rector. As the autumn days closed in, they waited eagerly for the snow that would turn their beautiful garden into a winter wonderland.

After a restful day in the garden enjoying the unseasonal warmth of a late Indian summer, they dined early and decided to retire to bed and hoped that the following day would be as warm as the day just gone. As the sister went to her room she happened to glance out of the window towards the church. For a moment she thought she saw a bluish light dancing between the tombstones. Shading her candle's light with her hand she peered intently towards the church, vaguely outlined by the rising moon, but there was no recurrence of the light so she assumed that what she had thought she had seen was just a reflection from her candle on the window pane.

She quickly undressed and climbed into bed but she couldn't sleep. The heat of the day still lingered and made even the light cotton sheets unbearable. She got up and threw back the shutters and opened the casement window. The slight breeze played deliciously on her body and she arranged the pillows on her bed so that she could sit and enjoy the coolness of the night. As she lay there reflecting on their good fortune in finding such a lovely place to live the moonlight became stronger and the gardens and the church took on the silvery chiaroscuro of a dream. She was jerked out

Dennis Price meets a grisly end in John Hough's 1978 *Twins of Evil*, released in 1971. Madelaine Collins stars as evil twin Frieda Gellhorn

of her reverie by a movement in the direction of the churchyard. Again she thought she saw a blue light but when she focused on the movement all she could see was the dark figure of a man coming towards the Grange. The unexpected sight mesmerised her. There was something innately evil about the way the figure, made grotesque by the moonlight, moved in a loping, sidling run. Try as she might to call out to her brothers sleeping in the next room, she was tongue-tied. She tried to jump out of bed and run for the door but the open window was right beside it and she couldn't force herself to move. Then, unexpectedly, the marauding figure vanished. Its disappearance was so abrupt that for a moment she couldn't believe her eyes. Movement flooded back into her limbs and without thinking she threw back the sheet and darted across the room and slammed the window shut. She thought of waking her brothers and telling them what she had seen – what she thought she had seen – she reminded herself. The doubt was enough to stop her. She knew what her brothers were like. They'd dismiss her fears as fanciful and not miss an opportunity to make fun of her for weeks. She was just about to slide back under the sheet when she heard a soft sound coming from the direction of the window. Fear struck her like a blow. Her heart pounded and for a moment she thought she would faint. With a supreme effort she pulled herself together. It was only the curtain flapping or a branch tapping against the window. She knew she was lying to herself but the alternative was too horrible to contemplate. Slowly, trancelike, she turned. Staring at her through the glass was a skeletal, brown face with malevolent red eyes and a gaping, sharp toothed mouth. A bony hand with long, dirty nails beckoned her and unbelievably she felt an urge to go and open the window.

Summoning up all her reserves of strength she resisted the impulse and tried to call and warn her brothers of her peril but her tongue refused to work. The bony hand began to scratch at the lead holding the window panes. Scratch... scratch... She thought that if she didn't do something she must surely die. With a tinkle of smashing glass a small pane fell away and the hideous hand reached in and released the latch. The window swung open and the terrible visitor climbed nimbly over the sill. The sister managed to let out a moan, a primeval mew of terror that couldn't be heard outside the room. She forced herself to back away but was stopped by the bed. Without warning the ogre surged forward, grabbed her by her thick brown hair and flung her on the bed. Before she could move his sharp teeth bit savagely into her neck and she heard an obscene sucking sound as he milked the blood from her body. Pain and fear were so intense that for a moment she regained control of her vocal cords and let out a loud and desperate screech. It seemed only a moment before her brothers were at the door, calling to her, reassuring her that they were on hand. But the door was locked and they wasted desperate moments breaking it down. The pause gave the hideous creature of the night the chance to jump out of the window and flee in the direction of the churchyard. The sister managed to point to the window before collapsing in a dead faint. One of the brothers rushed out of the house in pursuit of the attacker but was soon left behind as the ungainly figure loped frantically towards the churchyard and was lost to view amongst the grave stones.

The wound the sister had received in the throat was severe and for weeks she hovered on the brink of death. The doctor, apprised of her terrifying ordeal by her brothers, assured them that the wound would heal eventually but what the terrible experience would do to her nerves was another thing entirely. He suggested that as soon as she was able to move they all went somewhere, far away from the site of her harrowing experience, and hope that time would obscure the awful memories.

The three of them went to stay with friends in Switzerland. The sister was determined that the unfortunate event would not haunt the rest of her life and threw herself into exploring her new surroundings. Summer was nearly over when she called her brothers in and told them that she wanted to return to the Grange in Cumberland. When they demurred she overcame their protests by assuring them that she knew her mind and didn't intend to let an unfortunate incident with what was obviously an insane tramp, keep her away from the house they loved so dearly.

Back in the Grange the brothers tried to persuade her to take one of their rooms that faced away from the church and were easier to make safe. The sister pooh-poohed their concern. She would make sure that the shutters on her window were firmly closed and she would leave her bedroom door unlocked. The brothers were unhappy but knew their sister's disposition. Once she had made up her mind nobody could change it.

The summer passed without incident and the days began to draw in. The sister tried to reassure herself that what had happened before was a one-off incident and nothing like that could happen again. But she was still a little nervous about the fact that the stout shutters only went to about a foot below the top of the window. She knew her fears were foolish. It would be impossible for anyone to squeeze through such a small gap. Since the incident she had become a light sleeper and woke with a start in the night at any small sound. Mostly it was just the

sound of the house settling after the warmth of the day or the sound of a night bird. The sound that woke her was none of these. It was a sound from a nightmare. The soft scratch, scratch, scratch of nails on the window. In the gap between the top of the shutters and the frame of the window she could see the same hideous contorted face that was burned onto her brain, its monstrous eyes and a fang-filled mouth seemed to smile crazily at her, inviting her to open the shutters. This time she didn't wait to see what happened. There was no chance that her brothers would laugh at her this time. She screamed and screamed until she was exhausted. One of the brothers rushed into the room to protect her, a pistol in each hand. The second brother burst out of the front door, as had been planned. He saw the creature scuttling away across the lawn at an incredible speed. The pistol fired and the dark figure staggered but immediately regained its balance and continued on towards the churchyard at undiminished speed. The slight falter gave the brother a chance to gain a little and he saw the dark shape leap over the wall and disappear into a vault. The brother was tempted to follow but decided that it wasn't sensible to go blundering into a situation that he knew nothing about. He settled down in a position where he could see the door leading into the vault and waited for the dawn.

The next morning the brothers, the local vicar and a couple of gardeners from the Grange entered the vault. The sight that met their eyes was hideous to behold. Coffins were strewn about the dark vault as if thrown there by a maniacal child. Bones littered the floor and skulls grinned insanely from amongst the debris. Only one coffin remained undisturbed. When they lifted the lid they were amazed to see a perfectly preserved body stretched out on the satin

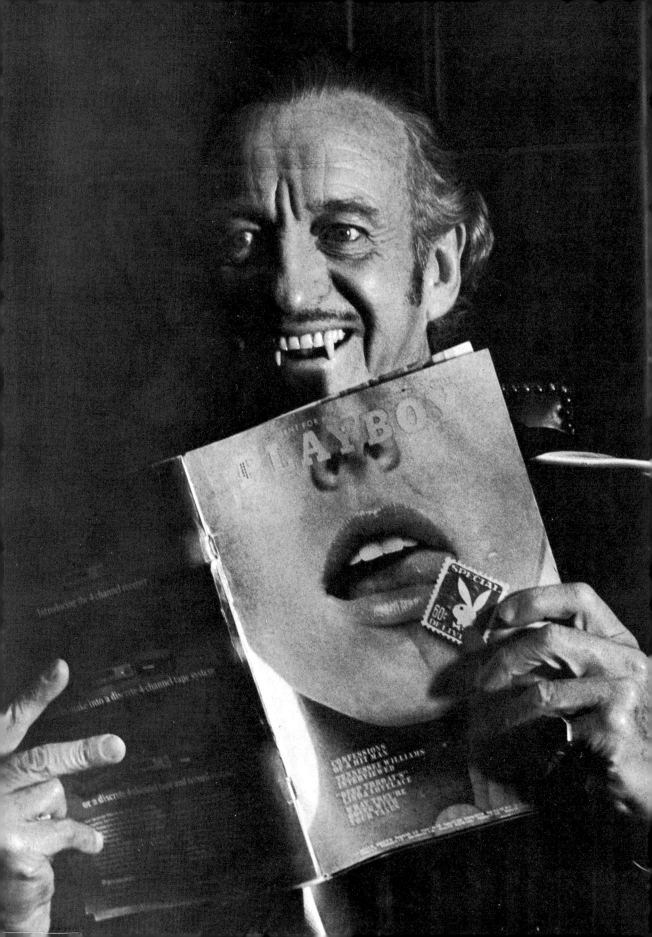

padding. The brown, hideously mummified face with craterous eyes and a shrunken mouth from which fang-like teeth projected, was instantly recognisable. It was the face that had filled their sister's waking nightmare. In one of the stick-like legs was a hole made by the bullet fired by the brother.

The brothers didn't wait to seek higher authority for what they were about to do. They sent for a spade and chopped off the head of the ghoul and then thrust the blade through the black heart. Just to make sure that the hideous revenant didn't walk again and bring disaster and fear to the village, they burnt the body and scattered the ashes to the winds.

The family stayed out their tenancy at Croglin Grange but it was never the same again and they were happy when their contract expired and they were able to move back to the quiet of the Swiss countryside.

The charm of the Croglin Grange story is that it is located firmly in the period when British writers were getting in on the horror market. It also set the story in a class that was to become the hallmark of practically every story that succeeded it. And some that preceded it by a decade or so. The vampire figure went for the neck, had incredible strength and was dispatched by decapitation and fire.

David Niven also gets in on the bloodsucking act in Clive Donner's *Vampira*, 1974

PART THREE
WRITERS AND TALES

Between about 1765 and 1820, something very strange happened to young girls everywhere – and especially in England. For some peculiar reason, they stopped imbibing at the fountain of reason and participating in the Enlightenment – that philosophical movement which gave us the French Revolution and that greatest of eighteenth-century inventions, the Noble Savage. (Where can I find one?) What did these young ladies do with the time they should have been devoting to Aristotle, Cicero or Voltaire? They read horror novels!

Or, more precisely, Gothic novels. Anne Radcliffe was supremo of the genre, and her bestseller was *The Mysteries of Udolpho* – a book so successful that Jane Austen devoted most of her novel *Northanger Abbey* to poking fun at it. The villain in Udolpho – Signor Montoni – is almost like a prototype for Dracula himself. Montoni lives in a castle atop a mountain, he consumes women (though he doesn't drink their blood), he is dark, sinister and exerts a sexual fascination over his female victims. Anne Radcliffe and fellow Gothic authors 'Monk' Lewis and Charles Maturin knew of the abominable writings of the notorious Marquis de Sade, hatched in the turmoil of the French Revolution, and the Sadean taste for violence

and sex – somewhat watered down for respectable readers – was a great success with the public until the sterner tastes of the Victorian era gained the upper hand.

The nineteenth century turned out to be the time when the vampire character migrated from Transylvania and points east and became almost exclusively British. True, two writers who were to promote the vampire character from a cross between a ghoul and a lycanthrope – with various demons mixed in for good measure – were Irish, but at that time the distinction wasn't as clear cut as it is today. Right from the start of the century the vampire became its own boss and, as the century advanced, British in all but accent. Why that should be is the sort of premise that Freudians could, and often do, wax lyrical on. Maybe it was the Empire, the British that is, which had grown like some gigantic vampire and was sucking the blood from the colonies and countries it subjugated and there was an unconscious revulsion for the power of the Imperialist monster. Or maybe it was an allegory on big business and how it drained the life force from all who came into contact with its financial fangs. Then again it could be a plot to reveal the inadequacies of the medical services, which, while claiming the ability to upstage God and cure anything with a bolt

of lightning or a snakebite remedy, were spreading death and destruction and feeding on the corpses in their futile surgical experiments. Or it could just be the British writers had the language and education, coupled with a vivid and slightly pornographic imagination, to be able to take the existing stories and fashion them into tales that would appeal to the general public – a public which was becoming increasingly literate with each passing government. The lives of the poor in their 'sinks' and 'stews' were being made famous by authors of standing such as Charles Dickens, Thomas Hardy, Disraeli, Elizabeth Gaskill, Charles Kingsley, Sir Arthur Conan Doyle and others. The clever trick they played was to set the poor in humble mode while the superior *bourgeoisie* and nobles inhabited a complex world of social mores which, contrasted with those dying in the workhouses and on the streets, seemed trivial and of little importance. Except, that is, as a permanent cork to stop the poor, dishonest but good people at the other end of the social pecking order from ever getting a good deal. As the writers, *per force* at this time, came from the middle and upper-middle classes, the characters they invented tended to be a patronising mish-mash of Shakespearean comedy characters and the perceived mannerisms of the downstairs staff as they related to the upstairs mob.

The classical birth of the modern vampire is usually attributed to Lord Byron via Dr. John Polidori, and the macabre antics of Lord Ruthven and his sidekick Aubrey. This is true only to the extent that Ruthven was from the aristocracy – at least he claimed blue blood. Others also trawled through the naive native tales of the last 6,000 years and began to develop the vampire to a point that, if it was going to stay around, it had to be available and

acceptable to the reading public. And at this time the lower, semi-literate classes were still stuck in a reluctant hero worship of anyone who could get his 'H' in the right place and talk down to the newly arrived 'Peeler'.

The century kicked in with a few stories that edged the basic vampire into the drawing room without infringing on the ladies' right to faint at the thought of anything untoward. The German writer Heinrich von Kleist wrote a feeble story about a noble woman, 'The Marquise of O –', finding herself unaccountably pregnant, discovering that the father was a Russian Count whom she had considered a saviour and friend, and freaking out. When the dastardly Count came back for more she dampened his ardour by dowsing him in holy water. This seemed to act as a redeeming crystal shower and the Count altered his evil ways and the two lived happily ever after. Not much of a vampire there, you might think. But the holy water gives it away. And the fact that the Count had committed his naughties while the innocent Marquise was in a fainting fit. Anyway, it was a start and enough to have the British authors who fancied themselves as horror writers looking to their wreaths of garlic.

It was during a fit of boredom and a bad batch of opium that the vampire story that was to underpin all later models of an undead anti-hero was born. The story is often told but for the sake of continuity: Dr. John Polidori, Mary Shelley (Godwin), Percy Bysshe Shelley and a sometime lover of the noble poet, Claire Clairmont (with child but bearing up wonderfully), met up in the Villa Diodati on the shore of Lake Geneva. The weather was foul and tempers were at volcano heat, not least because of the feud, the hatred almost, that had developed between Byron and Polidori. Polidori had been wished on Byron by his publishers who were tired of paying for Byron's extravagant lifestyle without getting anything sellable on paper. His lifestyle they could stomach. At the time that the mismatched parties were convening beside the waters of Lake Geneva, London was agog with speculation about the newly published novel by Lady Caroline Lamb which charted the amoral goings-on in society of one Clarence de Ruthven – Lord Glenarvon – the eponymous protagonist. Lady Caroline had not long broken off a notorious affair with Byron and it wasn't hard to make the connection between Lord Glenarvon and Lord Byron. Byron knew about the attempt at character assassination and like many who make a life-work out of belittling others, was worried about what exactly had been written. His clever little put-down before even seeing a copy of the book ran along the lines that the portrait it painted couldn't be very good because he hadn't sat for it very long. Whatever the rights and wrongs of the book the resultant publicity was Byron's publishers' dream promotion. The sixth Lord Byron already had a name for outrageous and scandalous behaviour and his voting public were up to buy anything that was penned by him. But he wasn't penning too vigorously and the publishers wanted Polidori to ride shotgun. They chose Polidori, not just because he was a bit of a writer himself but because he was a specialist in drugs. They had money invested in Byron and didn't want him taking a bad trip. Drugs, at this time, were thought to be mind expanding. Does anything change? Anyway, Polidori had ideas above his apparent station. Byron treated him like a servant and Polidori wanted to be a stout companion. At first amused by the doctor's pretensions, Byron began to hate him by the time they dropped their luggage in the hallway of their holiday home.

The other illustrious poet in the household, Percy Bysshe Shelley, had just dumped his wife and was having it away, prior to marriage with Mary Godwin. He was doped up to his eyeballs on laudanum for his headaches, and started fantasising. At one time he screamed and ran from the room when he fancied that Mary Shelley's breasts turned into huge, diabolical eyes. Maybe they had. Ms. Clairmont's station in the household was a little suspect. She laid claim to some classy relatives but with no visible means of supporting her lifestyle, was happy to do a favour for anybody who could buy her a frock, a glass of bubbly and silk sheets.

Mary Shelley (nee Godwin) seems to have been the only halfway ordinary member of the party – and she was about to pen one of the most successful stories, horror or otherwise, of all time – *Frankenstein – or the Modern Prometheus*. While the others are busy externalising their fantasies, Mary was finely adjusting hers to the edge of explosion.

So there were the five louche characters, in various stages of drug addiction and mental imbalance, trapped indoors by incessant rain with nothing to do but bitch and bicker at each other. Nobody could bitch and bicker like Byron. And nobody was so easy a target as John Polidori. But even Byron's sardonic baiting began to pall, so in desperation he suggested a story writing competition. A nightmare writing competition really – a ghost story. Something unusual and decadent. His 'all' didn't include Claire Clairmont, of course; her talents led in another direction. He probably didn't mean Mary either. Polidori was, of course, not even considered. It should have been between Byron and Shelley, but Shelley was having a series of turns and the best he could write was an introspective piece about his early life and the tragedy of being a supreme poet with no self-respect.

Byron dashed off a paragraph or two about a character who lived in and on genteel society and then went back to tormenting Polidori, amusing Mary, scorning Shelley, bonking Claire and taking increasing amounts of opium. By the end of the week the thought of a writing contest had been lost in the rain. Except to Mary, who wrote her nightmare scenario about a man-made man and his dire existence.

By this time the connection between Byron and Polidori was kept alive on bile. Polidori tried to hang on. His connection with the famous poet was opening doors that had been all but hermetically sealed before and he wanted to get as much out of his present humiliation as he could stand. When the break came it was dramatic and swift. With Byron shrieking obscenities at him the doctor packed his bags and left. Not all had been in vain. Before he left he managed to salvage the start of the ghost story Byron had written in the first flush of the writing competition. When the outside world got to hear about it the ennui-driven efforts at fantasy penmanship had the makings of a literary empire that would be deathless.

With nothing to do but sit and mope about the iniquities of the aristocracy, Polidori whiled away the time working Byron's 'fragment', as he later called it, of a story into a form that would attract publishers who only knew him as a writer of medical tracts. It was three years before it saw a bookshelf and then it was entitled *The Vampyre. A Tale*. At first it was ascribed to Byron himself. This was obviously a publisher's ploy to catch the attention of Byron's mesmerised public. That got right up the romantic lord's nostril. By now he was living on opium, mashed potatoes in vinegar and a growing fondness for seeing his name and antics in print. That Polidori should be

so bold as to think that he could write anything which could come anywhere near the cultured outpourings of the leading poet of the age bordered on blasphemy. The publishers took their time striking Byron's name off the by-line and substituting the little known Polidori. But when they did it made little difference to the weird tale's popularity. Polidori made very little out of his masterpiece in spite of it being translated into every civilised language. He died at the tender age of 25. The general opinion was that he committed suicide by drinking prussic acid but pathology at the time was a little suspect and it is now thought that he died of malaria which he contracted while on his wanderings around the Near East. Whatever the case, he was dead, but his story of a vampire in society lived on to breed and multiply.

The story starts with the sudden appearance in polite society of Clarence Ruthven – Lord Glenarvon. He is tall, handsome, witty, charismatic and suffers from halitosis. A condition which only seems to inflame the ladies more, particularly a certain Lady Mercer who is a well-known hostess at literary salons. She tries to get Ruthven's interest but he is more taken by a handsome and wealthy young man who has also taken Lady Mercer's eye. The attraction is mutual. Aubrey believes that the world and everything in it is beautiful. Isolated by his wealth and social position he can understand neither poverty nor the trauma of comparative wealth. Aubrey watches the effect Ruthven has on all those he comes into contact with and can see the difference between the way he is treated and the way the older man dominates those he is attracted to. Aubrey wants some of that unqualified adulation and when he hears that Ruthven intends to go on an extended tour of the continent he suddenly finds that, by sheer coincidence, he is also booked up for the same package. Ruthven, who has hidden his interest in Aubrey, graciously accepts Aubrey's suggestion that they should journey together and within a few days they set off.

At close quarters Aubrey finds his more worldly companion even more interesting. He notes that Ruthven appears to be sorry for the plight of the social outcasts and gives generous amounts of money to beggars and anyone who seems to live on the fringes of civilised society. But they have to be real, low-down, double-dyed villains. Respectable people, down on their luck, get sneers, ridicule and the boot. The remarkable outcome of those given a hand-out by Ruthven is that they all seem to come to a bad end. The money they are given, instead of helping them out of a bad situation, just embroils them deeper in whatever villainy they are into and leaves them to pay the price. Simple Aubrey takes note of the devastation Ruthven's charity creates and tries to explain to his new friend how he should and could be more helpful. Ruthven listens but ignores Aubrey's advice. Gambling is another of Ruthven's pleasures. The pleasure is not from the act of gambling but from the havoc he is able to cause. Against a villain he is happy to lose. With the extra money the villain can do more harm to more people. Ruthven prefers to show his gambling skills against those who can be ruined by a big loss.

In Rome Aubrey sees little of Ruthven. The gallant Lord is off being gallant to a wealthy Italian Countess. Aubrey spends his time looking at the monuments and avoiding the contamination of the prostitutes in the Via Veneto. Arriving back at his hotel after a day in the catacombs Aubrey is excited to find he has received two letters in his absence. One from his sister and the other from his guardian. The contents of his guardian's letter amaze him. It begs him to leave the evil influence of Ruthven and continue his tour on his own. The reason given is that since the two of them left England all sorts of unsavoury facts have hit the fan. Most of the women that Aubrey saw flitting around Ruthven and had inspired in him admiration for the way his friend had courteously handled them, have completely changed in character. Where before they were pious and dutiful mothers, sisters, daughters or wives, they are now little more than harlots. And it is all traced back to Ruthven who, while appearing to salute their virtuousness has been a vile seducer. Vile seducers being fairly common in those days, Aubrey isn't too put out by the description awarded his travelling companion. But it does fit in with his mood. He has already begun to be a little bored with the way Ruthven goes at every situation bullheaded and seemed to leave a wake of destruction behind him. But being a well brought-up lad and not wanting Ruthven to feel deserted, he decides to keep a closer eye on him and look out for an opportunity to break off their relationship more or less amicably.

So instead of wandering off by himself to brood on the beauty of past civilisations he positions himself to make a closer examination of the present one – and particularly the part that Lord Clarence Ruthven Glenarvon plays in it. Straight away Aubrey perceives that Ruthven is trifling with the affections of an innocent young girl and if he doesn't intercede immediately she is doomed to the original sin worse than death. There's nothing like a naive do-gooder on a do-gooding bender and it was inevitable that the virtuous Aubrey should rush in where a more experienced man of the world would fear to breeze through. So, with an 'avast and belay' Aubrey tells Ruthven to turn from his

Dracula in bat form was never quite like this. *Fright Night* 1985

evil ways or he, Aubrey, will have to intervene. Lord Ruthven laughs. Haughtily Aubrey returns to his room and writes a tame letter saying that he no longer wishes to be considered Ruthven's travelling companion. In a great huff he shifts his luggage to other quarters and then, before continuing on his journey, calls on the mother of the girl Ruthven has been seducing and puts the boot in. For the moment Ruthven's plans for lechery are shelved. He doesn't seem particularly put out and writes a polite letter back to Aubrey regretting but agreeing that their ways should part.

Aubrey's next stop is Greece where he gets his kicks, as he had done in Rome, looking at ancient monuments and feeling pious. Not so pious that he doesn't notice a beautiful and feisty young lady, the daughter of the innkeeper under whose roof he happens to be sleeping. Before long Aubrey is going on trips to the country for picnics and spending more time studying her pneumatic form than he is admiring the contours of the classic Grecian statues. The nymph that occupies virtuous Aubrey's thought is called Ianthe, and day by day he becomes more intoxicated with her physical beauty and transparent soul. She professes an appreciation for painting so Aubrey spends hours painting efficient watercolours while Ianthe stands intoxicatingly close making little sighs of pleasure. Almost unbelievingly she tells Aubrey of the wedding rites she has witnessed recently and gives the besotted traveller hope that she is thinking along those lines because she has hopes that they might some day be wed.

Aubrey, in spite of his infatuation, tries to keep up the pretence that he still has an interest in the country's antiquities. There is a site which he particularly wants to visit and he tells Ianthe's parents of his intentions. They beg him not to go as it is a notorious lair of *vampyres* and suchlike. Aubrey is too much a man of the world to be put off by peasant superstition and in spite of all they can do, he is determined to make the trip. When he is ready to go, Ianthe begs him to reconsider. He desperately wants to please her but feels that if he lets her change his mind she will despise him for a coward. At least, she persists, he should return before nightfall. This he is happy to promise. The day passes quickly and he is surprised to see the sun edging down below the distant horizon. He mounts his horse but before he has gone a few yards, there is a clap of thunder and lightning flashes and the rain begins to sheet down. The horse is completely spooked and Aubrey gets tired of the continued battle to stay in the saddle and dismounts. He trudges through the pouring rain until he sees what looks like a peasant's hovel by the side of the track. He's had enough. A shelter is a shelter, however humble. As he approaches there is a momentary break in the thunder and he hears a wild shriek of a frightened woman followed by a mocking chuckle. He gets no response when he knocks on the door of the hovel so he goes inside. It is dark but appears to be empty. Then, without warning, a pair of strong hands fasten around his throat and he is thrown to the ground. His unseen assailant drops his knee onto Aubrey's chest and clutches his neck in a stranglehold. The young man tries to fight back but he is no match for his enemy. As he is about to black out he becomes aware of lights and the cries of men crowding into the hut. The

unexpected invasion saves him. He feels the strong fingers relax and with a curse the dark figure flees. For a while Aubrey lies close to unconsciousness but then he remembers the woman's cry he heard before entering the hut. His rescuers don't believe him but agree to have a look around while Aubrey pulls himself together. He has almost done that when the searchers return. In their arms they carry the still, dead form of Ianthe. She is horribly pale and her neck and breasts are covered in blood. The villagers are in no doubt about what they have on their hands and set up a cry of `Vampyre! A vampyre!' as if naming it might in some way defeat it. Aubrey and his late muse, Ianthe, are carried back to the village. Aubrey, confronted for the first time in his life with events that his money, influence or innocence can't overcome, promptly falls into a violent fever and becomes delirious. You can imagine Aubrey's surprise when he recovers a week later to find Ruthven sitting beside his bed. In his fevered state Aubrey had singled out Ruthven as the slayer of his precious Ianthe and this made him, by local superstition – a vampire. Ruthven isn't at all put out by Aubrey's attitude towards him and insists on staying with him until he recovers. Ruthven is so attentive and appears to be so genuinely concerned with his health that by the time he is fit to travel he is willing to accept the older man's suggestion that they renew their trip together.

They travel through the mountains and have the ill-luck to be ambushed by bandits. Instantly the guides and bearers they have hired flee and they are alone with their attackers. Being a true Brit Aubrey draws his sabre and rushes forward in a suicidal attack on the robbers. Ruthven is a little more circumspect but takes a shot in the shoulder which knocks him to the ground. Overwhelmed by the robbers and with

Ruthven in danger of bleeding to death Aubrey takes the only course open to him and offers the brigands a reward if they deliver him and his friend to a place where his wounds can be properly attended. It is too late for Lord Ruthven. Two days later he dies. Before he dies he makes Aubrey promise not to tell anybody about what has happened during their travels together for a hundred and one days!

Aubrey is happy to take an oath on this. He guiltily remembers that his guardian has forbidden him to travel with Ruthven so the least that is made public the better. Ruthven then dies and Aubrey retires for the night. When he gets up in the morning he is amazed to find that Ruthven's body is missing. From one of the brigands he learns that Ruthven has paid them to carry out certain funeral rites after his death. They have taken his body up the mountain and laid it where the first light of the moon would strike it. Aubrey decides to go up the mountain and pay his last respects to the man whom he can't decide is either his enemy and the vile killer of his beloved or a boon companion with some unfortunate social habits.

When he arrives at the designated place there is no body nor clothes. Aubrey decides that the robbers have stolen the clothes and got rid of the body.

Aubrey's had enough of Greece and returns to Rome. There he hears that the lady whose honour was besmirched by Ruthven has disappeared and her parents have been reduced to poverty. Aubrey realises that the missing daughter has fallen a victim to Ruthven in the same way that his beloved Ianthe had and decides that the time has come to get away from the place that has destroyed his happiness and return home.

Aubrey's sister is very plain and not destined to be the belle of any ball. But she has a pleasant disposition and is only 18 so there was always a chance that nature might be kind and find someone who fancied her. Aubrey wants what is best for his sister so he starts taking her around the social circuit to give her a chance to find a suitable mate. He is standing looking over the gathered company when someone seizes his arm and a voice he remembers from a nightmare whispers in his ear. 'Remember your oath!'

He almost faints when he recognises Lord Ruthven, alive and apparently in rude health. Frightened out of his wits he dashes from the room and returns home. A few days later he is at the *soirée* of a relative with his sister. Again he meets the undead Ruthven, again he hears the hissed command.

'Remember your oath!'

Aubrey grabs his sister and hurries home. Aubrey doesn't know what to do. Chained by the oath he swore on the presumed deathbed of Ruthven he can't tell what he knows to anyone. Not even his sister – and it is driving him mad. A nervous breakdown ensues and when he recovers it is to find that his dear but dumb sister is about to marry the man whom Aubrey is now absolutely certain is a bloodsucking vampire.

The wedding date is set and Aubrey's hopes that he will still be able to save the day are dashed. The date set for the wedding is exactly one hundred and one days after Ruthven made him take the oath not to tell anybody anything he had learned about him during their time in Rome and Greece. Unfortunately his relatives, alarmed at Aubrey's response to the good news of his sister's betrothal, refuse to let him talk to her and warn him that he will be physically restrained if necessary, if he tries to interfere with the arrangements for the wedding. News of Aubrey's collapse amuse Ruthven. He is able to move on the climax of his plan to destroy his young acquaintance. (See extract).

Lord Ruthven had called the morning after at the drawing-room, and had been refused with everyone else. When he heard of Aubrey's ill health, he readily understood himself to be the cause of it; but when he learned that he was deemed insane, his exultation and pleasure could hardly be concealed from those among whom he had gained this information. He hastened to the house of his former companion, and, by constant attendance, and the pretence of great affection for the brother and interest in his fate, he gradually won the ear of Miss Aubrey. Who could resist his power? His tongue had dangers and toils to recount – could speak of himself as of an individual having no sympathy with any being on the crowded earth, save with her to whom he addressed himself; could tell how, since he knew her, his existence had begun to seem worthy of preservation, if it were merely that he might listen to her soothing accents; in fine, he knew so well how to use the serpent's art, or such was the will of fate, that he gained her affections. The title of the elder branch falling at length to him, he obtained an important embassy, which served as an excuse for hastening the marriage (in spite of her brother's deranged state), which was to take place the very day before his departure for the continent.

Aubrey, when he was left by the physician and his guardians, attempted to bribe the servants, but in vain. He asked for pen and paper, it was given him; he wrote a letter to his sister, conjuring her, as she valued her own happiness, her own honour, and the honour of those now in the grave, who once held her in their arms as their hope and the hope of their house, to delay but for a few hours that marriage, on which he denounced the most heavy curses. The servants promised they would deliver it; but giving it to the physician, he thought it

better not to harass any more the mind of Miss Aubrey by, what he considered, the ravings of a maniac. Night passed on without rest to the busy inmates of the house; and Aubrey heard, with a horror that may more easily be conceived than described, the notes of busy preparation. Morning came and the sound of carriages broke upon his ear. Aubrey grew almost frantic. The curiosity of the servants at last overcame their vigilance, they gradually stole away, leaving him in the custody of an helpless old woman. He seized the opportunity, with one bound was out of the room and in a moment found himself in the apartment where all were nearly assembled. Lord Ruthven was the first to perceive him: he immediately approached and taking his arm by force, hurried him from the room, speechless with rage. When on the staircase, Lord Ruthven whispered in his ear – "Remember your oath, and know, if not my bride today, your sister is dishonoured. Women are frail!" So saying, he pushed him towards his attendants, who, roused by the old woman, had come in search of him. Aubrey could no longer support himself; his rage not finding vent, had broken a blood-vessel, and he was conveyed to bed. This was not mentioned to his sister, who was not present when he entered, as the physician was afraid of agitating her. The marriage was solemnized and the bride and bridegroom left London.

Aubrey's weakness increased; the effusion of blood produced symptoms of the near approach of death. He desired his sister's guardians might be called, and when the midnight hour had struck, he related composedly what the reader has perused – he died immediately after.

The guardians hastened to protect Miss Aubrey; but when they arrived – it was too late. Lord Ruthven had disappeared and

Aubrey's sister had glutted the thirst of a vampyre!

Polidori's vampire, Lord Ruthven, almost met the criteria for a modern vampire. He's good looking, can pull the women without much trouble, is dead but refuses to lie down and has some sort of hypnotic effect on those he wants to use. There is also the suggestion that he can enter other people's thoughts. Where he still differs from today's aristocratic bloodsuckers is that he seems to have no ability to create vampires, doesn't change shape and there seems to be no known way of getting rid of him. It doesn't appear possible that he would succumb to a crucifix or holy water and he probably eats garlic for breakfast. The fact that he is able to move in daylight isn't so interesting. Only in the film versions of the vampire, some – not all, make a big thing of the all-powerful vampire shrivelling away to dust when the light of day hits him.

Once Lord Ruthven was let loose on the reading public there was no stopping him. Ruthven stories began to appear all over the world – few of them acknowledging Polidori's part in unleashing him into the world. Between 1819 and 1847 everyone with a pen and a spare sheet of paper wrote a vampire story but it wasn't until 1847 when James Malcolm Rymer anonymously wrote *Varney the Vampire* or the *Feast of Blood*, that the vampire character moved forward into a new era. But before we get into that it might be a good time to have a brief look at Byron's *Fragment* on which John Polidori based *The Vampyre'*.

byron's fragment

This was originally part of the story which Byron told in June 1816, as his contribution to the famous Villa Diodati ghost story session. He omitted most of the more 'vampiric' aspects of his original story in this published version, probably in order to highlight the differences between his *Fragment* and Polidori's *Vampyre*.

The reason Lord Byron published this *Fragment* at all (as an appendix to his poem *Mazeppa*, in 1819) was almost certainly self-defence – it was rushed out just after the appearance of Polidori's 'version' (which had been falsely attributed to Byron himself, partly because of a misunderstanding, partly in order to boost sales).

june 17, 1816

In the year 17--, having for some time determined on a journey through countries not hitherto much frequented by travellers, I set out, accompanied by a friend, whom I shall designate by the name of Augustus Darvell. He was a few years my elder, and a man of considerable fortune and ancient family: advantages which an extensive capacity prevented him alike from undervaluing or overrating. Some peculiar circumstances in his private history had rendered him to me an object of attention, of interest, and even of regard, which neither the reserve of his manners, nor occasional indications of an inquietude at times nearly approaching to alienation of mind, could extinguish.

I was yet young in life, which I had begun early, but my intimacy with him was of a recent date: we had been educated at the same schools and university; but his progress through these had preceded mine, and he had been deeply initiated into what is called the world, while I was yet in my noviciate. While thus engaged, I heard much both of his past and present life; and, although in these accounts there were many and irreconcilable contradictions, I could still gather from the whole that he was a being of no common order, and one who, whatever pains he might take to avoid remark, would still be remarkable. I had cultivated his acquaintance subsequently, and endeavoured to obtain his friendship, but this last appeared to be unattainable; whatever affections he might have possessed now, seemed to have been extinguished, and others to be concentred: that this feeling were acute, I had sufficient opportunities of observing; for, although he could control, he could not altogether disguise them: still he had a power of giving to one passion the appearance of another, in such a manner that it was difficult to define the nature of what was working within him; and the expressions of his features would vary so rapidly, though slightly, that it was useless to trace them to their sources. It was evident that he was a prey to some cureless disquiet; but whether it arose from ambition, love, remorse, grief, from one of all of these, or merely from a morbid temperament akin to disease, I could not discover: there were circumstances alleged which might have justified the application to each of these causes; but, as I have before said, these were so contradictory and contradicted, that none could be fixed upon with accuracy. Where there is mystery, it is generally supposed that there must also be evil: I know not how this may be, but in him there certainly was the one, though I could not ascertain the extent of the other -and felt loath, as far as regarded himself, to believe in its existence. My advances were received with sufficient coolness: but I was young, and not easily discouraged, and at length succeeded in obtaining, to a certain degree, that common-place intercourse and moderate confidence of common and every-day concerns, created and cemented by similarity of pursuit and frequency of meeting, which is called

intimacy, or friendship, according to the ideas of him who uses those words to express them.

Darvell had already travelled extensively; and to him I had applied for information with regard to the conduct of my intended journey. It was my secret wish that he might be prevailed on to accompany me; it was also a probable hope, founded upon the shadowy restlessness which I observed in him, and to which the animation which he appeared to feel on such subjects, and his apparent indifference to all by which he was more immediately surrounded, gave fresh strength. This wish I first hinted, and then expressed: his answer, though I had partly expected it, gave me all the pleasure of surprise – he consented; and, after the requisite arrangement, we commenced our voyages After journeying through various countries of the south of Europe, our attention was turned towards the East, according to our original destination; and it was in my progress through these regions that the incident occurred upon which will turn what I may have to relate.

The constitution of Darvell, which must from his appearance have been in early life more than usually robust, had been for some time gradually giving way, without the intervention of any apparent disease: he had neither cough nor hectic, yet he became daily more enfeebled; his habits were temperate, and he neither declined nor complained of fatigue; yet he was evidently wasting away: he became more and more silent and sleepless, and at length so seriously altered, that my alarm grew proportionate to what I conceived to be his danger.

We had determined, on our arrival at Smyrna, on an excursion to the ruins of Ephesus and Sardis, from which I endeavoured to dissuade him in his present state of indisposition – but in vain: there appeared to be an oppression on his mind, and a solemnity in his manner, which ill corresponded with his eagerness to proceed on what I regarded as a mere party of pleasure little suited to a valetudinarian; but I opposed him no longer – and in a few days we set off together, accompanied only by a serrugee and a single janizary.

We had passed halfway towards the remains of Ephesus, leaving behind us the more fertile environs of Smyrna, and were entering upon that wild and tenantless tract through the marshes and defiles which lead to the few huts yet lingering over the broken columns of Diana – the roofless walls of expelled Christianity, and the still more recent but complete desolation of abandoned mosques – when the sudden and rapid illness of my companion obliged us to halt at a Turkish cemetery, the turbaned tombstones of which were the sole indication that human life had ever been a sojourner in this wilderness. The only caravanserai we had seen was left some hours behind us; not a vestige of a town or even cottage was within sight or hope, and this 'city of the dead' appeared to be the sole refuge of my unfortunate friend, who seemed on the verge of becoming the last of its inhabitants.

In this situation, I looked round for a place where he might most conveniently repose. Contrary to the usual aspect of Mahometan burial-grounds, the cypresses were in this few in number, and these thinly scattered over its extent; the tombstones were mostly fallen, and worn with age: upon one of the most considerable of these, and beneath one of the most spreading trees, Darvell supported himself, in a half-reclining posture, with great difficulty. He asked for water. I had some doubts of our being able to find any, and prepared to go in search of it with hesitating despondency: but he

desired me to remain' and turning to Sulaiman, our janizary, who stood by us smoking with great tranquillity, he said, 'Sulaiman, verban su' (i.e.' bring some water') and went on describing the spot where it was to be found with great minuteness, at a small well for camels, a few hundred yards to the right: the janizary obeyed. I said to Darvell, 'How did you know this?' He replied, 'From our situation; you must perceive that this place was once inhabited, and could not have been so without springs: I have also been here before.'

'You have been here before! How came you never to mention this to me? and what could you be doing in a place where no one would remain a moment longer than they could help it?'

To this question I received no answer. In the mean time Sulaiman returned with the water, leaving the serrugee and the horses at the fountain. The quenching of his thirst had the appearance of reviving him for a moment; and I conceived hopes of his being able to proceed, or at least to return, and I urged the attempt. He was silent – and appeared to be collecting his spirits for an effort to speak. He began:

'This is the end of my journey, and of my life; I came here to die; but I have a request to make, a command – for such my last words must be. You will observe it?'

'Most certainly; but I have better hopes.'

'I have no hopes, nor wishes, but this – conceal my death from every human being.'

'I hope there will be no occasion; that you will recover, and – '

'Peace! it must be so: promise this.'

'I do.'

'Swear it, by all that – ' He here dictated an oath of great solemnity.

'There is no occasion for this. I will observe your request; and to doubt me is – '

'It cannot be helped – you must swear.'

I took the oath, it appeared to relieve him. He removed a seal ring from his finger, on which were some Arabic characters, and presented it to me. He proceeded:

'On the ninth day of the month, at noon precisely (what month you please, but this must be the day), you must fling this ring into the salt springs which run into the Bay of Eleusis; the day after, at the same hour, you must repair to the ruins of the temple of Ceres, and wait one hour.'

'Why?'

'You will see.'

'The ninth day of the month, you say?'

'The ninth.'

As I observed that the present was the ninth day of the month, his countenance changed, and he paused. As he sat, evidently becoming more feeble, a stork, with a snake in her beak, perched upon a tombstone near us; and, without devouring her prey, appeared to be steadfastly regarding us. I know not what impelled me to drive it away, but the attempt was useless; she made a few circles in the air, and returned exactly to the same spot. Darvell pointed to it, and smiled – he spoke – I know not whether to himself or to me – but the words were only, ''Tis well!'

'What is well? What do you mean?'

'No matter; you must bury me here this evening, and exactly where that bird is now perched. You know the rest of my injunctions.'

He then proceeded to give me several directions as to the manner in which his death might be best concealed. After these were finished, he exclaimed, 'You perceive that bird?'

'Certainly.'

'And the serpent writhing in her beak?'

'Doubtless: there is nothing uncommon in it, it is her natural prey. But it is odd that she does not devour it.'

He smiled in a ghastly manner, and said faintly, 'It is not yet time!' As he spoke, the stork flew away. My eyes followed it for a moment – it could hardly be longer than ten might be counted. I felt Darvell's weight, as it were, increase upon my shoulder, and, turning to look upon his face, perceived that he was dead!

I was shocked with the sudden certainty which could not be mistaken – his countenance in a few minutes became nearly black. I should have attributed so rapid a change to poison, had I not been aware that he had no opportunity of receiving it unperceived. The day was declining, the body was rapidly altering, and nothing remained but to fulfil his request. With the aid of Sulaiman's yagatan and my own sabre, we scooped a shallow grave upon the spot which Darvell had indicated: the earth easily gave way, having already received some Mahometan tenant. We dug as deeply as the time permitted us, and throwing the dry earth upon all that remained of the singular being departed, we cut a few sods of greener turf from the less withered soil around us, and laid them upon his sepulchre.

Between astonishment and grief, I was tearless.

VARNEY THE VAMPIRE

The *Varney the Vampire* stories were originally published in 109 weekly episodes and then condensed into a novel of over 850 pages. Because various writers wrote Varney stories there was a lot of argument about just who first invented the character and breathed the breath of death into him. Speculation was possible because writing for 'penny-dreadfuls' – '1 Penny plain – 2 Pennies coloured' – wasn't considered real writing. It

Blood and Roses 1960, based on Le Fanu's eerie tale, though given a thumbs-down by the author

sarcastic about the worth and standing of authors who wrote crap for the adult comic market. Forced by his terms of employment to add his pen to the industry of dodgy stories, he naturally decided to keep a low profile. The stories themselves were written in a prosy, arty manner that suggests he was going for the word count – being paid by the word and relishing every adjective. The sheer volume of Rymer's vampiric work not only strained the average unreinforced bookshelf but made sure that the only way to really write *'finis'* for a vampire was when he did the noble deed for himself. The length of the purple prose offering also ensured that it wasn't picked up and reprinted until the early 1970s. Even then it was against the advice of those in the know – and they were right. *Varney the Vampire* lost out to the public's shrinking attention span. Maybe someone will come up with a TV format that will permit Sir Francis back into the vampire world with a soap series.

Unlike the coldly handsome Lord Ruthven, Sir Francis sounds a nasty piece of work. From his description he doesn't seem to be the sort to have beautiful and virtuous maidens giving their all on a weekly basis. But if you can believe Rymer that's exactly what happened. Tall and lanky with huge watery eyes like polished metal, cold and clammy like a corpse, doesn't exactly fill a prescription for a Don Juan of the tombstones. Add (or subtract) from that his white, dirty skin, fang-like teeth, long dirty fingernails that appear to hang from his fingertips like talons and that infallible vampire trademark – dire halitosis – and it's a wonder he could get in the same carriage as a Billingsgate fish wife, let alone became an intimate of young, dainty girls. Obviously when Rymer dashed off the first episodes of *Varney the Vampire* he had no idea that it would still be talked about and analysed

was only possible to nail down the real 'culprit' when a researcher came across some notes in the early 1970s. J.M. Rymer was revealed in the light of day as the original chronicler of the dirty deeds of the vampire aristocrat, Sir Francis Varney. Before this time the Varney adventure marathon had been ascribed to the writer of the legendary but equally gory, *Sweeney Todd – the Demon Barber of Fleet St.*, Thomas Preskett Prest. The reason Rymer wanted to keep his part in Varney's inception a secret was that when he had been employed by another publishing house he had inadvisedly waxed

after 150 years. It was probably a bit like the record-breaking soap serial, *Coronation Street*. Half a dozen episodes and then think of something else. Both have proved to have legs that are the envy of marathon runners. The lack of conviction in Varney's longevity is obvious. No attempt was initially made to give him a background. Like Uncle Tom's Topsy he 'just growed'. Different writers saw him emerging from various backgrounds and his antecedence began to look like the 'truth' written by a newspaper columnist.

General opinion puts him in the Bannerworth family. The sort of relative from hell that you pray never knocks on your door and announces he is on holiday and in the area and he thought maybe he could... When the saga opens that's where he's located, although his exact status around the family hearth is never fully explained. He's there and falls for the beautiful young daughter of the household, Flora. Unable to control his lust he jumps on her, sinks his protruding fangs into her neck and sucks her dry. Henry Bannerworth, her father and presumably a saint among men, sees poor old Varney as a victim of his – admittedly, peculiar and deadly – passions and shields him when the villagers go on the rampage and want to discuss mortality at the point of a sawn-off stake.

Cynics say that there was only ever one Varney story and 108 copies with just the names changed to protect the guilty. That can be said about any long-running series. It would be patently silly to strike a rich vein and then decide to head off in another direction. As long as there were readers queuing up to buy the magazine there was someone to write the stories. It has also been pointed out that the opening episode owed more than a nodding acquaintance to the Croglin Grange story. This is true!

A young, obviously beautiful and virtuous maiden with long flowing chestnut hair is awakened by the sounds of a titanic hailstorm. Unable to get to sleep she becomes aware of a ghastly face peering at her through the window. Before she can do anything about it, Varney, for it's obviously he, leaps over the sill and makes a grab for her. She spends valuable screaming time squirming around on the bed trying to keep away from Varney's talons and halitosis before he darts in and grabs her by the hair. He forces her head back over the end of the bed and, ignoring all the fleshier parts now on display, sinks his incisors into her neck. Blood flies all over the place and at last the damsel, very much in distress, manages a few refined cries for help. By the time help arrives, Varney, flushed of cheek and blossoming from his fatal repast, is long gone. His victim dies, leaving a sorrowing sweetheart to beat his breast and declare his love for her even unto the grave. Before long there are rumours that a young girl bearing more than a passing resemblance to his ex-lover has been seen floating around the local churchyard in her white burial robes and a faraway look in her eyes. The boyfriend, obsessed with the thought that there might still be the chance of a little heavy petting, decides to hang out in the chapel and see what happens. While he waits he lapses into the sort of declarations of love that we usually find in Victorian novels and Spanish flicks. Just as he is running out of ways to convince himself that he will do anything for one more glimpse of his beloved she inconveniently appears. That has his hair standing on end and his libido taking a holiday. She disappears out of the chapel and he decides to follow her. If she has got a gill of warm blood in her – well, you never know what might happen. If, on the hand she turns out to be cold and clammy he can always stroll off as if nothing has happened. Still mouthing protestations of love he follows the white, ghostly figure. He calls her name. She turns her head, drawing him on, and disappears into a vault. In those days, of course, the general public likely to come into contact with the undead hadn't the benefit of cinema and TV and didn't know that when a beautiful figure in a white shroud throws you an encouraging look and disappears into a vault you give them the Italian digit and get back to your room at the tavern and read the good book. So our hot-panted friend goes blundering in, calling her name and expecting to be welcome with soft white open arms. He is greeted with large cold clammy hands – around his throat. All seems lost! But what's this? From afar comes the sound of peasantry on the move. The flickering light of their torches illuminates the scene. Varney unclamps his hands from around the young man's neck and makes off, but not before getting a bullet in the leg which makes his usual lolloping gait even more grotesque.

The villagers find the young lady in her coffin, in what is instantly recognised as a vampiric state. The village blacksmith, a noble man of culture and learning, eggs on his companions, explains that the poor girl's soul must be released. They agree. Then he spoils it by telling them that they must cut her head off. This isn't received too well and he grudgingly agrees to perform the therapeutic operation. They carry the coffin to the nearest crossroads, bang in the stake and get the customary lashings of blood and screaming, then they cut off the head and burn the body and scatter the ashes about the crossroads.

Meanwhile, poor old Varney is still hobbling across country, no doubt muttering about neighbours who can't mind their own business and looking for a vampire doctor. The doctoring comes in the shape of the moon. As it breaks free of the clouds and bathes Varney in its cold light the gunshot wound heals dramatically. Varney hops cheerfully on his way looking for a suitable site for his next episode.

The *Varney the Vampire* saga could also be said to set the pattern for many other books and TV series. Those old enough to remember David Janssen in *The Fugitive* will recognise the premise: an outcast, odd-jobbing around the country while every hand is turned against him. Janssen always managed to get away at the end of each exciting episode. Not so Varney. He usually ended up crippled, burned, hacked to pieces, squashed to death, beheaded, disembowelled or generally in a sorry state. His saviour was always the moonlight. No matter how much everybody seemed to get by without noticing his peculiarly death-like looks or blenching at a blast from his fiery breath, as soon as he got into a one-on-one situation with the girl of his choice, she started screaming and was rescued or she died and got given the vampire's farewell by a peasant staking party. It also meant that the villagers would then mount a major offensive against Sir Francis Varney and do him a great deal of brutal but ultimately ineffective, harm.

The first story, rambled through above, starts like Croglin Grange and finishes along the Universal Studio lines first used by Polidori in *The Vampyre*. With minor changes and historic flashbacks to try and sort out Varney's background, the plot stayed basically unchanged for the rest of the leviathan literary effort.

Varney was born around the beginning of the seventeenth or possibly late sixteenth century, and was a Royalist. He got bumped off by Cromwell's men and was revitalised a couple of years later to find himself in his vampiric state. This was wished on him because in a fit of pique he had struck and killed his son. Son killing was a sure-fire ticket of entry to vampirism. As Varney's life unfolded from the quill of Mr. Rymer, he developed a sense of honour. He also became more mercenary. His family home had been burned down by the Roundheads but Sir Francis was able to locate some treasure he had happened to bury before his death, as one does, and this set him up so that he could haunt in genteel society.

After a couple of years of having virtuous damsels screaming in his ear and never finding anyone willing to bring his pipe and slippers, Varney decided that enough was definitely enough. He would gladly have accepted the stake if it meant a bit of eternal peace but that damned moonlight kept interfering and making him whole again. He decided that he couldn't trust anyone to do a good job of finishing him off once and for all. He needed to find somewhere he could do himself in and not be resurrected by that old devil moon. So he went to Greece.

Let Jimmy Rymer take up Sir Francis Varney's tale from there.

We extract from the Allgemeine Zeitung *the following most curious story, the accuracy of which, of course, we cannot vouch for, but still there is a sufficient air of probability about it to induce us to present it to our readers.*

Late in the evening, about four days since, a tall and melancholy-looking stranger arrived, and put up at one of the principal hotels at Naples. He was a most peculiar-looking man, and considered by the persons of the establishment as about the ugliest guest they had ever had within the walls of their place.

In a short time he summoned the landlord, and the following conversation ensued between him and the strange guest.

"I want," said the stranger, "to see all the curiosities of Naples, and among the rest Mount Vesuvius. Is there any difficulty?"

"None," replied the landlord, "with a proper guide."

A guide was soon secured, who set out with the adventurous Englishman to make the ascent of the burning mountain.

They went on then until the guide did not think it quite prudent to go any further, as there was a great fissure in the side of the mountain, out of which a stream of lava was slowly issuing and spreading itself in rather an alarming manner.

The ugly Englishman, however, pointed to a secure mode of getting higher still and they proceeded until they were very near the edge of the crater itself. The stranger then took his purse from his pocket and flung it to the guide saying-

"You can keep that for your pains, and for coming into some danger with me. But the fact was, that I wanted a witness to an act which I have set my mind upon performing."

The guide says that these words were spoken with so much calmness that he easily believed the act mentioned as about to be done was some scientific experiment of which he knew that the English were very fond and he replied -

"Sir, I am only too proud to serve so generous and so distinguished a gentleman. In what way can I be useful?"

"You will make what haste you can," said the stranger, "from the mountain, inasmuch as it is covered with sulphurous vapours, inimical to human life, and when you reach the city you will cause to be published an account of my proceedings and what I say. You will say that you accompanied Varney the vampire to the crater of Mount Vesuvius and that, tired and disgusted with a life of horror, he flung himself in to prevent the

possibility of a reanimation of his remains."

Before, then, the guide could utter anything but a shriek, Varney took one tremendous leap and disappeared into the burning mouth of the mountain.

So Sir Francis Varney became a gallant by taking the typically stiff upper lip way out open only to British gentlemen and sex-mad lemmings. His method of disposing of his indestructible body by putting it where the moon doesn't shine is interesting and has the added value that it doesn't totally rule out a Reichenbach Falls type return. In a few million years when the volcano has cooled down a bit and wind and rain have weathered away the steep sides is it possible that moonlight could once again resuscitate the vampire and let him loose on a community which might not be *au fait* with the lore of the vampire. But that is for the future to worry about. The legacy Varney left for the vampire lover is a whole new set of neuroses for Bram Stoker to pick over, fillet and adopt.

CARMILLA

When Joseph Sheridan Le Fanu decided to produce the *oeuvre* for vampire literature he looked at 6,000 years of demons, ghouls, revenants and vampires and decided he liked none of them. On the principle that if you cast against character you can always blame the casting director if you finish up with a weak production, Le Fanu boldly struck out in graveyards new. He virtually discarded everything which made a vampire a vampire and came up with a vampire which set a new trend amongst portrayers of the undead. Vampires are male, cold, clammy and smelly – and usually ugly. Le Fanu produced a female vampire that was young, beautiful,

loving and innocent. She wasn't even feisty in ways that female baddies are usually expected to be. Carmilla was soft, doe-like and languid. Very languid. She appeared to be frail and made this an excuse to stay in her bed until the day was well advanced. Nothing unusual there. She did have a few odd habits – like turning into a black cat or disappearing when she found herself in a circumstance that demanded prudence rather than aggression. Also she didn't age – just changed her name to suit the situation. Le Fanu made it one of the rules of joining the vampire club. The name originally handed out to the novice vampire had to be retained. Not necessarily in its original form, though. Anagrams were allowed so Carmilla turns up as Mircalla and Millarca. Stoker never bothered to follow this foible in his vampire code but later imposters came up with various forms to try and outwit the lawyers. Alucard and Dr. Alcua were two that found some popularity.

J. Sheridan Le Fanu was the typical English gentleman – only he was Irish. Maybe Irish is a little too much. He was as Irish as Polidori was English. His grandparents were Huguenots obliged to leave France when Louis XIV slung out the Edict of Nantes which guarded the Protestants' right to protest. His family managed to get out with most of the family silver intact and it was enough to educate the young Joseph and send him to Trinity College. He was determined to be a writer and after being employed as a reporter on various journals he became editor of the *Dublin University Press*. This gave him an open platform for his own writing which he published under several *nom-de-plumes*. In 1872 he brought out an anthology of ghost stories, *In A Glass Darkly*. Arguably the best was 'Carmilla'.

The narrator of the story is 19-year-old

Ingrid with screen lover Sandor Eles in *Countess Dracula*

Ingrid in less
sinister mode in
*The Vampire
Lovers*

A scene from
*Countess
Dracula*
depicting her in
the stage of
disintegration

Laura. She lived with her father in a large rambling castle in Styria. They were reasonably well-off and had a handful of servants plus a governess living in the house. Laura was related to the Karnsteins on her mother's side. The nearest neighbour was General Spielsdorf, seven miles away. Between the castle and the General's place was a village but it has been deserted for years. At the start of the story Laura is expecting a visit from the General with his niece, Mademoiselle Bertha Rheinfeld. It is a visit long anticipated and Laura is excited at the prospect of someone of her own age to talk to. Meanwhile she reminisces about a dream she had when she was six years old.

Laura was lying in bed one night when she was visited by a beautiful lady. Laura didn't think it strange that she should come unannounced and when the visitor sat on the bed and caressed her she felt so relaxed she soon dropped off to sleep. She was jerked awake by the sensation of needles being dug deep into her chest. The pain was so intense that she screamed. Her nocturnal visitor was still there but, warned off by Laura's shrill cries, slipped off the bed and disappeared. When her nurse heard her story she examined Laura's chest but there was nothing to be seen. She also checked under the bed and was able to reassure Laura that there was nobody in the room who wasn't accounted for. Laura had to accept what she was told. The experience so frightened her that from that time until she was 14 years of age she insisted that a servant sleep in her bedroom. The experience was so vivid that she never forgot the gentle, sweet face that had disturbed her sleep.

The day for the General and his niece to arrive came, but instead of guests Laura's family received a letter. It was from the General saying that his niece had died and he was going to spend the rest of his life tracking down the monster who had killed her. The news had a sobering effect on both Laura and her father. In an effort to cheer her up her father suggested a walk. It was the night of the full moon and the familiar landscape looked beautifully different from the way it did in the sunlight. As they walked in the garden naming stars and quoting poetry they heard the rattle of a coach travelling at high speed on the track that passed close to the castle walls where there was a small humped-back bridge. The horses hit the bridge far too fast. As the coach keeled over out of control Laura heard the terrified scream of a woman. The coach crashed and turned on its side. The coachmen were unhurt and desperately tried to calm the horses and free them from the traces which held them between the shafts. A tall, distinguished woman climbed shakily out of the coach and directed the men in gently taking the inert body of a young woman from the wreck. The young woman revived but was in no condition to travel. Laura's father suggested they stayed for the night but the Countess – the young woman's mother – explained that it was vitally important that she continued her journey immediately. Laura's father insisted that the young lady, whose name was Carmilla, stayed with them until she was well enough to travel. The Countess appeared reluctant to leave her daughter but was finally convinced of the wisdom of this course of action. She warned Laura's father that her mission was so secretive that if news of it got out it could have unimaginable repercussions internationally. She begged him not to ask Carmilla to explain what was happening until the Countess was able to return and tell them all. Laura's father gave his solemn word and the Countess went off and Carmilla took up residence in the household.

When their guest had recovered

Ingrid in a clinch with Peter Cushing
in the *Vampire Lovers*

Anulka and
Marianne
Morris in
José Larraz'
Vampyres
released in
1976

somewhat from her frightening ordeal Laura went to see her. It was the first opportunity she had to see Carmilla in the light and she was momentarily struck dumb. It was the woman from her dream. Carmilla was also looking at Laura with obvious incredulity. She also had dreamed, at the same time as Laura, of their meeting.

Carmilla soon settled in and a deep, intense friendship grew between the two young women. It wasn't an easy bonding. Carmilla was described as being 'languid, very languid'. She didn't get up until the afternoon was well advanced and she rarely exerted herself walking. She preferred to sit quietly in the garden with Laura and read.

When Laura asked her anything about her life before the coach crashed and deposited her on their doorstep, Carmilla gave a sweet smile and promised she would reveal all when the time was right. Laura's father was happy to see the close relationship build between his lonely daughter and the beautiful stranger. The friendship between the two soon became very intense and Laura was completely dominated by the sweet Carmilla.

In the countryside around the castle the situation was not so happy. Within a short space of time four village girls died. The common symptom was a rapidly developing anaemia which surely and inexorably drew the life from them. Laura was also feeling unwell. She was listless and had lost interest in anything but her lovely companion. The relationship had now passed beyond the bounds of ordinary friendship and the lives of the two young women had become inextricably entwined. But still Carmilla kept her secrets and only promised that all would be revealed when her mother, the Countess, returned. Although their idyllic friendship was occasionally interrupted by spates of temper, these never lasted long. Carmilla always returned to her languid and slightly amused dalliance with her young friend.

Only once did her usual façade slip. Carmilla and Laura were sitting near the road that led to the chapel when a funeral party passed, singing hymns. Carmilla flew into a rage and swore the music was annoying her. Laura tried to explain that it was the funeral of a girl who had died of the wasting disease. Carmilla wouldn't listen. She said she wasn't interested in what the peasants got up to, dead or alive. Laura took her in her arms and kissed the mood away.

A tinker, a hunchback, arrived at the *Schloss* one morning and after sharpening the knives and mending the pots he suggested he file down Carmilla's pointed teeth. She was very upset and demanded that the tinker be thrown out. More deaths were reported around the area and Laura's father began to fear for the safety of his young wards. All the deaths that occurred were to girls of a similar age.

Soon after a picture cleaner arrived from Graz to restore some of the paintings that were hidden under years of soot and dirt. When cleaned, one of the pictures appear to be the spitting image of Carmilla. Carmilla's dialogue got a little fruity at this point. Example: 'Darling, darling, I live in you, and you would die for me. I love you!' The extent of her passion made Carmilla feel a little faint and she was put to bed. Laura sat with her and consoled her. Later that same evening Laura awoke to see a huge black cat prowling at the end of her bed. She was too frightened to cry out when it leaped on her bed and straddled her. The large, hypnotic green eyes watched her coolly from a distance of only a few inches. As Laura tried to break away she felt a stinging pain as if red-hot needles had been driven into her breast. With a scream she woke up and was aware of the figure of a woman standing at the bottom of the bed, black against the flickering candlelight. Without apparently moving the figure went to the door and disappeared from view. Supposing that it was Carmilla playing a trick on her, Laura got up and went to the door – it was locked on the inside as it always was when she slept.

Distraught, Laura hardly listened while her governess prattled on as they sat under a shading tree the following morning. The name Carmilla caught her attention. Her governess claimed that the trees under Carmilla's window were haunted. A ghostly white figure had twice been seen there during the night. When Carmilla appeared she looked tired and pale. Alone at last, Carmilla told Laura that she had woken in the night to see the dark figure of a woman standing at the foot of the bed. The figure had vanished when Carmilla held up a charm she had bought from the hunchback. Open-mouthed Laura listened, then blurted out her version of the very same story. For several days after that nothing happened. Carmilla claimed that it was entirely due to the efficacy of the charm she had purchased. It was keeping them both safe. Laura continued to sleep well but in spite of this awoke each morning feeling tired and out of sorts. She wouldn't admit she was ill so her father and doctor knew nothing of her condition. Carmilla never left her side during the day and they would lie for long hours entwined in each other's arms. The change in appearance from a bright healthy girl to a pallid invalid was gradual and although her father noticed the change in her, he accepted her reassurance that she was just a little off-colour and would soon recover.

However, Laura was sinking fast. One night in her dreams she heard a voice warn that her mother told her to beware of the assassin. A light sprang up and in it she could see Carmilla standing at the end of the bed in a white nightdress, covered in blood. Laura woke up with a shriek that brought the whole household scurrying to her room. She gave a garbled version of what she had experienced and insisted that they all go to Carmilla's room to make sure she was unharmed. Their consternation grew when they knocked on her door and got no reply. Laura ordered the servants to break down the door. Carmilla's room was empty.

It was past 4 o'clock by now. Laura insisted on sleeping in her governess's room. In the morning Laura's father ordered the servants to search the grounds and surrounding country fearing Carmilla had been kidnapped. Laura was inconsolable. After attempting to eat her lunch she returned to Carmilla's room and was amazed to see her in front of her dressing table. She explained her absence by telling a story about sleep walking and waking up only a few minutes earlier to find herself stretched out on a couch in her dressing room. Laura's father came up with an explanation for the strange incident which satisfied only if there was no scepticism. And there was none.

Meanwhile the father had finally woken up to the fact that Laura was looking more than a little peaky. Without consulting Laura he sent for the family doctor. As Laura told him her story he became more thoughtful. When she had finished the doctor talked to her father and what he told him upset him greatly. Laura was again called in and questioned about the feeling of having needles driven into her breast. When she was examined the doctor found a small blue spot at the base of her neck. He seemed to expect it. The doctor called in the governess and told her that, for the moment, she was not to leave Laura's side under any circumstances. Laura's father suggested that the doctor call back later that day to examine Carmilla and he agreed. Shortly after he left a messenger arrived with some letters for Laura's father. One of them was from General Spielsdorf who said he would be arriving on the following day.

At twelve o'clock the following day her father ordered the coach and invited the governess and Laura to accompany him on a trip to the deserted village of Karnstein where he had some business. Laura had never been there and was excited by the prospect of a trip away from her sick-bed. They had nearly reached the village when they met General Spielsdorf riding towards them. He climbed in the carriage and left his servants to go on to the house with his horse and luggage. As they rode towards Karnstein the General filled them in on the circumstances of his niece Bertha's death and what he had been doing in the ten months since.

He had made a point of introducing Bertha around and at one of the *salons* he had met two ladies, both wearing masks, one middle-aged but still remarkably handsome of figure, the other young and the most beautiful woman he had ever seen. Bertha was soon in deep conversation with the younger lady and the General struck up a conversation with the elder. He was amazed when she said she knew him and reminded him of certain events in his life. She refused to tell him who she was or to remove her mask. The younger woman, who was introduced as Mircalla, and Bertha were in deep conversation and Mircalla had removed her mask. The General was struck by the beauty of the girl and felt drawn towards her. He increased the pressure on Mircalla's mother to tell him who she was but she refused. A man in black came to her, addressed her as Countess, and whispered in her ear. They went out of earshot and the General saw them have an animated conversation. The Countess appeared agitated when she returned. Important business was calling her away. Unfortunately Mircalla was just recovering from a serious illness and was unfit to travel long distances. Prompted by Bertha, the General invited the beautiful girl to stay as a companion for his niece until the Countess returned. The Countess made the General promise that he would not try to find out her identity before she was able to reveal it to him herself. Reluctantly the General agreed and the Countess left. Somehow before they left the party, Mircalla went missing. In spite of

searching everywhere she couldn't be found. A couple of days later she turned up at Spielsdorf's home with a tale about having slept in the maid's room after losing them. The friendship between Bertha and Mircalla developed. But the girl was not an easy guest. There were reports that she had been seen wandering in the grounds at night and she never appeared until the day was well advanced. She explained it away by saying that her recent illness had left her very nervous and this displayed itself in her sleep-walking.

Other events were occupying General Spielsdorf's mind. Bertha was fading away before his eyes. She complained of strange dreams. Sometimes she fancied she saw Mircalla walking to and fro at the end of her bed. At other times it was a strange, black beast. Later she claimed that she felt as if two large needles had been stabbed into her breast. A few nights later she went into convulsions and lapsed into unconsciousness.

They were coming into the village now. Laura didn't know what to think. The events the General described were so like those she had endured that it had to be more than mere coincidence. They made their way to the vault of the Karnsteins in the ruined chapel but could not find the tomb of Mircalla. A passing woodsman filled them in on the deserted village history. The village had been plagued by revenants until a passing Moravian nobleman offered to put an end to their nightly marauding. He waited in the belltower and when they came out of their tombs, he stole their shrouds and took them up into the tower. When they returned the Moravian beckoned them up into the tower. As they reached the platform he cut off their heads with his sword. Next day the villagers impaled and burned the bodies and that should have been an end to it. But the nobleman removed the tomb of Countess Mircalla Karnstein and the new site where her coffin was hidden was forgotten. Spielsdorf bribed the woodsman to go into Graz and bring back a friend of his who could possibly help them uncover the tomb. The woodsman left immediately, leaving his axe in the care of the General. Spielsdorf continued his story while they waited.

Bertha was now in a very bad way so he sent for a physician but he didn't seem to be able to do anything for her so the General sent for an old friend from Graz. The two doctors could not agree on what was wrong with Bertha. As he was leaving the older one slipped the General a note and suggested he got in touch with a well-known ecclesiast who specialised in vampires. The General was sceptical, not believing in anything that wasn't normal. But he was worried enough to hide in Bertha's dressing room to keep watch through the night. Nothing happened at first, then he became aware of a black shadow surging up over Bertha's bed. Overcoming his surprise the General leapt forward, sword in hand. The black shadow returned to the end of the bed and turned into a snarling, ferocious Mircalla. Instinctively the General swung his sword but she wasn't there. She was standing by the door. Again he swung the sword but it passed right through her and shattered on the wall.

The General had just finished the tale when Carmilla arrived on the scene. On seeing her he gave a cry, picked up the axe the woodman had left behind and swung it at her head. The change in Carmilla was horrendous. From a sweet, smiling girl she had become a snarling monster. Effortlessly she caught the General's hand and forced him to drop the axe. Then she was gone! When the General recovered his breath he told them what they had already guessed. Carmilla was the slayer of his niece – the dreaded Mircalla!

Help was at hand. The woodsman returned with a curious-looking man who the General introduced to the others as Baron Vordenburg. Spielsdorf filled the Baron in with the latest turn of events and was assured that the evil Carmilla would soon be no more. He brought out some plans and studied the layout of the chapel. He led them along the aisle and with frequent examination of his plans tapped the plastered walls until he got the response he was looking for. Quickly they tore aside the ivy covering the spot to reveal the tomb of Mircalla, Countess Karnstein. The tomb opened they found Carmilla/Mircalla resting there, as sweet and angelic as the first time they met.

The next day officials arrived from the Imperial Court and having certified that Mircalla was a vampire a priest was called, a stake was driven into her body, she was decapitated and then burned.

Back at the *Schloss* Baron Vordenburg told them how he had discovered the site of Countess Mircalla's tomb.

"I have many journals and other papers, written by that remarkable man; the most curious among them is one treating of the visit of which you speak, to Karnstein. The tradition, of course, discolours and distorts a little. He might have been termed a Moravian nobleman, for he had changed his abode to that territory, and was, beside, a noble. But he was in truth a native of Upper Styria. It is enough to say that in very early youth he had been a passionate and favoured lover of the beautiful Mircalla, Countess Karnstein. Her early death plunged him into inconsolable grief. It is the nature of vampires to increase and multiply, but

according to an ascertained and ghostly law.

Assume, at starting, a territory perfectly free from that pest. How does it begin and how does it multiply itself? I will tell you. A person, more or less wicked, puts an end to himself. A suicide, under certain circumstances, becomes a vampire. That spectre visits living people in their slumbers – they die, and almost invariably, in the grave, develop into vampires. This happened to the beautiful Mircalla, who was haunted by one of those demons. My ancestor, Vordenburg, whose title I still bear, soon discovered this and in the course of the studies to which he devoted himself, learned a great deal more.

Among other things, he concluded that suspicion of vampirism would probably fall, sooner or later, upon the dead Countess, who in life had been his idol. He conceived a horror, be she what she might, of her remains being profaned by the outrage of a posthumous execution. He has left a curious paper to prove that the vampire, on its expulsion from its amphibious existence, is projected into a far more horrible life; and he resolved to save his once beloved Mircalla from this.

He adopted the stratagem of a journey here, a pretended removal of her remains and a real obliteration of her monument. When age had stolen upon him and from the vale of years he looked back on the scenes he was leaving, he considered in a different spirit, what he had done and a horror took possession of him. He made the tracings and notes which have guided me to the very spot and drew up a confession of the deception that he had practised. If he had intended any further action in this matter, death prevented him; and the hand of a remote descendant has, too late for many, directed the pursuit to the lair of the beast.

We talked a little more and among other things he said was this:

One sign of the vampire is the power in the hand. The slender hand of Mircalla closed like a vice of steel on the General's wrist when he raised the hatchet to strike. But its power is not confined to its grasp; it leaves a numbness in the limb it seizes, which is slowly, if ever, recovered from.

The following spring my father took me on a tour through Italy. We remained away for more than a year. It was long before the terror of recent events subsided; and to this hour the image of Carmilla returns to memory with ambiguous alternations – sometimes the playful, languid, beautiful girl, sometimes the writhing fiend I saw in the ruined church; and often from a reverie I have started, fancying I heard the light step of Carmilla at the drawing-room door."

Dracula

When Bram Stoker wrote *Dracula* it was as if six millennia of hit and miss attempts at formalising a popular anti-hero had coalesced on the point of his pen. The creature he wrought had the shape and the voice of man but the instincts and motives of an animal. When he fed he did it without any of the hang-ups that humans have now and have had since they gave up being hunter-gatherers and became farmers. Once these creatures had given up moving around the country eating anything that moved or wasn't likely to poison them, death became a prime motivation. Stick seeds in the ground, water them and stand back. All you have done is provide the natural flora with a chance to get bigger and juicier. But these are just the basic ingredients for the famous 'Hay Diet'. It produces a lot of wind and fertiliser but needs constantly topping up to provide motive power to sustain a day's work. It was

corralling what were to become the beasts of the field that freed up busy hands for other, non-dietary, tasks. Meat took longer to digest and built up muscle and reserves of energy. To get at those reserves of energy it meant killing. Man, in the non-sexist sense – became very proficient at killing. Assuming that cows, ducks and pigs could talk they would look on us very much in the way that humans would look at an entity that could farm us. Maybe humans are even less humane than the undead Dracula. At least

he puts on a bit of a performance. He dresses up like a head waiter, appropriately, mesmerizes with a look and only drinks the blood and leaves the messy business of feeding off the cadaver to his cousins the Ghoul Brothers. There is also the added comfort that the Count doesn't have it all his own way. He's very vulnerable really. That is, if Stoker's Dracula is taken as the definitive bloodsucker. He may be able to change his shape, disappear in a puff of smoke, fly, hypnotise gorgeous women and climb down

An unrecognisable Gary Oldman menaces Keanu Reeves in *Bram Stoker's Dracula* from 1992

walls upside down but think of the disadvantages. As soon as dawn peeps over the horizon, unless he is in a claustrophobically sealed coffin, his goose is cooked. Once he is in the coffin anyone with a ball-peen hammer and a hawthorn branch can dent his starched shirt front in a decidedly lethal way. He can't cross over water except at certain times. This makes a well earned holiday in Venice or Amsterdam out of the question. Holy water, communion wafers and crucifixes give him a severe attack of curling lip and gyrating eyeballs and the sight of an exposed cleavage supporting a vibrating epiglottis drives him mad with lust. Just lying on a mattress of dirt and expecting every creak and rustle to be the introduction to the lid being thrown back and a stake hammered through the blood-rich heart could put the average vampire in trauma counselling for years.

So why did Bram Stoker compose the deathless Dracula the way he did? It's reasonable to assume he wanted his vampire to be the natural progeny of all the ghouls and demons that had gone before. Vlad and Erzebet had given the gore a touch of class. Plogojowitz and Paole had brought them to official notice and their investigators had provided authenticity. St. Germain provided the mystery. Ruthven took the vampire into contemporary society and made it palatable and Carmilla gave a vinegared dose of compassion and romanticism. Stoker picked and mixed, taking the elements that he liked, embroidering and enhancing where necessary and discarding anything he found too hard to draw into the story. The Count he took from Polidori's Ruthven – based on Lord Byron – strained through Rymer's Varney. The location was selected through travel brochures, timetables and travel books but located by Le Fanu's Carmilla in the Carpathian mountainous area. Stoker

acknowledged his debt to Le Fanu and had, without doubt, read the other two great vampire writers of the nineteenth century. He did for the vampire what Anne Rice did for it in the present century – took all that had gone before and reshaped it for a contemporary readership. Anne said that her books were shaped by the films and books pumped out as cheap thrillers by an industry that largely disdained the genre. She never managed to finish Stoker's *Dracula* – she's not the only one – but the images in her head and her unique view of what a vampire is all about have thrust the story forward in the same way Stoker did a century ago.

Where did Stoker's inspiration come from?

He was an Irish man, born in Dublin in 1847. He was a sickly child and spent most of his childhood in bed staring at the shadows on the ceiling. There seems to be no medical reason for his weakness but he wasn't beyond throwing a tantrum if anyone suggested he was skiving. He doted on his mother who spent long hours at his bedside telling him stories of leprechauns, will-o'-the wisps and demons that trod the pride of the Irish into the fields. Quite suddenly, in his teens, he decided that bed was for wimps, got up, won a place at Trinity College, the alma mater of Le Fanu, and became involved with Oscar Wilde. Egged on by his adoring maternal parent, he started to write and preferred sitting at his desk to getting out there rubbing palms and pontificating on the ways of the wicked world. Bram wasn't exactly pleased when his father found him a sinecure in the civil service. He had already met the great actor, Henry Irving, and felt more than a little drawn to the world of footlights and curtain calls. To express his literary bent he became the drama critic for the *Dublin Evening Mail*. This led to the job of editor of the *Irish Echo*. He wasn't happy there, resigned at the first opportunity and begun to write short stories which he was able to float with chums he had made in the newspaper game.

Stoker had built on his acquaintanceship with Henry Irving, turning up at theatres when the great man was on tour or writing laudatory pieces on his performances in the newspapers and bringing them to Irving's attention. He was lucky. Although big and bear-like Stoker was at heart a prim Victorian. This suited Irving. He wanted someone willing to take on all the dirty jobs that were beneath the dignity of the leading thespian of the day. The need for a front man became even more acute when, in 1878, Irving took on the Lyceum Theatre. Before he had time to snap his fingers twice Stoker was at his side. The relationship, as it developed, was that of a shepherd and dog. Irving whistled and Stoker rushed around doing what had to be done. If he got it wrong Irving was there with a kick and a snarl. The relationship rubbed along, both men getting what they wanted, both men getting closer but more separate in their views. In the few moments he got when he wasn't playing spear carrier, Stoker returned to his first love – writing. A couple of books were published but Irving wasn't impressed. Stoker then conceived the idea of writing a vampire story. He had the perfect role model in his boss and it would be a safe way to stick two fingers up behind his back. It took nearly eight years of research, writing, revising and editing to come to a point were he felt confident to present it to a publisher.

Still Irving wasn't impressed, so Stoker decided to stage a 'reading' using the members of the Lyceum company. He hoped that his master, Henry Irving, might be enticed into the lead role but it was not to be. Irving came to the reading, huffed through it and then told Stoker not to give up the day

job – the story was too far-fetched and boring to ever attract an audience. This was in an era renown for big promises that didn't quite work out. Victoria celebrated 60 years as head of the British Empire on which 'the sun would never set.' Lumière had shown his magic moving picture show on the end of a New Jersey pier and it was generally accepted that 'it was interesting but not something that would last!' The *Titanic*, the unsinkable liner that sank on its maiden voyage, was on the drawing board; the Olympic Games were revived in Athens with the pious hope that the games would supplant war as the world's main confrontational interest; Alfred Dreyfus was pronounced guilty by a court of his peers and enemies and the South Sea Bubble had long since burst.

Bram Stoker's time as Irving's kicking boy was cut short in 1898 by a fire at the Lyceum Theatre which destroyed everything. Irving's health at this time was not good and when the theatre was forced to close permanently in 1902 he took the loss of his home base badly and died a couple of years later. Bram threw himself into writing full time. *Dracula* was doing reasonable business but at this time there was no hint of the phenomenon it was to be in later years. Stoker stayed mainly with the fantasy genre, producing a novel every two or three years until 1911 when he wrote his final horror story – *The Lair of the White Worm*.

Stoker's declining years were not easy. He had a stroke in 1902 and then developed Bright's Disease, a degenerative illness of the kidneys which has an effect on the human body much like the vampire manifestations wrought by his creation.

Bram died in 1912 without seeing his major work performed on stage or in the new medium of film. He missed the controversy that the plagiarism by F.W.

Murnau with his trend-setting *Nosferatu* brought to his widow, Florence, in her later years when she fought like a fury to preserve his copyright interest. Murnau opened the the floodgates and before long there wasn't a soul in the film watching world that hadn't seen the monster that Bram Stoker had envisaged after a heavy supper.

Dracula begins with a solicitor's clerk going to Transylvania to oversee the purchase of a manor house in Purfleet in Essex for a nobleman called Count Dracula. His journey is described in some detail, then the locals get edgy when he tells them where he's going and the coachman is not prepared to go all the way. As Harker prepares to hump his carpet bag up the hill to the distantly glimpsed castle, a coach and four

140

thunders out of the mist and reins in alongside. The horses are as black as night and perched on the box is a tall man, his face half hidden by a wide-brimmed black hat, even in the dark the man's remarkable eyes are visible. Harker climbs aboard, the horses are lashed up and at breakneck speed they plummet along the rocky trail, skid over a stone bridge and rein to a halt in the courtyard.

Harker wanders around for a bit and is startled by a figure on the stairs who introduces himself as the host and wishes him a happy stay. Knowing what we know, this could possibly be interpreted as a black-humoured joke, if it is its only attempt at humour in the whole book.

Dracula has a big, strong face, clean shaven with a long, white moustache. He is dressed in black from head to foot without a speck of colour anywhere. He greets Harker with 'Welcome to my house. Enter freely and of your own will and leave some of the happiness you bring!' When Dracula shakes hands he has a grip that makes the conveyancing clerk wince. He notes that the hand is as cold as ice. Over supper Harker studies his host more closely and notes his high intelligent forehead and his bushy eyebrows which almost meet above his nose. And his mouth! This is hard and cruel with sharp white teeth that protrude over his lip. His chin is broad and strong and his ears are pointed like an animal. What upsets Harker most are Dracula's hands. They have hairs in the palms and he had been told at school that there was only one way to create that phenomenon. And his awful breath! Harker should have been warned by that alone but there hadn't been a lot of vampires in the west country where he hailed from and he hadn't caught up with modern ways yet. Even next morning when Harker can't see Dracula in his shaving mirror he doesn't

seem to twig. Then the give-away. Dracula takes an ill-tempered lunge at his throat but cools down when he sees a crucifix hanging from a chain around his neck. Harker recalls that the locals back in the village had been giving him a hard time and insisted that he wore the crucifix. He wishes he hadn't been so offhand about their simple superstitions and listened a little more closely to what they had to say.

Harker decides to find out more about his host and questions him about Transylvanian history. It was a long time since anyone had wanted a fireside chat with Dracula and he can't resist the opportunity offered by a captive audience. Dracula claims to be a *boyar*, a feudal lord and a member of the Hungarian royal family. His ancestors, Szekelys, had been brought into Transylvania as mercenaries to protect the Hungarians from invasion. They stayed and became the power that propped up the throne. It was Dracula and his relatives who were responsible for giving the Turkish invaders a bad time and ultimately driving them out of the country. He also claims a hold on that well known prankster of old – Vlad Tepes. Count Dracula ends his discourse with a tragic 'I am the last of my kind!' although this proves later to be a bit of truth manipulation as he has a cellar full of women – all his kind.

The Count goes through the rules and regulations for guests at Castle Dracula. Don't make a nuisance of yourself, don't try to find him but wait until he is available – shades of *Bluebeard* here – don't go in the locked room. Harker settles down and does whatever estate agents do when they are arranging the sale of Carfax Abbey and Harker hopes that, mission accomplished, he will soon be on his way back to Exeter.

Harker goes to his room and is looking out of his window enjoying the afterglow from the setting sun when he sees his host going out for the evening. Nothing unusual in that except that he is climbing down the castle wall – head first. Harker begins to have severe doubts about his position in the household. This happens on a number of occasions and Harker decides that he must find out more about his peculiar host. Forgetting what happened to Bluebeard's bride, Harker creeps around trying all the doors in the castle. At first he is lucky and finds them all locked and bolted. This doesn't discourage him and he persists until he finds an open door. A sense of defiance overcomes Harker and he sits in the room beyond the open door and writes his diary. He also forgets the Count's warning about sleeping around. He nods off and when he awakens he can't believe his eyes. Standing in front of him are three scantily dressed nymphettes giving him the eye and flashing their small, pearly white teeth set in wide, voluptuous mouths. Harker tries to insert the image of his fiancée, Mina Murray, between him and the sirens but the Yorkshire lass loses out. Two of the women push the fairer and younger one forward, urge her on by telling her that Harker is young and strong and 'there are kisses for all of us!' The blonde glides forward and bends over him. He abandons all thought of Mina. She drops on her knees before him and he hopes for the best. As she moves in, her white teeth gleaming against her scarlet lips, he waits with bated breath. Just as he can bear the waiting no longer the Count turns up and spoils it. He walks in, throws the women about and in a manic whisper gives his keynote speech finishing with 'This man belongs to me!' The women aren't too happy about being thwarted and give him a bit of lip, asking him what he has got for them. The Count throws a bag on the floor which moves as if there is something alive in it. The women fall on the bag and Harker hears the half stifled cry of a baby. As he looks on in horror the women and the baby disappear. There isn't anywhere they could escape but they went. Harker is getting more upset by the moment and when the Count fixes him with his blood-red eyes he faints. When Harker wakes up he is in bed, his clothes neatly folded beside him and the room looks the same as it had when he left it the previous afternoon to go on his little fact-finding adventure. For a moment he is relieved. The horrendous scenes of the night before have just been a nightmare brought about by too much eating and too little exercise. The only clue that maybe it wasn't a dream comes when he finds his watch has stopped – he is a meticulous watch winder.

Increasingly agitated by his feeling of danger and the strange actions of the Count, Harker, having noted that he has never seen his host during the daylight hours, makes a determined effort to seek him out. What he finds frightens him to death – almost. In a locked cellar he finds Dracula, stretched out in a coffin on a bed of earth. Around him are about 50 more coffins. The Count lies on his back, his eyes staring and death-like. His cheeks are white and his lips are red with fresh spilt blood. Getting bolder by the minute Harker makes a thorough examination of the body and finds that there is no pulse and it is not breathing. There is no sign of life, yet Harker still believes his host is alive. Maybe it is wishful thinking, not wishing to lose a useful fee, no matter what. He notes that there has been a remarkable change in the Count's appearance, however. The hair and moustache have become darker and the skin plumper.

Even the deep, burning eyes seemed set amongst swollen flesh, for the lids and pouches underneath were bloated. It seemed as if the whole dreadful creature were simply gorged with blood; he lay like a filthy leech, exhausted in his repletion.

Rather harsh criticism for his host and client maybe, but in the circumstances understandable. Harker picks up a shovel and is about to bash in Dracula's face with it. As he swings the shovel the Count turns his head and looks at him. Harker's aim is effected and he cuts Dracula's head with the edge of the spade. The blow knocks the coffin lid back into place and Jonathan is relieved not to have to face the maliciously smiling face again. Next day Harker watches as gypsies come to the castle and carry away the undead body of Dracula and his 50 boxes of earth which were to sustain him in England.

Dazed and half out of his mind Harker wanders around until he is picked up by some locals who are courteous enough not to say 'I told you so,' and begins trauma counselling.

Meanwhile the trauma causer has boarded a ship called the *Demeter* and set sail for England. He spends his time at sea judiciously sucking the blood out of the sailors one by one until they are all dried out husks. It probably accounts for the fact that the ship missed the Essex coast completely and landed up a couple of hundred miles north. When he catches sight of Whitby he calls up a storm to drive him ashore and then abandons ship in the shape of a big black wolf.

Now the story shifts away from the Count and his peculiarities and moves in on a local family that happens to be connected to the missing Jonathan Harker. Lucy Westenra is a flighty piece who is no better than she should be and in complete contrast to the ambitious Mina Murray who is

engaged to Harker and has learned to type.

Meanwhile, in another part of the town, a lunatic, Renfield, under the supervision of Dr. Seward, is having one of his turns. His peculiarly distasteful trick is catching and eating flies. Or anything else that is unfortunate enough to seek shelter in his wall-to-wall padded cell. The reason he is agitated now is that the master he has been waiting for is coming. The doctor finds him an interesting specimen but doesn't have a clue what his ravings are all about. And he also seems clueless as far as Lucy Westenra is concerned. They have a bit of a misunderstanding. When she begins to look pale and interesting he thinks it's a matter of diet. Only the efficient Mina thinks something might be wrong. On a moonlight night she sees what appears to be Lucy with a man in black sitting on a seat on the clifftop, a seat known locally as the 'suicide seat'. By the time Mina gets around the bay Lucy has been taken over and Mina gets a glimpse of a hellish face with red staring eyes. Lucy goes into decline and Dr. Seward, who rather likes her, is puzzled by her symptoms. He calls in his old mentor from Amsterdam, Professor Abraham Van Helsing. Lucy's fiancé, the Hon. Arthur Holmwood, fusses a lot but doesn't really do anything at this stage. Another would-be suitor, Quincy P. Morris, an American, still has feelings for Lucy and promises to do anything possible to help her recover her health.

Back in Transylvania Harker has evaded the three vampire brides and ends up in a hospital in Budapest. He writes to Mina. Mina is nursing her friend Lucy but as she appears to be recovering she decides to go to Harker in Hungary. Mina's departure opens the door for the Count and he moves in on the already half-vamped Lucy. Van Helsing departs to consult his books which he has

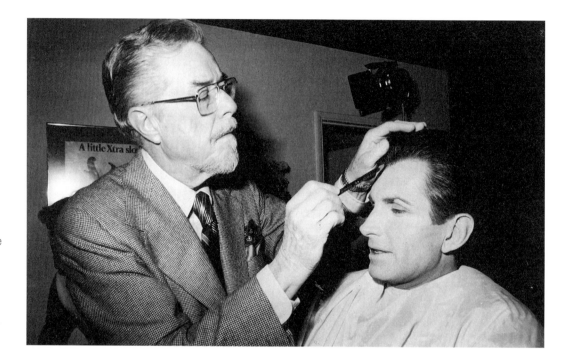

William Tuttle makes up George Hamilton as Dracula for *Love at First Bite*, 1979

...and the finished product

in a vain effort to counter the virulent vampire blood now coursing through her veins. Lucy succumbs and Van Helsing convinces Holmwood, now elevated to the peerage through the death of his father, Morris, and Seward that Lucy has now become a vampire. They stake out the family vault and see her swanning off (or should it be batting?) in the obligatory white gown to return later with a plump baby that she is obviously putting by for high supper. The four leap out and contain her with a great display of crosses and other vampire-inhibiting symbols. Van Helsing keeps Holmwood up to the mark and he drives a stake, opportunely provided by the doctor from Amsterdam, through his beloved's heart. She screams and gouts blood until Van Helsing cuts off her head and stuffs her mouth with garlic. Naturally everyone is very upset now and Van Helsing calls together the liberators of Lucy's immortal

inconveniently left back in Amsterdam and by the time he returns it is virtually all up with Lucy. He desperately tries to revive her by pumping blood out of her human suitors

soul and tells them what he knows about vampires and, in particular, Count Dracula. After what they have gone through with Lucy's unusual funeral rites they are more than convinced that something less than kosher is lurking in the cemetery.

Mina, now married to Harker, is equally upset by the death of her best friend and feels guilty that she left her unguarded. She takes on the role of collator and gathers together the information fed to her by Van Helsing and Dr. Seward. Renfield, by this time in a regular frenzy of excitement and under constant restraint in the asylum, is babbling about the 'Master' who is coming and whose feet he is not worthy to kiss. Slowly it dawns on Dr. Seward that Renfield is not the religious maniac he had him committed for but the 'master' he awaits is, in fact, Van Helsing's vampire, Dracula! This puts a whole different angle on the affair. Mina is now having problems and exhibiting the same sort of symptoms that Lucy had. Unbelievably nobody seems to notice until Van Helsing pays a visit to the 'zoophagous' Renfield. Renfield is a little peeved that the awaited Master hasn't come through for him and has left him languishing, strait-jacketed, in a padded cell, and lets slip Dracula's interest in Mrs. Harker.

Van Helsing rushes back to find that the Count has already started the process of turning the delectable Mina into a card-carrying vampire. In the nick of time Van Helsing bursts into Mina's bedroom. Dracula has just unzipped the front of his chest with one of his chisel-sharp fingernails and Mina is lapping up the flowing blood like its mother's milk. With cross and holy water Van Helsing drives off her attacker and then marks her forehead with a holy wafer. The holy biscuit burns her skin and proves that she is well on the way to becoming another vampire.

Dracula, foiled in his major plan, visits Renfield in his cell but doesn't give the madman the power he had been expecting. Instead he bangs him around the walls for a while and then leaves. Seward calls in Van Helsing and, with his dying breath, Renfield tells him of the 50 coffins filled with soil from Transylvania that Dracula has scattered about the country so that he is never far from a rejuvenating bit of his old homeland.

Mina is a stronger character than Lucy and realises that, if she doesn't do something constructive, and soon, she will also end up screaming as a stake is pounded through her décolleté. So when Van Helsing suggests he hypnotises her in an attempt to track down the Count who, through the exchange of blood between them, is now mentally attached to Mina whether he likes it or not, she agrees immediately. One by one they find the coffins and Van Helsing sanitises them with Eucharist wafers and holy water. One coffin is missing and, through Mina, Van Helsing is able to ascertain that the Count has now left the country and is heading for the safety of his homeland in Transylvania aboard ship. The doctor organises a posse and they set off after him. Travel arrangements were, even then, a bit dodgy and it is soon obvious that the vampire king will be safe in his castle if they don't do something fairly drastic. He has now transferred to a wagon driven by his gypsy friends and making good time. The pursuers split up. Seward and Morris, armed to the teeth go on horseback, Harker and Holmwood take a steamboat and follow the Count's voyage up river and Mina and Van Helsing take a carriage.

Van Helsing and Mina Harker arrive at Dracula's castle first. She is in a bit of a state. The proximity to the vampire's power source is doing all sorts of things to her hormones and she has become untrustworthy. The professor draws a circle and sanctifies it with Eucharist wafers and places Mina in it with grave warnings about what will happen to her if she tries to get out. Satisfied that he is not going to have any bother from the vampire-in-waiting, he breaks into Castle Dracula and gives the three beautiful vampires who gave Jonathan Harker a bit of a surprise – an even bigger surprise. He cuts off their heads. Then he searches out Dracula's regular hidey-hole and purifies it with wafers and crucifixes. Lastly he seals all the entrances to the castle with garlic, crosses and wafers – which happily he has thought to bring with him. When he gets back to Mina she is in more of a state than when he left. Not only is she getting a headache from the castle vibes and the holy relics scattered about but some of Dracula's soul mates, a pack of ravaging wolves, have moved in and are eyeing her up as a potential source of protein. He moves her to a more secure place and they await the arrival of the others. It's a close-run thing. The gypsy wagon with the Dracula coffin lashed on board is in a race against the setting sun. The professor tries to hold the gypsies with a rifle but it is Quincey Morris and Jonathan Harker who get to the coffin first. Morris doesn't muck about with garlic or hawthorn stakes, he whips out his Bowie knife and plunges it into the heart of Count Dracula while Harker chops off his head with a *kukri*. It is only then that the vampire slayers realise that the gallant Quincey P. Morris is mortally wounded.

By this time the gypsies, seeing themselves covered by the Winchesters, and at the mercy of Lord Godalming and Dr. Seward, had given in and made no further resistance. The sun was almost down on the mountain tops, and the shadows of the whole group fell long upon the snow. I saw the Count lying within the box upon the earth, some of which the rude falling from the cart had scattered over him. He was deathly pale, just like a waxen image, and the red eyes glared with the horrible vindictive look which I knew too well.

As I looked, the eyes saw the sinking sun, and the look of hate in them turned to triumph.

But, on the instant, came the sweep and flash of Jonathan's great knife. I shrieked as I saw it shear through the throat; whilst at the same moment Mr. Morris's bowie knife plunged in the heart.

It was like a miracle; but before our very eyes, and almost in the drawing of a breath, the whole body crumbled into dust and passed from our sight.

I shall be glad as long as I live that even in that moment of final dissolution there was in the face a look of peace, such as I never could have imagined might have rested there.

The Castle of Dracula now stood out against the red sky, and every stone of its broken battlements was articulated against the light of the setting sun.

The gypsies, taking us as in some way the cause of the extraordinary disappearance of the dead man, turned, without a word, and rode away as if for their lives. Those who were unmounted jumped upon the leiter-waggon and shouted to the horsemen not to desert them. The wolves, which had withdrawn to a safe distance, followed in their wake, leaving us alone.

Mr. Morris, who had sunk to the ground, leaned on his elbow, holding his hand pressed to his side; the blood still gushed through his fingers. I flew to him, for the Holy circle did not now keep me back; so did the two doctors. Jonathan knelt behind him and the wounded man laid back his head on his shoulder. With a sigh he took, with a feeble effort, my hand in that of his own which was unstained. He must have seen the anguish of my heart in my face, for he smiled at me and said: – "I am only too happy to have been of any service! Oh God!" he cried suddenly, struggling up to a sitting posture and pointing to me, "it was worth this to die! Look! Look!"

The sun was now right down upon the mountain top, and the red gleams fell upon my face, so that it was bathed in rosy light. With one impulse the men sank on their knees, and a deep and earnest "Amen" broke from all as their eyes followed the pointing of his finger as the dying man spoke:

"Now God be thanked that all has not been in vain! See! the snow is not more stainless than her forehead! The curse has passed away!"

And, to our bitter grief, with a smile and silence, he died, a gallant gentleman.

"It could be YOU..." *next*. Lugosi as Our Man in Transylvania

PART FOUR
AT THE MOVIES

The cinema and vampires were made for each other. When Stoker penned *Dracula* the Lumière Brothers were projecting flickering images onto the screen that, by their crudeness, became the pre-ordained carrier for tales of the undead. Although there was plenty of material about for the movie pioneers to work with, the vampire was not stylized on film for over a decade. There were a few films which seemed to be about vampires but none of them took up Count Dracula or Lord Ruthven or even dear old Sir Francis Varney at first. The early films were all about journeys to the moon, or digging tunnels under the English Channel. A lot of celluloid went on watching naked men and women run, jump or get undressed. The entrepreneurs soon caught on to the idea that a dozen or so middle-aged men huddled together in the dark watching a woman take off her clothers or being mounted by an Alsation was worth a bob or too. Magic also went down well. Cutting a man's head off and joining it onto a woman's body was only a matter of stopping the camera, adjusting the mirror and starting all over again.

When finally someone did get around to the idea of a little blood letting mixed with heaving bosoms and high-pitched ululation it was a German film maker, Fritz Murnau.

Murnau had cut his horror dentures in the trenches of the First World War. Anything after that seemed tame but he did his best. His first shy at the fictional horror film came with *Der Janus Kopf* – the two-faced man – the story of Jekyll and Hyde starring Conrad Veidt and Bela Lugosi. Murnau wasn't too keen on paying royalties and, having made a nice little pile out of Robert L. Stevenson, turned his attention to the popular, best selling British fantasy novel – *Dracula*. He tried a tentative approach to the publishers, Constable, but walked off whistling when they started quoting telephone numbers at him. The rebuff by the sordid British who could only think in terms of money and didn't realise what an artist they were turning down, only made Murnau more determined. He went back to Germany, turned up the wick and set about altering the story so that he could claim it as his own. Murnau's vampire went back to its Romanian roots, jumped a couple of hundred years and became Nosferatu. The location in Transylvania, 'the land beyond the Forest' was good, but Germany was better. They had forests. And mountains. Vampires and things weren't unknown either. Dracula re-emerged as Graf Orlock and the seaside resort of Whitby became Bremen.

Stoker's Dracula was not the urbane character he has now become. He was a thing of the cemetery. A vault dweller. Dracula preferred the shadows. The night was his time for business! If he needed to broach the sunlight, he could do so without ending up fit only for the vacuum cleaner. There was also a problem with a shadow. Dracula didn't have one. Nor a reflection. Which is probably the reason he looked so repellent. If you can't see your reflection how do you put your make-up on or make sure your kiss-curl is in place? There was the thing with animals, as well. Dracula was especially close with bats and wolves. Murnau's Orlock, on the other hand, was big with rats. The playtime for Nosferatu was 1830s when Bremen was having a particularly bountiful time, rat-wise, and it was either get rid of Orlock or bring in the Pied Piper who had done so well in Hamelin.

Graf Orlock was more like the Dracula described by Stoker. He had the long dirty nails, a sallow complexion and halitosis but differed teethwise. Orlock's teeth protruded out front like a cobra while Dracula stuck to his lycanthropic roots with the enlarged canines of his pet wolves. Orlock's misfortune was that he could see his reflection in a mirror. And he cast a shadow. The sun is the real saviour. The best way to get rid of a Nosferatu – according to Murnau – was to get some buxom wench to come forward and while she is trifling with his affections, the sun will come up, Graf Orlock will fry in the ultra-violet and, *et voila*, the plague of vampires and rats is over – until next time. A climax rescheduled for Dracula by later film makers!

The story of Orlock, played by Max Schreck, runs along similar lines to Dracula. Waldemar Hutter, the plagiarised Jonathan Harker character, leaves his wife Ellen to go to Transylvania to put through the sale of a house in Germany. He is met on the road by a carriage driven by a mysterious coachman. Hutter is a bit put off by his host, Graf Orlock, but a sale is a sale and he sticks it out even after he has to fight off the advances of the evil Graf when he attacks him in his bed. When Hutter rises in the morning and goes to look for Orlock, he realises that he is too late. The ghoulish Graf has left for Germany.

Hutter, suffering from amnesia and halitosis shock, is hospitalised. His boss, Herr Knock, has meanwhile gone around the twist and been committed to an asylum. Professor Bulwar, the renamed Van Helsing, is experimenting in his laboratory with meat-eating plants (shades of the *Little Shoppe of Horror*). Orlock, en route for Bremen aboard ship, is experimenting with a little meat-eating himself – on the crew. With Orlock's arrival in the city comes a plague carried by the rats. Hutter, in his hospital bed, has been doing a little research on the odious Orlock and has come up with a surefire remedy to put him out of business. All you have to do is find some virtuous woman who will put up with the ugly, evil-smelling little toe-rag for the night and then, when the dawn comes, he will die – really, finally and irrevocably. A virtuous woman willing to share her bed with Orlock seems a bit of a contradiction but Hutter is not downhearted. After all, didn't the delightful Ellen stay true and virtuous while he was away having his breakdown in Transylvania? Ellen decides to help out and when the Graf sidles into her room, bald head glistening in the moonlight, fingernails clicking like crickets, she throws back her head and bares her all. Orlock hasn't had anything this good – or this willing – for a moon or two and dives in. Keeping one eye on the sundial, the virtuous and ridiculous Ellen gives Orlock a good time until the sun's up, then does frenzied things with her arms and eyes while he disintegrates. Noble husband Hutter rushes in to congratulate the wife on a good job well-done – and possibly negotiate the terms of the divorce settlement for adultery – only to find her giving a lingering farewell performance which for sheer energy, belies her dying state.

Unfortunately for Murnau, the changes he made to Stoker's script in 1922 were not enough to buy off Stoker's zealous widow, Florence. She pursued him through the courts and cinemas of the world and largely succeeded in getting the picture banned and burned. Murnau didn't put up much of a defence. He kept his head below the battlements and picked off what he could when the watchful Florence had her attention elsewhere. He really didn't know what all the fuss was about. The result was that very few copies of the Pana Films *Nosferatu* survived the twenties. Some did, however, and the plagiarised screenplay has now become a classic not just of the horror genre but of films in general. Murnau set a trend, which still exists, for spooky lighting and Gothic sets that encapsulate the mood and add as much to the style of a movie as the music score and the dialogue.

the cape that made the monster

Although *Nosferatu* can claim a prominent place in the archive of seminal films it had one drawback – at least to a cinema audience which was becoming more sophisticated by the reel. Moody shadows and eyeball gyrating histrionics work fine when there is nothing to off-set and refine them but sound and rapidly advancing technology only illuminated the unnatural style of the movie. Whatever the reason for the lack of

enthusiasm to jump on the hearse set in motion by Murnau, the cinema was not to see a major portrayal of the Undead for a decade. It was left to the theatre to come up with the next step in the vampire's evolution.

There is something in the water around the Dublin area that breeds literary types interested in drinking blood and working in the Lyceum Theatre in London. Hamilton Deane grew up on his family estate in Ireland. The Stoker grounds shared a common border with the Deanes and although the young Hamilton had no more than a nodding acquaintance with his worldly neighbour, Bram, he devoured anything he could read about him and his famous friend and master, Henry Irving. At this time our Henry was the most famous actor in the world, revered in America and the colonies as the 'new' type of thespian. A sort of precursor of Stanislawski and Marlon Brando. What he couldn't do with a line like 'The bells, the bells...' wasn't worth doing. Against his family's wishes, naturally, Hamilton saved enough cash from his pocket money to board the ferry and brave the Irish sea. By the time he made it to London he had already spiked his soft Dublin brogue and could put on a reasonably flat-vowelled imitation of a British gent. He sought out Bram Stoker and made himself known. Bram, flattered by the youngster who had made the perilous journey from Dublin to be with his hero and needing a confidence transfusion after Henry Irving had been less than complimentary about his attempt at staging 'Dracula' at the Lyceum, took him under his wing.

Hamilton couldn't believe his luck. Here he was in the legendary capital of the theatrical arts, cheek by jowl with two of the theatre's most honoured practitioners. By judiciously working on the weaknesses of both, Hamilton had time to work out what

The first
stage version
of *Dracula*
with Raymond
Huntley in
obligatory
cloak

he wanted to do. He inveigled his way into a production or two but he wasn't satisfied. He wanted to be more than a hollow vessel waiting for someone else to fill and give the motivation.

The death of Henry Irving in 1905 and then Bram Stoker in 1912 acted as the catalyst. Deane put together his own touring theatre and went on the road. This also wasn't what he wanted. *Dracula* was what had drawn him to Stoker. He felt that the novel held all the elements needed to arouse a captive audience and make his name in the theatre. Mindful of the problems that Murnau had with his film, *Nosferatu*, Hamilton went to see Florence, Bram's widow, and tried hard to negotiate the stage rights. His puppy-dog eyes and sensuous mouth did the trick and he looked around for someone to adapt the book for the stage. There must have been a lot of work for writers at that time because he found it impossible to get anyone interested. He had broken the book down into what he saw as the prime elements but had been reluctant to take on the writing job himself. It's always a

problem for an entrepreneur. If he stages his own work and it fails he is ridiculed for lack of artistic and fiscal judgement and his authority suffers when he negotiates with other playwrights and actors. London wasn't the healthiest place to live at that time. Influenza stalked the streets and came in through the box-office. Stricken, Deane retired to his bed and, doubtless, remembered that his mentor's great inspiration came while he was in bed nursing a bout of indigestion. By the time he had snuffled into his last handkerchief, the first draft of his stage play was lying on the eiderdown. It hadn't been an easy job. Getting 'the land beyond the forest', Transylvania, onto a stage wasn't easy – so he dropped it. Lucy's admirers came in for a little pruning or had a sex-change. The pistol-packing Quincy Morris, who succumbed in the final chapter of the novel, was transformed into a female to cut the cost – actresses then, as now, being less expensive to employ than actors.

Originally Hamilton had intended to play the lead role of Dracula himself but when he counted up the lines he found that the more verbose Van Helsing had more stage time than Dracula so became the vampire's mortal nemesis. When he started to block the play he realised that flailing around in churchyards and driving stakes through heaving breasts was all very well but it wasn't easy to get over to the audience. What it needed was flair. A lot of dramatic movement – the sort dear old Irving had been so good at. Dracula was a problem. Ghosts the theatre could do. Gauzes and mirrors and a bit of groaning and chain rattling was enough to get most audiences on the edge of their seats. But Dracula wasn't a ghost. He had qualified for the first stage by dying, but instead of mouldering away and coming back in a white sheet and walking through walls, he was in a much too substantial form. Besides, the plays that were putting bums on seats were drawing-room'comedies and dramas. Galsworthy was big. Wilde was using his notoriety to pull in audiences, and *Charley's Aunt* was never off the stage for long. A stinking, shuffling, socially inadequate degenerate wasn't likelyto have the matrons of Tunbridge Wells making the day trip to Shaftesbury Avenue in their thousands.

Hamilton thought long and fruitfully about his presentation of the main man – Count Dracula. Dracula was high born, had lived for centuries and was undead. Undead meant bloodless. Stoker's Dracula had been red-faced, bucolic when flushed with rich, fresh blood – a very unflattering complexion at that time. It was still a decade away from the fashion of a fortnight's holiday a year grilling in the hot, unfamiliar rays of the seashore sun. Pale was aristocratic. So Hamilton Deane got out the pan-stick and whited up his leading man, Raymond Huntley. It was good, stood out well against the shadowy surroundings but it still didn't produce the ecstatic reaction that Deane wanted. Aristocratic also meant rich, fine clothes. A starched white shirt-front, maybe a cordon or two, tails and of course, a cape – an opera cloak!

That did it!

Not only did it swirl majestically in the hands of an enthusiastic actor but it could be used to hide all sorts of tricks. Appearances and disappearances, particularly through the 'vamp-trap', became ten times as dramatic enhanced by a swirling cape.

Although Hamilton didn't realise it at the time he had created the perfect prototype for the cinematic vampire which has even survived Anne Rice's revitalised image.

At last Hamilton Deane was ready to show his hand. He wasn't sure exactly what

he was holding so decided to give it an out-of-town premiere at the Little Theatre in Derby. The show went on in 1924, exactly 20 years after Stoker had published the novel and, in spite of the critics who were universally unimpressed, played to packed houses. Encouraged, Deane made the transfer to the Duke of York Theatre in London in 1927. Again the crits were unhelpful but, in the style of the great Barnum, Deane pulled off a publicity stunt that has been repeated at regular intervals ever since. He advertised that medically qualified personnel would be in attendance at every performance to succour anyone overcome by the horror of the show.

The show went from success to success. Not only was it a staple of the London stage but it was opening all over the provinces.

The fame of *Dracula* – the stage play – swept across the Atlantic and before long Florence Stoker was having her hand squeezed by American producers anxious to stage her money-spinner in the States.

A Mr. Liveright – maybe an apt name for the man who was going to foster the Undead in the New World – secured the rights and, in what was to become true Hollywood style, decided to rewrite the Hamilton Deane version.

A newspaper man, John L. Balderston, was contracted for the job and he took Deane's script, tore it up and rewrote it. Hamilton Deane was less than a happy lad when he saw the new version, but Florence controlled the property and all he could do was smile and take it. At least they kept his name on the cover.

Bela Lugosi welcomed the audience to his castle on opening night and with his thick Middle-European accent, melodramatic declaiming and swirling cape, set the scene for 70 years of blood-sucking.

Hamilton Deane finally persuaded

himself to perform the less verbose but more memorable role of Dracula in 1939. Sentimentally he took it home to the Lyceum Theatre where 40 years earlier Stoker had given a reading of his own stage play to establish copyright.

In the development of the screen vampire, no-one did more than Hamilton Deane. It is entirely credible that if he hadn't had the inspiration of taking Count Dracula out of the decaying castle and dirt-filled coffin and re-establishing him in the drawing-room that Lord Ruthven had disgraced nearly a century before, the money-spinning extravaganzas of the modern vampire image would not exist. When, at last, the Hollywood moguls decided to cash in on the success in the Theatre of Bram Stoker's *Dracula* it was Hamilton Deane's lead they followed and summoned Bela Lugosi to the East Coast, starched shirt front, swirling cloak, widow's peak and pointy teeth included.

Bela Lugosi

Before we get into the metamorphosis of the literary and theatrical monster that was, and is, Dracula, a brief look at the man who strained the product of thousands of years through a spider's web and leapt onto the stage, undead: Bela Lugosi!

That English was not his native language is apparent to anyone who has stared in fascination at his flickering image on the screen and listened to slow, tortuous pronouncements like 'I... am... Dracula...' or the archly camp 'I... never... drink... wine!' His foreignness, not just from the English-speaking world but from humanity, is what makes him special – and hugely fascinating. Exclusive to Lugosi were also his extravagant, and, at times, seriously suspect,

and overly theatrical gesticulations. Probably because he was never exactly fluent in English, he found it impossible to speak without exploiting gestures which ranged from something which looked like a mimed strangulation of a fractious chicken to an evil-eye motivated arm extension that was uncomfortably like the result of a severe bout of arthritis.

The crude black and white movies, in the present era of digital television and glorious colour, while comparing unfavourably on a technical level, bring something to the ambience of the films that post-Hammer productions lack. Coppola's *Dracula*, Branagh's *Frankenstein* and Rice's *Interview with the Vampire* were magnificent creations. There was an earnestness and need to please absent in the old Universal films. In the twenties through to the forties horror films were potboilers, thrust out on the market by an uninterested studio to feed the taste of the lowest common denominator patrons who could be relied upon to belly up to the box office and sit through breaking films, terrible sound and excruciating acting as they waited for the main feature of the double bill to come around again.

Bela Lugosi fitted into this niche like a crab into a discarded shell. This isn't to denigrate Lugosi's acting skills. He had an air which guaranteed that on the stage he was a wow. Unfortunately, the very tools which served him well on the stage, coupled with, at first, only the vaguest idea of what his dialogue meant, did not initially serve him well on film. Then Lon Chaney, due to appear for Tod Browning in the first kosher production of Dracula died and Lugosi, fresh from stage success in the role, was issued with his cape and fangs and set in front of a camera. From those first scratchy seconds when Lugosi appears at the top of the dramatically over-designed castle steps

and announces his presence to the world to the last gurgling, phlegm-retching moment of the final reel, Lugosi is dramatically, indulgently and wonderful the vampire King.

For a poor uneducated boy from a small town in Hungary it was a triumph. At the tender age of 12 he had given up any chance of a formal education and, when a travelling theatre show came to Lugos, he decided to dedicate his life to the thespian art. His father, a baker, disapproved. He wanted his son to be an ornament for the Blaska name. An accountant or a solicitor. This was at a time before the jokes about there being some things that rats wouldn't do had become popular and book-keeping and pleading were considered honest professions. In spite of Bela's dedication to his new profession he spent a lot of time serving soup and mending fences before he changed his name from Blaska and adopted the name of his natal village of Lugos.

Gradually he began to get work on the stage and in films, usually as the short-lived villain, until in 1922 he got fed up with grotty productions and unappreciative audiences and invested in a ticket to the land of the moving image, America! He soon discovered that his early retirement from academia had left him with a problem. Amongst the smart set, babbling on about Shakespearean concepts and the real meaning of life, his roots made him the butt of a lot of what passed for humour. To better his standing he went on a crash course of self-improvement. In silent films he strutted the haunting shadows with panache and conviction.

His big break came when Raymond Huntley, the British actor who had played the part in London in Hamilton Deane's stage production, decided he had had enough of the undead and refused to play in the revised Balderston Broadway production. Bela's roles in third-rate productions coupled with his established stage career and interesting vocal delivery got him the job. Predictably the critics were not impressed. How wrong can you get? They described the script as 'turgid and nonsensical' and predicted the players would be taking an early bath. *Dracula* played to packed houses for 40 weeks and then toured successfully throughout the States. In spite of his success on the boards and his expertise with cape and fangs, Lugosi was not originally cast for the lead role. Tod Browning, the producer, wanted Lon Chaney, the man of a thousand faces and the leading horror actor of the day. Unfortunately, when the time came to roll, Chaney had more than qualified to play Dracula in one respect but was uncompromisingly obtuse in the second, a serious miscalculation. He died but didn't make it to the 'undead' stage. Browning had already filmed with Lugosi on *The Thirteenth Chair* and the actor made sure that his recent success on Broadway didn't go unnoticed. Browning, for some reason, wasn't convinced that Lugosi's performance would make the transition to film and dragged his feet. Lugosi wasn't to be denied. He didn't exactly offer to work for nothing but it was the next best thing. Even in 1930 $500 wasn't a fortune and was way below what other cast members were picking up. Lugosi's belief in the film, and his own ability to make it work, was more than justified and when it opened in February 1931 it became a roaring five-stake success.

It was the high point of Bela Lugosi's career. Never again was he able to touch that particular nerve that had the public crying for more. Or maybe, in Lugosi's case he never made it with the producers for some reason. Whatever effect he had, or didn't have, on the producers was more than compensated for amongst the ladies in the audience. According to Lugosi, 97 percent of his mail came from ladies offering to open a jugular for him. Parts were still offered him but he was becoming a little picky, a mood that only lasted long enough to tarnish his success as a vampire. He could have had the part of the monster in Frankenstein but declined and left the door open for British ex-pat actor Boris Karloff to virtually eclipse him as the number one horror icon for the next quarter of a century. He did get some reasonable parts. Igor in a couple of *Frankenstein* films, a variety of bloodsuckers in unnoteworthy films and a couple of good outings in *The Black Cat* and *The Raven* with Karloff. But the fang and cape genre was beginning a downward spiral which soon became uncontrollable. Abbott and Costello links at least kept him in the mainstream although these were embarrassing for the man who had practically invented the horror film industry. What was to come was even worse. Arthur Lucan and his wife had been pushing out nil-budget films for a long time and the humour had never got higher than the crotch. By the time Lugosi got an invitation to appear with them in a comedy film (*Old Mother Riley Meets the Vampire,* 1952) the main production cost was the crew's bacon butties. By this time Bela was hooked on prescription drugs and hardly knew what time of the year it was. Worse was to come. Ed Wood – now a cult icon but in those days simply infamous for being the worst film-maker ever – decided to resurrect Lugosi's film career. Wood believed that anything put on film had a magical power to turn dross into sparkling art. Nothing mattered but pointing the camera and capturing an image. He used Lugosi for *Glen or Glenda* and *Bride of the Atom*. All his filmic philosophy

came to fruition in the unbelievably inept *Plan 9 from Outer Space*. Wood had promised it as a giant step for Bela Lugosi but it proved to be a step too far. It is believed that Lugosi's death may have been an indirect consequence of an incident that occurred during the shooting of *Bride*. A stand-in was needed for Lugosi in *Plan 9* – Wood's wife's chiropractor, playing Lugosi's role with his cape drawn, yashmak-wise, across his face. Even in this Wood couldn't get it right. The stand-in looked nothing like the principal.

Bela Lugosi was buried, as he requested, dressed in the Dracula costume, complete with the cape that had brought him such phenomenal success and then been the cause of his dive into debilitating obsession as it became increasingly difficult to separate his own psyche from that of the twisted characters he was forced to play. In many ways Lugosi could have been a role model for Norma Desmond's character in *Sunset Boulevard*. Like her, he was always waiting for the next great part that would catapult him once more into the limelight.

For Bela Lugosi the end was an anti-climax, but not the end. Lugosi is still the definitive Dracula, the foundation on which actors, writers and directors have built all later productions of vampiric tales.

Dracula – the movie

Tod Browning's idea of taking the Deane-Balderston stage version of *Dracula* as a template came with built-in flaws. These flaws have been exaggerated by time and make the film so slow and talkie that it is almost a life-sentence to sit through it. I know that sort of remark could get me burned at the stake but what can I do? I must call it as I see it. When Browning finally got

Mike Raven and Barbara Jefford in Hammer's *Lust for a Vampire*, released in 1971

his head together and got Lugosi's signature on the dotted line he found the idea of having a well-rehearsed cast so therapeutic that he thrust contracts in front of the rest of the stage production and sat back and waited for the film to make itself. There was a little judicious pruning amongst the cast but basically the plot remained true to

Stoker by reinstating scenes cut from the stage version. Mina Murray, Jonathan Harker's intended in the book, gets Dr. Seward as papa and becomes Mina Seward, played by Helen Chandler. Lucy Westenra becomes Lucy Weston and Frances Dale gets the part. Jonathan Harker, played by David Manners, feels the cut of the blue pencil.

Instead of Harker making the perilous journey to the Carpathians to meet the bloodthirsty boyar, it is Dwight Frye's oddly repellent R.N. Renfield that makes the trip. Dr. John Seward, one of the provocative Lucy's suitors originally, becomes domesticated and a little surplus to requirements. Which leaves Abraham van Helsing. Edward Van Sloan revamped the part for the movie but could never convince himself that what was good for the stage was a little over-ripe for the screen.

What actually demotivated Tod Browning when he had started the film is not known. But something – or someone – obviously did pull the plug. The film opens promisingly enough with a neatly under-scored version of Tchaikovsky's *Swan Lake* as Renfield makes his journey across Europe to the Carpathian mountains and Castle Dracula. There Renfield, costumed like a silent movie comic with facial twitches to match, is confronted by Lugosi but never gets near having a meaningful relationship with the scantily shroud-clad ladies of the night. Dracula is in a hurry to get away. His supply of hot, on the hoof nourishment is scarce in the area due to serious over-culling. He takes a quick snack off Renfield and gets the poor bloke in a tizzy of overacting as they board the ship, and through mountainous seas and a lot of shadow play make sail for England.

From the time the death-ship hits the beach the film, like the vessel, loses its momentum. It's almost as if Browning and his cameraman Karl Freund had a falling-out, an artistic difference of opinion. It has been suggested that Tod Browning's role of director was usurped by Freund, possibly with the backing of Universal Studios who had reportedly paid $50,000 for the film rights from Bram Stoker's widow, Florence. Tod Browning was at a stage in his career

where he wanted to move up a gear, make a statement. A statement for which Universal Studios didn't want to pay. Browning gave a show of petulance only bettered by Shirley Temple and sat the rest of the film out. Karl Freund became equally obtuse and shot what the actors presented. As their ideas had been ingrained by repeated performances on the boards, the film, after an entertaining ten minutes or so, returns to its roots. The actors mouth the story to each other, throwing in a few theatrical moves for good measure, and then stand around and stare politely as Dwight Frye pulls out all the melodramatic stops in his effort to put over the fact that Renfield might be a bat or two short of a belfry. Frye's bombastic performance was well received at the time but it's a bit embarrassing now. It did help to put Lugosi's act into perspective, though. Without Frye's scenery chewing, Dracula's peculiarities of speech and gesture would be more suspect. The two of them together make Van Helsing look positively boring. There are a few oases in the desert though. The dialogue, infused with the immediacy of the stage, fairly crackles in some of the exchanges between the Count and the Professor and it's not all due to a crappy soundtrack.

Further evidence of Tod Browning's lack of interest comes at the end. Dracula gets his come-uppance in Carfax Abbey, on a set that Busby Berkeley would have been pleased to design. He is overcome by the righteous Professor Van Helsing, Dr. Seward and the vapid Jonathan Harker. Having talked the plot to death for the last 60 minutes, it would have been nice if Browning had tailed his film with another spectacular trip through the Carpathians to Dracula's castle for the showdown. But no! In some versions the rather weak ending is given balls by Van Helsing solemnly telling the audience that vampires really do exist and to watch out for

the signs of infection. A pity really, but did it matter? *Dracula* with Bela Lugosi is *the* vampire film. Everyone who took to the fangs post-Lugosi relied heavily on his interpretation. And, for once, it was the actor that made the difference – in spite of the efforts of the director.

exclusive hammer

Although Lugosi cornered the Dracula market in the thirties and forties, the films that appeared were, very much like the vampire's victims, anaemic and slumping towards an undistinguished demise. The Hammer film company was formed to give to Exclusive Films, a distribution company owned by Jimmy Carreras' father Enrique and Will Hinds, something to distribute. Hammer Films, a family-owned cottage industry, became well known as a maker of low-budget films. These were often based on successful radio series or plays. *PC 49*, the story of a British bobby on the beat, *Dick Barton – Special Agent*, a radio series which cleared the streets every evening at a quarter to seven, and *The Man In Black* with your story teller – Valentine Dyall – are good examples. The format was repeated endlessly. Get a fading American actor in the lead and build the story around him with a cast of reliable English actors and technicians. The formula worked but the studios weren't exactly making MGM look over their corporate shoulder. They discovered science fiction with *Spaceways* in 1953 and were encouraged by the reaction of the audience to take a closer look at the fantasy genre. Up until this time the American studios had led the way in this type of film and the British had mainly stuck to underworld and down-and-out but cheerful movies. Jimmy Carreras liked the

idea of taking on the Americans but hesitated to launch an all-out attack on the market. So it was back to what was pulling the audience on the airwaves. *The Saint* with Louis Heyward playing the title role and turning the uniquely British hero/villain into just another hard-bitten Joe with a tender ego. More Americans, although ex-pats living in London, were pulling the ratings on the wireless. The Lyon family with Bebe Daniels and Ben Lyon had a loyal audience and their mid-Atlantic voices were instantly recognisable. Their credentials were good enough to get them on the Hammer set.

One break came in 1955 with *The Quatermass Xperiment* with Brian Donlevy as the Professor. The TV series had been another street sweeper. The series was so good, in fact, that Jimmy Carreras had been a little wary about taking on the expectations of an audience that had so recently sat through a six-part TV series. He need not have worried. This was a time when a ten-inch television screen was considered a bit above the Joneses and an H-shaped aerial on the roof was practically a national monument. The grainy, barely discernible picture had to be viewed in a darkened room and a 'breakdown in transmission' was as much a part of the evening's entertainment as the potter's wheel that endlessly turned during the 'intermission'. On the screen the pursuit of the returning astronaut, who was now mutating into a cactus, was riveting. Especially when it ends up on scaffolding inside Westminster Abbey and London's electricity supply is diverted through the steel rods to fry it. It was another vampire in some respects. The astronaut was absorbed by something out in space and turned into a monster which in turn went around absorbing other life-forms until the Van Helsing character, played by Donlevy, overcame it.

Opposite: Grisly and gruesome 1960 – Andree Melly and Yvonne Monlaur in *The Brides of Dracula*

William
Marshall plays
Blacula 1972

Hammer had touched a pulse and discovered the x certificate. *X the Unknown* was a film cobbled together in 30 minutes by the Hammer luminaries, Tony Hinds, Michael Carreras and Jimmy Sangster. Sangster got the job of writing the script and Hinds produced. *Quatermass 2* followed quickly with Brian Donlevy playing the undaunted Professor and many of the Hammer Repertory Company filling the minor roles and crew.

The runaway success of x-rated horror films made the Hammer hierarchy take another look at what they were doing. A new version of *Frankenstein* looked a good bet. The old Universal films were still doing good business in the flea-pits and the story was out of copyright. Universal didn't quite see it that way. In the end it was agreed that Universal had no more right to Mary Shelley's monster than anyone else, but Boris Karloff's make up was a different matter. So a new persona for the creature was invented and the hunt was on for a suitable actor. First choice was six foot five inch stuntman, Peter Brace. Brace was actually in the chair having the make-up applied when Jimmy Sangster broke the news to him that they had decided to use an actor. *The Curse of Frankenstein* (1957) was the start of a sinister career for Christopher Lee. *The Curse* was a great success so Jimmy Carreras decided to pull the other leg and follow Universal's lead with another character dating back to the Villa by Lake Geneva – Dracula! – a decision that was to make the Hammer name an

international institution and Christopher Lee the new King of Horror.

christopher lee

The story of Hammer Horror is in many ways the story of Christopher Lee. Lee's interpretation of the sexy Count carried the films in which he appeared into realms untouched by former essays into the Gothic underworld. Lugosi's Dracula had been strange and, to pristine English ears, so alien it was easy to believe that he was not human. The same attitude applied to the Americans. Although a country made up of the huddled masses of basically European countries, they were so desperate to be American with a big

Once again Dracula (Lee) lurks in the dark to catch someone unawares

'A', as Phil Harris put it, that they also were willing to see Lugosi as a creature from another world.

Chris Lee wasn't having that. As he said, he was tall, dark and gruesome with a cut-glass British accent and he wasn't going to start 'zedding' his THs and 'v-ing' his Ws. He tipped his hat to Lugosi in the wardrobe department, high-collared cloak and white starched shirt front. The widow's peak stayed and the canines were enlarged but that was about it. Lee was left to produce a character for his monster and this he did splendidly. Lee's Dracula had no redeeming factor. Nothing that would make him hesitate at the last moment and let a potential victim escape the fate worse than Dracula's halitosis that was in store for them. In fact, with Lee's characterisation, it was unlikely that he had bad breath. That would have been a weakness that he didn't possess.

The basic character of Lee's Dracula was probably culled from the background of the actor. He only appeared on screen in *Dracula* (1958) for six minutes but it was the confirmation of the old acting adage that there are no small parts – just small actors. In the film, for those six dynamic minutes, Lee *is* Dracula. Peter Cushing, as Van Helsing, had a lot more to do and did it magnificently but Lee carried off the honours and switched on the Hammer Horror era.

Lee was born in London on 27 May 1922 to an Italian countess and a British colonel in the Kings Royal Rifle Corps. He followed his father into the army in the Second World War and served with distinction. Rank were the main studios in England at that time. They made a virtue out of spotting potential talent, getting a signature on a dotted line, and squeezing it through the sausage machine of the Rank Charm School. Charm

wasn't what they injected into the lanky Lee. He had that in abundance. His family had moved amongst the crowned heads of Europe and the Middle East for years and had learned when to curtsey and when to command. What they got from Lee was intensity and drive. And an aristocratic attitude which, even if it was spurious, got results. He claimed a seven-year contract and in 1947 he made his movie debut in a pot-boiler – *Corridor of Mirrors*. And at this time there was still a chance that he might decide to take off at a tangent and exploit his greatest asset – his voice. Fortunately he soon became an actor in great demand and during the Fifties appeared in 13 films. Then Christopher Lee merged seamlessly with Dracula, and, as they say, the rest is history.

the horror of dracula

Hammer Films badly wanted to confirm their new-found, and surprising, role as the top brick in the Horror chimney. Originally they intended to make the film 'as she were wrote'. Jimmy Sangster, who was engaged to write the script following the success of *X the Unknown* and the recent *Frankenstein*, soon realised that a massive pruning job was needed if the constricting budget was to be met. Out went the trip to darkest Transylvania and most of the action was confined to the Count's castle and the Holmwood estate which was conveniently re-located so that there weren't any time-consuming trips and Count and victims could communicate without having to explain their itinerary. It is also reasonable for Jonathan Harker to appear in the guise of a librarian ostensibly taken on by Dracula to catalogue his library, although the thought of the short-tempered bloodsucker curled up in front of the fire with a good book does

take some swallowing. What Harker is really there for is to rid the world of a nasty piece of work that has terrorised the countryside for far too long. In spite of warnings not to get too nosy Harker can't resist the temptation of a little judicious poking around when the opportunity presents itself and, wouldn't you know it, runs into a simpering siren who begs him to help her. Everyone knows that if you are wandering around in a creepy castle and you're approached by a succulent young woman in

a diaphanous cheese-cloth and a cleavage that would get homage from a building labourer's butt, you purse your lips and walk off whistling Dixie. Not our Jonathan, though. Providing a shoulder to cry on develops into a deadly wrestling match when the doe-eyed seductress tries to sink her prehensile fangs into his suitably bronzed but vulnerable neck. Rescue comes in the red-eyed and snarling shape of Dracula himself who, jealous of finding someone having a good time without inviting him to

Lorrimer Van Helsing (Peter Cushing) rescues his granddaughter Jessica (Stephanie Beacham) from the arch vampire in Hammer's *Dracula A.D. 1972*

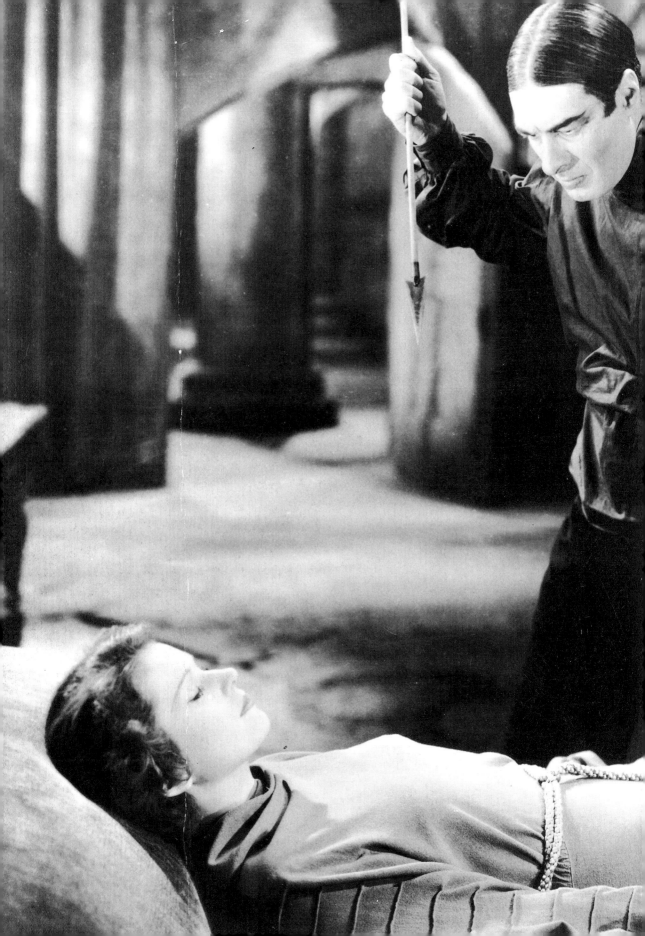

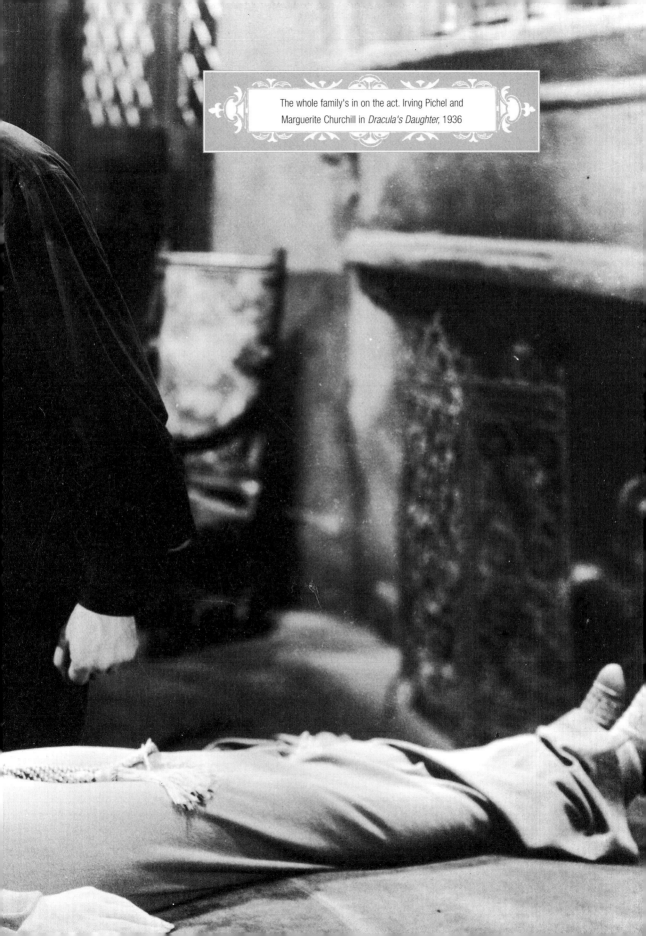

The whole family's in on the act. Irving Pichel and Marguerite Churchill in *Dracula's Daughter*, 1936

join them, strangles the wanna-be vampire lady and renders Harker out of action as a reward for his gallantry. Dracula can't pass up a good suck when it's offered to him on the hoof and helps himself to a little aperitif so that when Harker recovers he finds the incontrovertible evidence that his life is not his own – teeth marks on his jugular.

A dedicated man, Harker pushes aside the evidence that he will soon be sucking blood with the best of them and he sets out to find where Dracula gets his head down during the sunlight hours and discovers a crypt with coffins. The first one he opens contains his former seducer. This Harker doesn't need Van Helsing to give him a course on vampire dispatching. He gets a stake and mallet and turns the beautiful young woman into an old hag with a few well aimed blows. Tactically it was a bad, bad move. The time it has taken to sharpen up the stake and reflect on life's little iniquities has given the sun time to sink below the western horizon and Dracula to work up a thirst.

Doctor Van Helsing arrives in a village. What and where the village is isn't important. It could be in some fold in the moors of Yorkshire or a tiny hamlet in the west country. Wherever it is, it has the familiarity that all the other villages have in all the other films where someone turns up looking for information. Nobody is willing to talk to the stranger except the buxom barmaid. She has found Harker's diary at the crossroads when she was out walking the dog and held on to it knowing that someone would be making enquiries about the young gentleman now he had disappeared. A quick flip through the pages brings Van Helsing up to date and after the usual lack of co-operation from the hotelier he arrives at Dracula's castle only to be nearly hedge-hogged by a flying hearse and six. In the castle all is quiet. As Van Helsing moves

through the huge, deserted rooms his attention is drawn to a discarded photograph frame. He recognises it as belonging to Harker. The picture that it held of Harker's fiancée, Lucy, is missing. Van Helsing is too late to save Harker and does the decent thing by hammering through his heart one of the unused stakes that Harker brought. Finding no clues which might help him locate the vampire, Van Helsing journeys on to the home of his friend, Arthur Holmwood. Holmwood, in this version, is married to Mina. The happy couple are upset. They have been waiting for Harker to return so that they can make a decision about what they should do with his fiancée Lucy who has taken to her bed and refuses to help with the washing up. Van Helsing instantly ventures that a vampire is on the loose and this is verified by socking great big holes in Lucy's alabaster throat. Huge strings of garlic bulbs and garlands of garlic flowers are conjured up and hung around the room. All the Doctor's security is brought to nought by the maid who opens the window and removes the garlic flowers and lets in Lucy's supernatural lover.

It's the end for Lucy as a warm, vibrant human being and the beginning as a cold, bloodsucking demon. She is seen flitting around the churchyard and through the trees like a large white cabbage butterfly and with the help of Arthur Holmwood, Van Helsing pins her in her coffin with a wooden stake through the heart. Van Helsing and his newly initiated assistant, Arthur, get on the trail of Dracula's hearse and trace it to an undertaker's. They arrive too late. Dracula and his coffin have again disappeared. They go back to Holmwood's place for a council of war. As a precaution Arthur puts a crucifix around Mina's neck and his stiff upper lip crumbles when she gives a mournful moan and faints. The cross has marked Mina as a victim of Dracula and an embryonic vampire.

Van Helsing, well up on all the latest medical practices, gives Mina a blood transfusion. But how did Dracula get into the house? The answer is soon discovered. Dracula doubled back and, unseen, installed his coffin in the basement. While Van Helsing is trying to make up his mind as to whether he should use holy water or garlic to dampen Dracula's ardour, the old marauder grabs Mina and elopes. It's still dark but with Mina in a state of almost vampirehood it's no time to hang around waiting for some insomniac cockerel to welcome the dawn.

While Dracula scoots around the castle dragging the semi reluctant Mina, Arthur and Van Helsing close in. The Doctor distracts the vampire with a display of altar effects, Arthur Holmwood grabs his wife and beats it. Van Helsing now has a free run at the vampire but soon finds that being bounced off the walls by a supernatural being with supernatural strength is no way to finish a picture. Just when it looks as if the next Dracula might be without Van Helsing, the astute Doctor notices that dawn has come to the rescue. He races along the huge table with Dracula in close pursuit, leaps onto the curtains and pulls them to the ground. Just in time! The light barbecues Dracula to a frazzle and only his ring with the distinctive Dracul emblem, and a pile of dust remains to mark his passing.

The end, although pretty terminal for Dracula, proved to be the start of a whole new career for the pallid gentleman from Transylvania. James Bernard with his haunting 'Dra-cu-la' theme must also share in the round of applause for producing an atmosphere of menace and doom not often experienced in films. And what about Dracula? He was now a man of the world, owing a passing allegiance to Transylvania but now grown far beyond the constrictions of the Carpathian mountains.

For me, Christopher Lee *is* Dracula. Bela Lugosi must be saluted as the man that made the monster what it became, but his over-ripe diction and hammy performance make sitting through his seminal film a battle against slumber and that fatal lid flutter that precedes a full-blown snore. Hammer's *Dracula* does drag a little – now. It didn't 40 years ago and it held its own until quite recently. Even if the film, in total, does have its slower moments, no-one nods off while Chris Lee is doing his bit. Despite his other films like *Dracula Prince of Darkness,* to me his six riveting minutes in that film have never been bettered and it is for that brief performance that I think he edges out the malefic Lugosi. It's easy to imagine Lee's cool voice charming the cross off a virtuous maiden but it takes a huge suspension of belief to imagine Bela Lugosi, with the stone-wall killer eyes, persuading even a well-used lady of the night with a predilection for kinky men into doing anything but laugh when Bela comes on strong. Heresy I know, but you've got to tell it how you see it.

It still took nearly four decades to cross the Atlantic in the chronicles of Anne Rice. That it should be the vampire trio of Lestat, Louis and Claudia that move the central story of the vampire on rather than Coppola's *Dracula* is easily explained. Rice explains away the old vampires and moves the story on to a new level. Not necessarily a level I wish to be seen on but nevertheless a genuine development of the vampire on its journey from a leech-like fantasy in a foreign language to a god image on an inverted cross.

Tom Cruise and Brad Pitt in *Interview with the Vampire*, 1994, based on Anne Rice's novel on the bloodsucker's point of view

lestat and all that

The idea of having a tortured vampire constantly questioning his immortality came to Anne Rice when she was sitting at a typewriter idly trying to think of a theme for a short story. 'How', she thought, 'How would a vampire see itself if it had to justify its references in real life?' Dracula may have been born of a nightmare brought on by a surfeit of lobster thermidor but Lestat's genesis was of a far more poignant nature. Anne had already written a number of

books and a few years earlier had produced a short story detailing an interview with a vampire, Louis, by a young journalist. Unable to find a publisher, vampires not being, in the early Seventies, the high profile literary figure they are now, she stuck the manuscript in the drawer all writers keep for stories they know will one day attract the end of the rainbow their way. In this early effort neither the vampire Lestat nor the infanta vampire Claudia made even a footnote. Anne Rice lost her daughter Michelle and so her thoughts turned from the merely erotic which had made up much of her output til then, and turned to a darker vein. She took out the discarded *Interview with the Vampire* manuscript and probed the nature and sensibilities of creatures once human, who had become virtually indestructible.

In many ways the vampires of Rice owe more to Le Fanu's *Carmilla* than Stoker's *Dracula*. The main protagonists are more rounded characters who not only question their immortality but, at times, revel in it. Claudia, a sophisticated woman trapped in the body of a six-year-old child, is one of the spookiest and best drawn figures in the vampire iconography. This invocation, Rice admits, is a direct product of her feelings when she lost her baby. In the first draft Claudia survives to join vampires more in touch with the feelings of her trapped psyche. Once Anne had distanced herself from the tragedy she rewrote the story and exposed Claudia to the sunlight – and disintegration. Louis, the interviewee, also had a personality change. Originally he was a cocky vampire telling it as he was and revelling in it. Rewritten Louis becomes a querulous, doubt-ridden, don't-wannabe vampire with a Lestat complex. Lestat is the vampire brought into the short story to give it weight and legs. And legs he certainly has. Since *Interview With The Vampire* was published in 1976 Anne Rice has exploded onto the 'undead and loving it' market with *The Vampire Lestat* (1985), *Queen of The Damned* (1988), *The Tale of a Body Thief* (1992) and *Memnoch The Devil* (1995).

These make up *The Vampire Chronicles* and are set to grow and grow. In spite of the non-appearance of Lestat in the original story it is this character that has moved the vampire forward into what could be a new era. That claim is qualified because I'm not sure that the old devil Dracula isn't lurking in the tomb waiting for a dose of invigorating blood to revitalise the parts that Coppola's Dracula exposed to the sun and undid all the phlegmatic work that vampire-loving directors have done over the years.

Although *The Vampire Chronicles* are, obviously, a literary work, the apotheosis of this is what was done to the ongoing legend by the cinema. Tom Cruise, who plays the vampire Lestat, didn't get everyone's vote as an example of clever casting. Even Anne Rice herself spent a year seizing every opportunity to denounce Cruise as a wet-haddock compared with her literary superman. She recanted when she was shown early rushes of the film and became a vociferous champion of Lestat/Cruise. If I were a cynic I would be inclined to think the whole episode was a marvellous piece of PR opportunism. Brad Pitt also had his detractors. Marlon Brando's legacy of mumbling his dialogue is, like a virus, still deeply imbedded in the body thespian and Brad's soul-less soul searching needs an effort on the part of the audience to be believed. The permutations and extraordinary sweep of *The Vampire Chronicles* are too complex to mull over here. All we need to know is how the history of the vampire has reached the present day and its possible projection into the future.

The story goes that Louis (Brad Pitt) meets a boy reporter in a hotel room in San Francisco. Louis has been a vampire for 300 years and still doesn't seem to know what it's all about. He wants to get all his angst and self-doubt out into the open so that he can start to love himself. So far it sounds like one of Oprah Winfrey's less original shows. Regression being the buzzword, Louis does an ace piece of regression without having to resort to hypnotism – he was actually there. In the deep South, depressed by the untimely death of his brother, Louis catches the eye of

Lestat (Tom Cruise) who is a practising vampire with a brightly polished shingle. He inducts Louis into the clan and takes him to live on the plantation where there is always a ready supply of nubile slaves to titillate the bloody appetite. Louis feels he was bred for higher things and tries to keep off the human juice, pigging out on rats, cats and, I guess, pigs. Lestat doesn't give Louis an easy time and he decides to leave. Lestat takes that as a personal slight and when Louis, in a moment of emotional weakness, feeds off a young girl, Lestat seizes the opportunity to keep Louis in close attendance. Lestat seeks out the child and finds her unfed and undernourished with a newly dead mother in a sewer-side hovel. He completes the job of making her into a vampire and presents her to Louis. This does the trick and Louis gives up thoughts of leaving and they settle down to an uncomfortable *menage à trois*. Uncomfortable because nobody seems to know who is supposed to be putting it to whom; Louis continues to exhibit an advanced stage of vampire melancholia, while Claudia, the newly created child vampire, rails against the injustice of being bitten into undeadedness while still in the underformed body of a six-year-old. She gets so fed up in the end that she decides to do away with her vampiric father. Claudia feeds Lestat poison and then with the help of Louis, chucks him into one of the swamps that make New Orleans such a paradise for mosquitoes.

Louis and Claudia go to Europe where they find most of the vampires are nothing more than rotting corpses. This does away with the post-Polidori concept of drawing-room vampires and reverts to the revenant days of Peter Plogojowitz and Arnold Paole. Louis knows he is better than that and they finally meet up with an old vampire queen, Armand, who has been cruising vampire bars for the last four centuries looking for someone just like Louis. Claudia, in spite of her physical childishness, has also put a century or so under her liberty bodice. She realises that Louis is more than a little interested in the charms of Armand. The last thing she wants is to find herself on the scrapheap at the age of six going on 300, and forces Louis to create a mother vampire out of a doll-maker she has met – Madeleine.

Then Lestat inconveniently returns from his watery grave and shows his extreme displeasure at being marginalised by the ancient child. By now the odd trio of Louis, Claudia and now Madeleine have been introduced to others of a similar persuasion by Armand at the Theatre of the Vampires in Paris. These are a new breed of vampire who live by a strict code and probably sign on for social benefits when free blood gets a bit short. When Lestat tells them that Claudia tried to get rid of him – him, her creator – the vampires throw Claudia and the vampiric surrogate mother, Madeleine, in a pit where they are fried by the midday sun. The vampire theatre offers some neat visuals and moody lighting. There is also a set-piece where a naked lady is paraded around the stage before the supporting vampires sink their fangs into her. It turns out to be a swan-song for the theatre. Louis understandably miffed that his long-time companion has paid the ultimate price by being bathed in sunlight, burns down the theatre and all the coffins with their occupiers in them, before setting off on his travels again. Lestat rather fades away towards the end of the film, but it is Louis' story and who can blame him for wanting to portray himself as a poor bitten creature of the night who is not necessarily a bad person.

The boy reporter seems to take it all in as a matter of course. When he leaves to turn in his story he's not too sure about the reception he'll get with his hard-nosed editor. His fate is decided for him when Lestat drops into the back seat of his convertible.

Lestat brings the historic vampire to its climax. What started as assorted bloodsuckers with various hang-ups has reached the summit from which all future vampires will be invited to leap. Whether the New Age vampire will hit the spot or whether the change from a two-dimensional leech to a multi-dimensional god-head will finally drive a purifying stake through the legend is yet to be determined. Sartorially it could be a good thing. Instead of Goths lurching around in stygian black they can open out to the florid fashions of the eighteenth century and still stay within the genre.

FILMS THAT MADE A GENRE

Hundreds of films have been made based on the vampire. Few of them have anything original to say. Reviewing vampire films is like chewing gum – you keep on doing it but after the first five minutes the flavour's gone and you just keep on chewing. Occasionally there is a story with something original to say or one that offers a different aspect on the same theme.

In this last section I've taken what are, for me, the vampire movies which made a difference. Not everyone will agree but then there are those who don't like pistachio ice cream. There's no accounting for taste.

Let's start with the grand-daddy of them all...

nosferatu – 'eine symphonie des grauens' (1922)

Nosferatu is as famous for its litigation as for its place in cinematic history as the first major vampire film. The director Murnau, known affectionately as Fred, plagiarised Stoker's *Dracula* to pull off a filmic coup. The storyline vaguely follows the original; some even claim that it is more faithful to the original than most of the later attempts. This depends how generous you are. I recently sat through the film at a festival. Jaded by 50 years of cinema going, I found the sets tacky and too stagey without really adding anything but ennui to the film. The storyline also needed a lot of swallowing. Stoker made it seem probable that in that far off, away-from-the-tourists part of Europe, there might just be a creature who shinned down walls headfirst and got his vitamins without the chore of chewing. Count Orlock, the made-over Dracula of *Nosferatu*, is just unbelievable. And Ellen, Hutter's wife, scheming to bring about the evil Count's demise, and her own, by giving her all is laughable. But it must get its due. It was the first vampire film and even if it did die the death and warn production companies off the subject for a decade, no one can take that away from it. It also provided generations of latter-day film fanciers the opportunity to nod sagely and pontificate on the hidden meanings, symbolism and metaphysical aspirations of the progenitor of the genre.

Production Company: PRANA FILM
Director: Friedrich Willhelm Murnau
Scriptwriter: Henrik Galeen
Cameraman: Fritz Nagner
Designer: Albin Grau
Leading Actor: Max Schreck

London after midnight
(1927)

The most imposing thing about *London After Midnight* is the amount of uncertainty surrounding it. Not just the reels of film themselves but also the story. It's one of those films that is 'lost' – though by no means forgotten. Few books or magazines on horror get by without including photographs of Lon Chaney, in ludicrous make-up, gagging it up with some poor member of the cast with not enough pull to get out of it. Now, it is claimed it has been found and is undergoing rehab in any of a dozen or so studios you might like to name. What's more, it's not a *real* vampire movie at all. It was America's answer to the suspect subject of the Undead. Not quite sure how to angle it, they located it in London – everyone knew, even back in 1927, that anything could happen on the gas-lit, fog-bound streets of London. To make it a bit respectable Lon Chaney plays a Scotland Yard detective – Detective Inspector Burke. Jack the Ripper was still fresh in people's minds and Burke and Hare had introduced a suitably macabre element to the 'resurrectionist' art to provide a Gothic wash to the overall picture.

Inspector Burke, with his insipid daughter, sets up a ludicrous scam to try and capture a murderer. By pretending to be a vampire and frightening the life out of anyone who might have anything to do with it he reduces the suspects to two. These look like resisting his fried-egg eyes and Joker mouth until he puts the hex on them and the culprit reveals himself as... the one everybody suspected in the first place. All I can say is that I'm glad Chaney didn't get his prosthetics on the real Dracula.

Production Company: MGM
Director: Tod Browning
Scriptwriter: Waldemar Young
Cinematographer: Merrit B. Gerstad
Leading Actors: Lon Chaney, Marceline Day

Dracula (1931)

After Tod Browning's outing with *London After Midnight* it took him a while to screw up his nerve to take a tilt at the rapidly growing legend of the deadly Count from the Carpathians. Although Tod's original choice for the Count was Lon Chaney, we can only count our blessings that the man of a thousand faces conked out before he had a chance at vampire's numero uno.

Bela Lugosi's Count is delicious and believable. The shortcomings of script and acting in the minor roles can be corrected through the prism of time. But it is still difficult to sit through the film without thoughts straying to what to cook for dinner or whose birthday have you missed.

It stays fairly faithful to Stoker except it is edited by cash register. Bela Lugosi saves the film – just – but it is another eyelid-dragger and only remains as an iconic masterpiece because it defined the Dracula persona upon which later movie makers were happy to draw.

Production Company: Universal
Director: Tod Browning
Script: Garrett Fort
Cinematographer: Karl Freund
Leading Actors: Bela Lugosi, Helen Chandler, David Manners

Footnote:
Using Tod Browning's script and sets, Universal set up a Spanish version of *Dracula*. This is often cited as being the film that Lugosi should have made. The story is

Bela Lugosi as the Count in mesmersing form in *Dracula* 1931

almost a scene-for-scene copy of the Browning version (pun intended) but the Spanish director manages to get an extra something out of the story and the actor who plays Dracula, Carlos Villarias, a more muted and believable character.

ÐRACULA'S ÐAUGHTER (1936)

This is a film which fails to fulfil the promise of the first reel. The idea of opening as an extension of the end of *Dracula* is great. Like a Western where death strikes haphazardly from the barrel of a gun, no questions asked, the denouement of a vampire film often begs the question of what happens to the newly

staked body, if it doesn't conveniently disintegrate. Here the answer is provided. Van Helsing, again played by Edward Van Sloan, is arrested. His defence sounds decidedly weak. Especially as Dracula has inconveniently stayed in a too substantial form.

Enter Countess Zaleska, the delicious but distant Gloria Holden, who turns out to be Dracula's daughter. She uses mesmerism to spirit the body of papa away and gives him a decent incineration in what looks like a wilder part of Epping Forrest. But the daughter is a good girl and doesn't want to follow in her father's toothmarks. Unfortunately along the way she has taken on a butler from hell, Sandor (Irving Pichel) who has a vested interest in the Countess getting toothsome. He wants to become immortal. Don't we all?

All the Countess wants is to have her paintings exhibited in the Royal Academy. And sleep with psychologist Dr. Jeffrey Garth (Otto Kruger), an ex-student of Van Helsing who the Professor hopes will convince Scotland Yard that he is not a homicidal maniac. Since a lasting relationship is not on the books, tempted by the wild Sandor, the Countess has a mood change, vamps a girl Sandor has found as a sacrificial model for her lethal paintbrush and then has a go at a toff she meets on London's foggy streets.

Van Helsing lets out a 'view hello' that would waken even the undead and follows the coffin to Transylvania when the Countess kidnaps Garth's secretary, Janet, in a vain attempt to get a romance going with the psychiatrist. Sandor can see his chances of being a permanently unwelcome guest at Gothic weekend parties diminishing and gets petty and ventilates the Countess's magnificent bosom with a hickory shafted arrow and is himself done to death by a local copper.

Van Helsing, done out of a good staking by one of the extras, is given the last words as a consolation prize. 'She was very beautiful when she died (pause for dramatic effect), a hundred years ago!'

Could have been wonderful but somehow ran out of blood-sugar along the way.

Production Company: Universal
Director: Lambert Hillyer
Script: Garrett Fort
Cinematographer: John P Fulton
Designer: Albert D'Agostino
Leading Actors: Otto Kruger, Marguerite Churchill, Edward van Sloan, Gloria Holden

house of Dracula (1945)

The war years produced a rash of vampire films without really moving the basic thesis on. Lon Chaney Jr. turned out for *Son of Dracula* (1943); 1944's *House of Frankenstein* was an ugly parade that trotted out all the usual monsters and then John Carradine donned the cloak and topped it with an oversized topper to appear as a vampire looking for a cure. Dr. Edelman (Onslow Stevens) understandably sceptical at first, is soon convinced that he has stumbled on a new branch of medical research that will get him on the front page of *The Lancet*. Coincidentally Edelman's secretary, Miliza, happens to be an old acquaintance of Dracula who narrowly escaped a vampiric role by landing the job as secretary.

Then Lawrence Talbot (Lon Chaney Jr.) arrives on the scene and tries to explain to the doctor, now on credibility overload, that he is a suffering, fur-faced werewolf. The good doctor is less than enthusiastic about getting further involved with a creature who could be bad for his health and shows him the door. Talbot leaves and finds himself a susceptible member of the constabulary who promises to bang him up for the full moon. The police then send for the famous Doctor Edelman. Obligingly Talbot puts on an end of the month hirsute performance for the doctor. Edelman takes him home and gives him an X-ray examination which reveals anomalies in the Wolfman's brain. Always up for a risky experiment the doctor has a go and Talbot goes bananas and jumps over a cliff. Washed ashore by the incoming tide, he ends up in a cave. The doctor, not willing to lose a good experiment, follows. Eventually the moon wanes and Talbot is himself again. Friends once more, Doctor Edelman and amateur werewolf Talbot are on their way home when they discover the body of, wouldn't you know it, Frankenstein. Unable to believe his amazing luck, the doctor has the body taken to his lab and disturbs Dracula trying to have his evil way with Nurse Miliza. It was her the evil bloodsucker had been after all the time.

The plot, as well as the blood, thickens, Edelman has found an enzyme in Drac's blood which he thinks he can eradicate with his antitoxin. The Doc injects himself with the antitoxin and persuades Dracula to have a transfusion. The vampire appears to agree but when the Doctor becomes a little illl from loss of blood, he reverses the process and the doctor gets a wellie full of blood type Dracula. The Doctor Dracula goes on the hunt and kills a villager. Talbot, now a soulful ex-werewolf, is the only one to suspect the medical man. Meanwhile, Edelman has revived the Frankenstein monster which does what monsters to best and ambles around tossing police and peasants all over the place. This causes huge explosions in the laboratory. Edelman, now completely around the twist, tries to shoot Talbot and the ululating Miliza but is de-franchised by a blazing timber which also does for the monster.

Talbot and Miliza escape to a life of moonlight walks and happy memories.

Love the film. It is all so banal and piles coincidence on coincidence until, in true Feydeau fashion, everyone runs into everyone else and the plot goes up in smoke.

Production Company: Universal
Director: Eric C. Kenton
Script: Edward T. Lowe
Cinematographer: George Robinson
Art Director: John B. Goodman
Leading Actors: Onslow Stevens, John Carradine, Lon Chaney Jr., Glenn Strange, Lionel Atwill, Martha O'Driscoll

Dracula (1958)

Vampire films got sillier and sillier post-war, the nadir being the 1952 *Old Mother Riley Meets the Vampire*. Poor old Bela Lugosi would have done well to give this one a miss but he needed the money. It was left to Hammer Films, cashing in on the previous year's success with *Curse of Frankenstein*, to pump blood into the moribund corpse of Dracula.

After a few liberties were taken with Stoker's story, Harker (John van Eyssen) goes to Transylvania with the purpose of piercing the Count's starched shirt front and gets sucked to death for his temerity. Van Helsing (Peter Cushing) arrives in the nearest village to be met with the usual over acting. Only the publican's wild-eyed daughter will speak to him and she reveals she has found Harker's diary which she just happened to find at the crossroads. Heartened by this sign of story progress, van Helsing goes to the castle. Dracula (Christopher Lee) has left, but he finds Harker's still warm though bloodless body in the crypt. Ominously he finds the photograph frame of Harker's fiancée, *sans* photo, lying on the floor. Barely pausing to drive a stake through Harker's heart, Van Helsing is off to London, arriving there to find the luscious Lucy has already been abused by the vampire. He gets Mina, Arthur Holmwood's wife in this version, to deck out the fading Lucy's bedroom with garlic, crucifixes and other vampire repellents. It's all to no avail. Gerda, the au pair, gets rid of all the detritus cluttering up the room and Dracula returns and finishes Lucy off. They bury Lucy but she refuses to lie down and before long becomes a nuisance. A stake through the heart settles her down and Arthur and Van Helsing get serious about taking Dracula out. Now Mina becomes a problem. While hubby and the professor from Amsterdam have been out sorting Lucy's after-death problems poor old Mina has been getting it in the neck.

The money saver on this film now comes into play. Instead of needing to dash all over the place looking for Dracula's coffin they find it in the basement of the Holmwood's residence. Discovered, Dracula grabs Mina and makes for his castle where Holmwood and van Helsing trap him. Holmwood grabs his wife while Van Helsing confronts Dracula. Dracula throws Van Helsing about for a bit and it looks as if the fearless vampire hunter is picking up too many lumps to be able to do himself justice as a prince amongst men... when the sun comes up. Van Helsing sprints along the conveniently placed refectory table, leaps onto the huge velvet curtains and pulls them from whatever keeps huge velvet curtains in place. Sunlight streams in and with a little help from candlesticks held in the shape of a cross by van Helsing, fries Dracula until only his ring and a hank of hair is recognisable. Mina is released from the Dracula's spell and the three weary vampire vanquishers head off into the morning sunlight, another good night's work done.

Christopher Lee was only on film for about six minutes but it was enough to establish him as the answer to the increasingly fading charms of Bela Lugosi. Lee was Dracula in all the colour and deft direction that was a Hammer trademark.

Production Company: Hammer Films
Director: Terence Fisher
Script: Jimmy Sangster
Cinematographer: Jack Asher
Art Director: Bernard Robinson
Music: James Bernard
Leading Actors: Peter Cushing, Christopher Lee, Michael Gough, Melissa Stribling

the last man on earth
[1961]

Interesting because this film switched the vampire story and came up with a look at the world from the other side. Probably had something to do with all the trouble going on in the Southern states where black citizens were trying to get a fair crack at the Constitution.

Only Vincent Price, playing the beleaguered scientist Morgan, is alive in the normal sense. Everyone else has been turned into a vampire by the usual catastrophic scientific cock-up. Morgan is okay by day and travels around delivering resting vampires from the burden of their undeadedess. Understandably they, the Undead, aren't too happy about this situation and spend the nights trying to repay the compliment. Price is on a loser from the start. He plays the doctor in peril with his foot so hard on the soft pedal that you just know he's not going to make old bones. Sure enough, a little carelessness in his personal relationships exposes him to the vampires and he must pay the price. What the vampires feed off with their only milch-cow gone is anyone's guess. It isn't a great film but at least it puts another notch in the vampire legend. Originally it was going to be a Hammer film but they showed the script to the then censor who advised them that he would not pass a film with such violence and it made the rounds, eventually getting made in Italy by AIP. Pity, it could have done with the magic Hammer touch.

Production Company: La Regina/ Alta Vista/AIP
Director: Sidney Salkow
Leading Actors: Vincent Price, Franca Bettoia

ɒracula prince of ɒarkness (1966)

Why this film? Because my publisher told me to... Well, it's a bit of an odd one. Christopher Lee takes up the cloak for Hammer after eight years – and doesn't say a word. And, to make it even more surreal, there's no Van Helsing doing his darndest to stake anything that looks pale and moves. Instead, we have the late Andrew Keir, a monk with a very secular lifestyle who carries a gun and hasn't a kindly word for anyone. He also bears the name of the evil manservant from *Dracula's Daughter*, Sandor.

Jimmy Sangster claimed to me that the reason Lee kept his lip buttoned all through the film was because he refused to say the banal lines in the script. I suppose he can say that – he *wrote* the script.

Another oddity is that Dracula doesn't get staked in this one. Nor garlicked or Holy Watered to death. He falls foul of that little known vampire decimator – running water. Why did Hammer wait so long to exploit the filmic benefits of Lee after the success of *Dracula*? Some say it was Christopher Lee trying to avoid being typecast as a vampire. I guess he lost that one. Others claim that, Van Helsing having deaded the Count fairly terminally in 1958, no one could come up with an acceptable way to revive him. As if we cared. The film had problems with the censor. What was left was pretty gory so what was cut must have been sensational.

Dracula Prince of Darkness is sometimes cited, as arguably the best vampire film Hammer ever made. If it is, I'm not sure what that says for the other films about the unceasing battle between good and evil as exemplified by Messrs, Cushing and Lee.

Directed with his usual verve by Terence Fisher and based on a story by John Elder, who was actually Antony Hinds, and scripted by John Sansom, hiding the identity of Jimmy Sangster, it makes one wonder what went on behind the scenes to bring out the nommes de plume?

A special mention must be made of the transmogrification of Barbara Shelley from the demure, newly widowed gentlewoman into a bosomy, blood-obsessed monster up to the final scene the acting honours are fairly evenly distributed between Lee's dumb vampire and Keir's vociferous monk. Then the Hand of God handed the final scene to the Spawn of the Devil in no uncertain terms. It is one of Lee's hammiest performances, but still one of his most unforgettable.

Production Company: Hammer Films
Director: Terence Fisher
Script: John Sansom (Jimmy Sangster)
Cinematographer: Michael Reed
Music: James Bernard
Leading Actors: Christopher Lee, Barbara Shelley, Francis Matthews, Andrew Keir

the vampire lovers (1970)

I have to include this one. It springs from one of the fountains of vampire lore – Sheridan Le Fanu. There have been almost as many variations on Le Fanu's story as there are on Stoker's *Dracula*. *Vampire Lovers* gives us a vampire with soul. Not just a wham-bam, that's-your-jugular-ripped-out monster. Not a monster that isn't aware either, which is definitely one up for the monster clan. Carmilla can love! She knows that her love is fatal to the loved one. She falls in love with what will eventually be her victim, knowing that the relationship won't last.

What I find fascinating about the

Ingrid Pitt feels a little light-headed. *The Vampire Lovers*

Carmilla story is that she is practically a complete counterpoint to everything a vampire has become. She goes out during the day, sups her nourishment from the breast rather than the neck, has lycanthropic tendencies but only uses them in a dream-like state. She can induce thoughts and reactions in those around her and can disappear or appear at will. To be finished off she still needs a good staking but you feel compassion for her. You feel that she would be a good Christian lady if she could but she's been dealt a hand that's a lot more fun and hasn't the will to say 'sod immortality and all these sexy young women throwing themselves at me'. And who can blame her. It all boils down to a hickory stick in the cleavage and Peter Cushing painting another set of fangs transfixed by a stake on the side of his brougham.

Production Company: Hammer Films
Director: Roy Ward Baker
Script: Tudor Gates, Michael Styles
Cinematographer: Moray Grant
Art Director: Scott McGregor
Music: Harry Robinson
Leading Actors: Ingrid Pitt, Pippa Steele,
Madeline Smith, Peter Cushing,
George Cole, Jon Finch, Dawn Addams
Kate O'Mara

Dracula a.d. 1972

Everything was against this film being a success. Well, maybe not everything. It still had Christopher Lee and Peter Cushing at the height of their power. And Stephanie Beacham's cleavage – and Caroline Munro's wholesome athletic attraction. What it had against it was the early seventies – all flares, kipper ties, fanny fringes and bouffants. Dated before it left the bath.

It starts a 100 years before the main story. Dracula impales himself on a wheel and dies. Van Helsing follows his old adversary across the dark divide. A young man arrives on the scene, takes some ashes from Dracula's desiccated body and his ring. The same young man turns up at Van Helsing's funeral and buries his Dracula mementoes near the grave.

A hundred years and we're in the salivating seventies. Everybody is emancipated and doing their own thing by dressing in the same shiny plastic and wearing the same make-up and hairstyle – men as well as women. The old ways have been forgotten by all but Jessica Van Helsing (Stephanie Beacham) and her grand-dad (Peter Cushing). Jessica is running around with a way-out bunch led by one Johnny Alucard (Christopher Neame). They put on what passed for an orgy in the seventies – a little grass, bouncy music, introspective swaying and calling everyone 'man', regardless of sex. Alucard brings out Drac's ring and ashes and mixes them with his own blood to bring Dracula back from the ash-can. Obligingly Dracula springs up, fully clad, and immediately gets his reanimated choppers into Laura (Caroline Munro). This brings grand-dad Van Helsing back into the action and from now on it's a straight fight between Dracula in the red corner and Van Helsing in the blue. The final shoot-out with Dracula and Van Helsing with Stephanie Beacham in the middle – not sure who's side she's on – is the best bit of the film. Van Helsing, as always, comes out on top and he and a reformed Jessica live happily ever after.

At the time of its release it was panned by the critics but time has lent it a substance that wasn't there in its first run. Nostalgia is selling big and what's more nostalgic than flares, mini skirts and armless sheepskin jackets.

Production Company: Hammer
Films
Director: Alan Gibson
Script: Don Houghton
Cinematographer: Dick Bush
Music: Michael Vickers
Leading Actors: Christopher Lee,
Peter Cushing, Stephanie Beacham,
Chirstopher Neame

martin (1978)

Is he or isn't he? The ambiguity of just what or who Martin is makes this film interesting. In spite of the sustained effort of the music director to kill it off with an unrelenting out-of-tune piano and a nerve-grating penny whistle.

We see the vague looking, apparent teenager, getting ready to sup blood. No cloak, fangs or metamorphosis is involved -

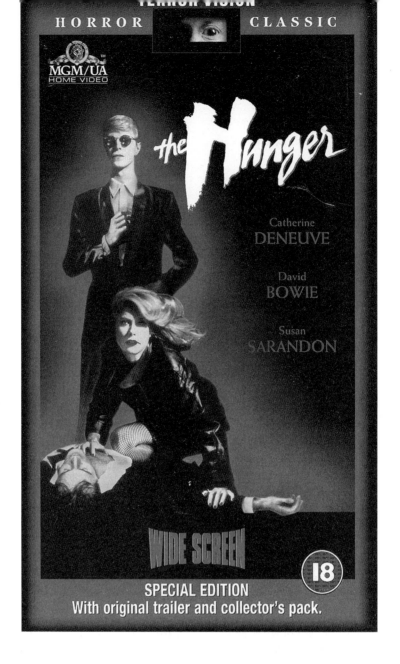

just a syringe and a razor blade. No one seems to be too concerned that he leaves a blood-drained corpse in the Pullman coach on a train.

Except, that is, for his cousin who keeps calling him Nosferatu and claiming that the fresh-faced, monosyllabic boy is 84 years old. For a low budget movie (witness the music score) it is a surprisingly intriguing film. Whether Martin is a paid-up, founder member of the vampire union is doubtful –

maybe unlikely, but it takes all sorts to make the world of the Undead and if he doesn't make it on the first application maybe he might be inducted as an honorary blood-sucker.

Production Company: Laurel
Director: George Romero
Script: George Romero
Cinematographer: Michale Gorrick
Music: Donald Rubinstein

Leading Actors: John Amplas,
Lincoln Maazel, Christine Forrest,
Tom Savini

love at first bite (1979)

This is a hard one to call. It starts off a bit slapstick, desperate to touch all the vampire icons. It also wants to be contemporary so pokes a finger at the communists, although what is meant by the confrontation of cool, rejuvenated Count (George Hamilton) Dracula and the cardboard cut-out commissar of the Soviet Republic is, to say the least, a little pathetic. More slapstick in New York with the Transylvanian coffin getting mixed up with one on the way to Harlem nearly sinks the movie without trace. Renfield (Arte Johnson), Dracula's long-time associate of many guises, gives the part a sort of restrained Dwight Frye performance. Richard Benjamin plays a descendent of Van Helsing, a psychoanalyst who is trying to get it together with the object of Dracula's affections, a cover girl played wonderfully by Susan St. James. L'amour does it. When Susan appears the picture picks up. She turns the tables on Dracula by biting him into an orgasm – the first in six centuries. Hamilton's Bela Lugosi voice holds up and the suave persona that Lee tacked onto Lugosi's boiled shirt front gives the film that taste of the classic thirties movie when a hero worth his salt would rather be seen dead than appear after sunset without his white tie and tails. Just one other thing. Did the whole film have a New York Jewish flavour, or was that Benjamin's influence?

I started off not impressed but by the end I was liking it – at second bite!

Production Company:
Simon Productions

Director: Stan Dragoti
Script: Robert Kaufman
Cinematographer: Edward Rosson
Music: Charles Bernstein
Leading Actors: George Hamilton, Susan St. James, Richard Benjamin, Arte Johnson, Dick Shawn

the hunger (1983)

So you've been vampirised and are now immortal. But who says you're going to stay young and juicy forever? Certainly not beautiful blood-sucking Catherine Deneuve, who is good at handing out eternity but gives no guarantee that you are going to like it. David Bowie finds this out fairly early on in the film and dutifully starts ageing in a matter of hours. This brings in Susan Sarandon who plays a scientist studying, would you believe, the cause of ageing. With Bowie out of the way it is time for a good whack of some erotic sex scenes and blood-smeared walls. Before Bowie fades completely Deneuve helps him into a coffin and puts him with the other crumbling immortal lovers in the attic.

Sarandon outgrows her mentor and foists on her a death suitable for a lady who keeps an attic full of rotting lovers. For me the film worked because of Catherine Deneuve. I suppose it's an idle tale with a few moments of genuine horror, as when the rapidly ageing Bowie kills the trusting teenage girl whom he has been teaching to play the piano. Or when Deneuve lowers Bowie into the coffin and closes the lid. But she's not in the true Dracula vein. For one thing she has no trouble going out in the daytime. For another, she hasn't got the teeth for an intrusion straight into the jugular and has to use a cute little knife she carries around for the job. Nor is she into sleeping in a coffin.

And she has a conscience and feels a deep sorrow for her desiccated lovers. Not deep enough for her to stop recruiting more attic fodder but then, if we all controlled our desires what a boring old world it would be.

Production Company: MGM/UA
Director: Tony Scott
Script: Ivan Davis, Michel Thomas
Cinematographer: Stephen Goldblatt
Leading Actors: Catherine Deneuve, Susan Sarandon, David Bowie

gothic (1986)

Whether this film fits into the framework of a vampire movie is arguable. It has got a lot going for it. For one thing, Lord Byron is posited, courtesy of Lady Caroline Lamb, as the template for the aristocratic leeches that followed. In *The Giaour* he wrote about the vampire/revenant which returns from the grave to cause problems for his family. Then there is the location – the infamous Villa Diodati on the misty shores of Lake Geneva and Shelley going mad on pint mugs of laudanum. Poor, misguided Polidori trying to suck up to the ignoble Lord and doing belly churning things with leeches and prussic acid. Clair Clairmont doesn't come out of it too well, but in that steamy, thunder shattered household who does?

This film got a terrible panning when it came out – unfairly, I think! If ever there was a *total* horror movie I think this must be well up in the queue for recognition. When I saw it seven or eight years ago I knew nothing about the shenanigans in Switzerland so dismissed it as high camp. Then I read up on the beginnings of the genre and came across a lot of accounts of what went on. Shelley's reaction to Clair's nipples becoming eyes,

Mary (Shelley) Godwin's idea to create a man who denies his creator and Lord Byron penning his *Fragment* that Polidori embellished into an industry – all come within the framework of this movie. The cast is almost unbelievably fantastic in a situation which must have put a lot of strain on relationships. Gabriel Byrne is the perfect Byron and Natasha Richardson, as Shelley's impulsive paramour, couldn't be bettered. But maybe it is Timothy Spall who is most remembered as the repellent Polidori, guzzling live leeches and trying to do himself a bit of mischief with a bottle of acid.

The camera work, the lighting, the sense of disorientation that Ken Russell brings to it. The entire design of the film, the sound, everything about it... What can I say? I'm a fan and this picture does it for me! Byron, the mental vampire.

Production Company: Virgin Vision
Director: Ken Russell
Cinematographer: Robert Southon
Script: Stephen Volk
Music: Thomas Dolby
Leading Actors: Gabriel Byrne, Julian Sands, Natasha Richardson, Myriam Cyr, Timothy Spall

the lost boys (1987)

J.M. Barrie would have been proud of this little lot. It is not exactly *Peter Pan*, but the stories had a lot in common. Where they differ is the wrapping. These lost boys are vampires and proud of it. They have grown away from the Stoker mould and are reaching towards the more fun side of vampiric immortality. I liked their sleeping arrangements – upside down in the remains of a fairground that got razed in an earthquake. The film doesn't take itself too

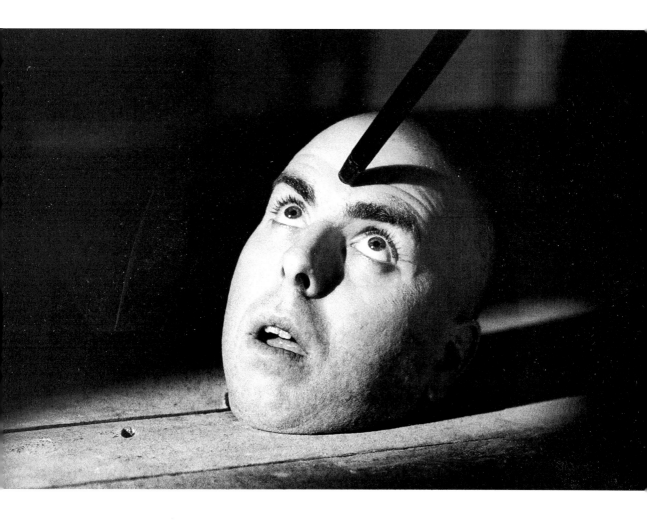

seriously – which is wonderful. The wannabe Van Helsings are a couple of loopy teenagers, dressed like Ninja turtles – the Frog Bros. They have only one answer for anyone tainted by vampirism – stake 'em!

Although entertaining, with a committed cast lead by Donald Sutherland's son, Kiefer, the film does paint itself into a bit of a corner with some of its ideas and there is a big cheat at the end when all the boys have been undeaded but the vampire infestation stays. When the head vampire is revealed it isn't exactly an amazing moment as the script so desperately tries to sell you a red herring

that has a decidedly suspect sell-by date.

Still, it's a fun movie that looked at a few side issues which can inconvenience your neighbourhood undead.

Production Company: Warner Bros
Director: Joel Schumacher
Script: Janice Fischer, James Jeremias, Jeffrey Boam
Cinematographer: Michael Chapman
Leading Actors: Jason Patric, Corey Haim, Dianne West, Jami Gertz, Bernard Hughes, Kiefer Sutherland

Timothy Spall as Polidori in Ken Russell's *Gothic* is having a little headache

THE LOST·BOYS

Sleep all day. Party all night. Never grow old.
It's fun to be a vampire.

WIDE SCREEN

15

SPECIAL EDITION
With original trailer and collector's pack.

BRAM STOKER'S DRACULA (1992)

I feel I have to tell the truth; this film left me as cold as a newly uncovered revenant in Siberia. Why? Don't expect me to be rational. Something to do with the colour and hype I suspect. This was hyped as the *real* Dracula and it wasn't. It was supposed to bring what is a rather boring book to some sort of halcyon realisation. Then they go and stick a piece up front that has nothing to do with the *real* Dracula. Next Coppola goes over the top and tries to justify it. Dracula doesn't have to be justified. Like being a Christian or a bungee jumper, it takes an act of faith. That's why when I come into contact with a modern theme on an old tune, I act like a sea anemone and recoil. All that brilliant colour and earnestness is too much. It's not that I disliked the film – it's just that it didn't serve up what I wanted – and anyone who knows me knows I like my steaks bloody without all the trimmings which defuse the flavour.

Production Company:
Columbia/American Zoetrope/Osiris
Director: Francis Ford Coppola
Script: James V. Hart
Music: Wojciech Kilar
Cinematographer: Michael Balhaus
Leading Actors: Gary Oldman, Winona Ryder, Anthony Hopkins, Keanu Reeves, Richard E. Grant

INTERVIEW WITH THE VAMPIRE (1994)

Funny old one, this. I did a review for the *Evening Standard* when this came out and I must admit I was less than generous about it. I thought it was very much like *Bram Stoker's Dracula* as visualised by Francis Ford Coppola. All colour and flair and no trousers. I saw it again while writing this book and my perception has changed. I still like my real Dracula done on a shoestring and with a plot line that idealises illogicality. But then, Lestat (Tom Cruise) is no Lugosi and Brad Pitt definitely is a lot more toothsome than Dwight Frye. And, I suppose, while I'm quoting negatives – there is a world of difference between Stoker's uptight Victorian narrative and the free-wheeling style adopted by Anne Rice.

My second viewing of *IV*, as it is conveniently abbreviated, was without a Dracula hang-up, comparing this self-justifying story with any other is an object lesson in futility. The good thing about the film is that it does pay homage to the old-type vampire. For a while there, Lestat is little more than a Plogojowitz with attitude. The sun is still the nemesis of the undead and they still drink the blood of anything which moves, straight from the pumping artery.

Production Company:
Geffen Pictures/Warner Bros.
Director: Neil Jordan
Script: Anne Rice
Cinematographer: Philippe Rousselot
Music: Elliott Goldenthal
Leading Actors: Tom Cruise, Brad Pitt, Antonio Banderas, Stephen Rea, Kirsten Dunst

SOURCE MATERIAL

The Illustrated Vampire Movie Guide by Stephen Jones/Titan Books
Horror edited by Phil Hardy/Aurum Press
The Hammer Story by Marcus Hearn and Alan Barnes/Titan Books
Vampire – The Encyclopaedia by Matthew Bunson/Thames and Hudson
Dracula by Bram Stoker/Everyman
The BFI Companion to Horror edited by Kim Newman/Cassell
Hammer Films by Tom Johnson & D. Del Vecchio/McFarland
V is for Vampire by David W. Skal/Robson Books
Chronicles of a Vampire by Manuela Dunn Mascetti/Bloomsbury
Dreadful Pleasures by James B. Mitchell/Oxford University Press
Bram Stoker by Barbara Bedford/Weidenfeld & Nicholson
The Vampire in Legend & Fact by Basil Cooper/Robert Hale
Hammer – House of Horror by Howard Maxford/Batsford

Dracula, The Vampire Legend by Robert Marrero/Fantasma Books
The Vampire Book by J. Gordon Melton/Invisible Ink Press
The Vampire Cinema by David Pirie/Hamlyn
Horror Movies by Carlos Clarens/Secker & Warburg
The Dracula Myth by Gabriel Ronay/W.H. Allen
Dracula was a Woman by Raymond R. McNally/McGraw Hill
The Vampire Lovers by J. Sheridan Le Fanu/Fontana Books
A–Z of Horror by Howard Maxford/ Batsford
Countess Dracula by Tony Thorne/ Bloomsbury
Vampyres by Christopher Frayling/Faber & Faber
The Vampire Companion by Kathrine Ramsland/Little, Brown & Co.
Science Fiction, Fantasy & Horror Film, Sequels, Series and Remakes by Kim Holston & Tom Winchester/McFarland

INDEX